REA

NEW HISTORICAL VOICE CONTEST FINALIST!

A DARING DANCE

"Maybe I'd like to see this hula-hula dance." Jefferson's voice deepened over the words, and Sinclair felt as if he'd caressed her. She was staring up at him as he gently reached down to curl a strand of her hair around one finger.

"I really can't perform the hula-hula. I only read about it once." Her voice sounded breathless to her own ears and she couldn't seem to turn away from the heated look in his eyes.

"You've got a pretty good imagination, Sinclair. I bet you could do it, if you really put your mind to it."

Sinclair shook her head violently. "I really couldn't. It sounded so . . . primitive and sensuous."

His finger traced an imaginary pattern down the side of her cheek to rest at the lace edge of her gown. "Sensuous?"

She closed her eyes as his arm encircled her waist and pulled her toward him.

"The women perform it nearly naked." Her breath was coming in small bursts now and her blood felt heated. "The men dance with them." She was swaying on her feet as his warmth enveloped her.

He tightened his hold, pulling her hard against him. "If that's the truth, I'll be thinking about taking a trip to those islands, because that must be a sight to see."

His mouth claimed hers.

BENEATH A SILVER MOON

DEBORAH SCHNEIDER

LEISURE BOOKS NEW YORK CITY

LOVE SPELL®

September 2002

Published by

Dorchester Publishing Co., Inc.
276 Fifth Avenue
New York, NY 10001

ISBN 0-8439-5105-2

The name "Love Spell" and its logo are trademarks of Dorchester Publishing Co., Inc.

Printed in the United States of America.

Visit us on the web at www.dorchesterpub.com.

With special thanks to the men in my life: Dave, Derek, Garth and Colin—because they believed in me.

To Sheryl Hoyt and Jesse Petersen, who told me the truth, even when it was painful and I didn't want to hear it. Without their help, this book would not exist.

BENEATH A
SILVER MOON

Chapter One

Montana Territory, 1883

"The Blue Willow? Could you direct me there, please?"

Sinclair Readford was beginning to wonder if the men in Montana were even more tiresome than the ones in Philadelphia had been.

The ticket agent stood staring at her, blinking behind his thick wire-rim glasses, but obviously incapable of formulating an answer to her very simple question. She was trying with great difficulty to remain polite, even though she was bone-tired, filthy dirty and impatient to finally meet her aunt Tilly. And this man couldn't seem to remember where the Blue Willow Hotel for Young Ladies was, in spite of being in a town that consisted of no more than one main street, a handful of stores and a train depot.

The man blushed and looked away, stuttering about his wife being a decent, upstanding woman who wouldn't tolerate something. His downcast eyes and mumbling response made Sinclair frown. It was an unusual reaction to such a simple question, but then she surmised this man must be one of those reticent westerners she'd read about—men who would stammer when speaking with young ladies and blush at any sort of interchange with a female. Not that she was paying any special kind of attention to him.

Sinclair Readford was a most proper and dignified young lady. Or at least, she tried to be.

Tapping her parasol on the counter daintily, she turned at a slight angle so her head dipped to one side and gave her a better view of the man.

"Just the general direction, perhaps?"

She pointed toward the east. The man shook his head, so she pointed toward the west, and he nodded.

Sinclair gave him a cool smile, murmuring her thanks, then picked up her alligator leather Gladstone bag and briskly walked out into the late-afternoon sunlight.

Glancing down the street, she wondered if she might need to hire a carriage to take her to her aunt's hotel. But noticing that there didn't appear to be any carriages in town and the only horses she could see were hitched in front of the saloon, she decided it was likely more expedient to walk.

To escape the glare of the sun, she paused to adjust her parasol. The horses shifted, made an awkward, frightful sound and Sinclair wrinkled her nose. Smelly, unpredictable creatures as far as she was concerned. Stepping down off the depot steps, she fol-

2

lowed the wide, dusty street across the tracks.

The combined odors of manure and sawdust assailed her and she tossed her head at flies buzzing lazily in a pattern, circling the dark blue hat she wore.

Passing several small, shedlike structures, she noticed there were names painted on the doors. A frown creased her brow as she wondered why these small buildings would be called *Dirty Sal, Frenchie, Maybelle* or *Big Gert*?

The West was certainly turning out to be a different sort of experience, and she found herself nearly giddy with excitement as she realized she was finally in Montana territory. Her father would have a fit when he discovered she'd managed to get there all by herself. But, of course, by the time he returned from Egypt, she'd be back home safe and snug in their huge old house on Walnut Street. It would serve him right for not taking her with him, and spouting all that nonsense about what a respectable woman could and could not do.

She glanced down at her Gladstone, remembering she had tucked all of Aunt Tilly's letters in the bag. She'd been shocked to discover those same letters several months ago as she was sorting through some old papers in the attic. Sinclair had never been told she had an aunt, much less one who was a successful businesswoman in Montana. Some of the letters were only a year old, and were addressed to her. A fact that had infuriated Sinclair, then made her coldly determined to find her mother's sister, and to do so without interference from her overprotective father.

Sinclair paused to study the building before her. There was a small sign hanging from the porch that

3

read, BLUE WILLOW, IT'S A PLEASURE TO SERVE YOU. The hotel was painted in various shades of blue, and a massive willow tree graced the front yard. It didn't take much imagination to figure out the name. The place looked prosperous and well cared for, obviously a sign that business was good.

Standing on the porch, Sinclair tried to shake the dust from her traveling gown, adjusted her hat, then pulled the bell. Almost immediately she found herself facing a tall black woman in a starched gray uniform. The woman raised an eyebrow and took in her appearance from the tips of her boots to the feathers on her hat.

Despite all of her planning, her careful preparations and the endless travel to get there, Sinclair felt a tremor of fear ripple through her body. For the first time she wondered what would happen if her aunt was displeased to see her. She knew she should have sent a telegram, but then she'd talked herself out it, acknowledging she was afraid the response would be a message to remain in Philadelphia. For once in her life Sinclair had wanted a taste of adventure, and she'd spent months planning this trip and scheming to save the money to make it a reality.

"You looking for somebody, honey?" The woman had a wide smile and friendly demeanor.

It helped Sinclair find her courage again.

"I would like to speak with Matilda Haynes, if you please." Her voice was soft and pleading, and sounded a bit shaky to her own ears.

The woman frowned down at her. "Madam ain't here right now. Mayhap you should come back some other time." The woman glanced over her shoulder, as if she expected someone to be listening, then her voice dropped an octave.

"Right now, it ain't the best time to be coming on, if you know what I mean."

Sinclair stared at her in bewilderment. She had no idea what this woman meant. And she had never thought to make a contingency plan if her aunt was not at the hotel. Her heart started to beat faster and she could feel her hands growing damp in her gloves.

"Might I wait for her, in the lobby? You see, I'm . . . family." Sinclair was afraid to divulge too much information to a servant, but she didn't want to spend the evening huddled in a doorway either.

She'd read about wild frontier towns in novels and serial stories in the newspaper. When night fell, cowboys rode into town, drank liquor, challenged one another to gunfights, then did despicable things to the women they found on the streets. A shudder of revulsion wracked her slim body.

The woman shook her head sadly. "I don't know when Madam is getting back, but if you're family, I imagine she'd want us to look out after you. I'll tell Hank you're here, and he can figure things out." Turning her back on Sinclair, she headed toward the rear of the house, shaking her head and grumbling to herself as she went.

Sinclair didn't know what to do. Kicking her bag into the hallway ahead of her, she stepped forward and tried not to think about her predicament. To distract herself, she took note of the furnishings. There was a huge chandelier hanging from the center of the ceiling and a mahogany staircase that swirled up at least two more stories. The walls were papered in a soft nature print that Sinclair recognized. A design from William Morris. A bowl of flowers sat on a marble-topped table in the center hallway next to a small glass jar that held coins.

Glancing about and seeing there was no one to ask for permission, Sinclair decided to investigate. Picking up a coin, she was delighted to find a small heart stamped in the middle. She turned it over in the gloved palm of her hand, but couldn't seem to recall ever seeing anything like it. Perhaps it was used within the hotel to purchase food and small toiletries. She wondered if there was a small commissary for the girls to organize and run. It would make sense, as her aunt had indicated that she supported young ladies in becoming financially independent.

She heard laughter as a pocket door opened and a young woman with bright red hair piled on top of her head appeared with a gentleman. Sinclair dropped the coin quickly back into the jar and backed away in embarrassment. She didn't want the woman to think she was stealing. But the redhead didn't seem to care as she brushed past the gentleman to stand in front of Sinclair and examine her from top to bottom.

"You the new girl, then?" Her look was impertinent, but Sinclair tried not to take offense.

"Yes, I suppose you could say that."

The woman walked around her slowly, studying her as if she were a specimen in one of Sinclair's father's many insect collections. Sinclair noticed that even though the woman wore a dress with a scandalously low-bodice, the style of the gown was the latest cut and the fabric of excellent quality. She must have interrupted the ladies when they were holding a party or gathering of some sort.

Sinclair blushed at the woman's frank perusal. Her blush deepened when she realized the man had paused and was studying her with the same intensive scrutiny. The woman caught his look and narrowed her eyes.

"Too fresh and young for the likes of you, Stanley. A man like you needs a woman with experience and stamina."

Before Sinclair had time to decipher the rather rude comment, the woman waved a soft white hand toward the doors.

"My name is Miss Dauphine. I'm the hostess this evening. Why don't you go in and introduce yourself to some of the others?" She tucked her arm into the crook of the man's elbow and winked. "It should give everyone a little jolt to see you, Sister."

Sinclair started to pick up her bag, then realized it would be foolish to carry it around the hotel with her. Likely the porter would put it in her room when this mysterious Hank appeared. Perhaps Hank was the manager and would know when to expect Aunt Tilly's return.

Stepping through the doorway, Sinclair found herself admiring the furnishings in the next room. A fire blazed in a huge marble fireplace, and the room was painted in Pompeii red, a perfect shade to match the bright floral upholstery and velvet couches, of which there seemed to be an extraordinary number, along with love seats and chaises. Perhaps this was a salon, where her aunt gathered her guests for conversation and literary readings. She wanted to pause and examine the furniture more closely, but she could hear voices in the adjoining room and she continued. With all the grace and poise she could muster, she opened the door and entered.

She stopped in awestruck wonder at the scene before her. While this parlor was identical to the previous room, it wasn't the furnishings that astounded her, it was the occupants of the room. Most of them were young women, of a variety of sizes, shapes, hair color and features. But the most outstanding characteristic of the group was the state of their dress. Or more precisely, the state of their undress.

All of the women were garbed in their underwear. They were indecent, and there were men in the room. Yet none of the women seemed self-conscious or ashamed. In fact, they stared at Sinclair as if she were the one out of place, and she glanced down at herself to be sure that in walking into the room she hadn't suddenly discarded most of her clothing.

The men sat in comfortable overstuffed chairs or shared seating with some of the women, and everyone held heavy crystal glasses. Sinclair could see a collection of decanters on a silver tray on the large oak table stationed beneath the chandelier, and she could smell the combination of cheap perfume, liquor and overheated bodies, which suffused the room.

She tried to smile graciously. "I'm sorry, I seem to have stumbled upon a private party. I beg your forgiveness and hope you'll excuse me."

A well-endowed blonde perched on the lap of one man raised a hand languidly and waved it in Sinclair's direction.

"Lookie here, ladies. It's Queen Victoria come all

the way to Ghost Horse Gulch to have tea with us."

The other women tittered, and Sinclair felt the heat rush to her cheeks. She bit back a quick retort about having some tarts with that tea and attempted to regain her composure. She started to back out of the room.

"I've obviously made a mistake, this . . . cannot be where I'm supposed to be."

A plump brunette waving a brightly decorated Japanese fan laughed hoarsely. "This place ain't where any of us is supposed to be. Just the luck of the draw, ain't it, your majesty?"

Sinclair had backed nearly to the door when she heard a deep voice behind her.

"Lily, where else could you sleep until noon every day and drink champagne all night? You're much too spoiled now to ever go back to a humdrum life."

Sinclair spun around to face a tall man with dark, thick hair combed back and falling well below his starched white collar. He wore a fancy silk vest, an elaborate tie and dark gray trousers. His black boots were so shiny, Sinclair could see her reflection in them. Raising her head, she found herself staring into the darkest, coldest eyes she'd ever seen. She felt chilled to the marrow with his gaze.

He started to walk around her slowly, and Sinclair felt frozen to the spot from his perusal. She swallowed and finally found her voice.

"I'm Sinclair Readford, from Philadelphia. I'm looking for Matilda Haynes."

The man smiled thinly. "Of course you are, but I'm sorry to inform you Matilda has taken an extended holiday, and I don't know when she'll be returning.

For now, I'm in charge of the Blue Willow."

Sinclair nearly collapsed from disappointment. She'd traveled all these miles, spent almost all of her money, and her aunt wasn't even there. Tears prickled her eyes.

The man gave her another long glance, in what was becoming a familiar routine, beginning at her toes and ending when he once again caught her eye. Sinclair blushed as she had a sense that he could almost see through her clothing. She felt as exposed as the women lounging about the room.

He held out a large, smooth-skinned hand. "I'm Hank Borscht, and of course, we'll make every effort to accommodate you until Matilda gets back." His voice was oily, and had a false ring to it. Sinclair had an intuition things were not as she had supposed at the Blue Willow, and that maybe she should hurry back to Philadelphia just as soon as possible.

Unfortunately, the train only came to Ghost Horse Gulch once each week, and she'd heard the whistle blowing as it left while she walked to the hotel. Like it or not, she was stuck.

Sinclair's mind whirled. The women sat staring at her, waiting to see what would happen next. Hank towered over her, then grasped her arm as if escorting her onto a dance floor.

"We have the perfect accommodations, don't we, ladies?"

There was giggling behind her, and several girls made rude comments. Sinclair tried to pull away from Hank Borscht, but his grip tightened. "And we have entertainment every night, don't we, girls?"

Hank didn't loosen his grip on Sinclair's arm as he

10

pulled her through the two rooms toward the second floor. She nearly screamed, but didn't think it would do any good. No one looked surprised to see him forcing a woman up the stairs, and she sensed she'd get no help from the other members of the household.

A young woman wandered out of one of the rooms on the third floor. She was wearing her corset, pantalets and a nearly transparent gown. Her face was heavily painted and her dark hair tightly curled.

"Polly, put this one in the blue room. And make her undress. I doubt she'll try to escape if she's naked. I'll be up later to sample the goods." He laughed heavily as his eyes raked Sinclair's body again. "Should be a long, hard night of riding. Breaking in a new filly is hard work."

Sinclair couldn't summon a response. Her heart was thumping so hard in her chest, she imagined they could hear it. She thought she had a pretty good idea what the man was talking about, or at least, perhaps she did. She could taste something metallic in her mouth, and she realized it was fear. Then Hank was gone and she stood staring at the woman named Polly.

Polly pushed her along a hallway until they came to a doorway painted blue. She opened it and pointed. "I guess this is going to be your room. It ain't so bad. Nellie liked it real well, till she took the ague and died."

Sinclair stared into the small blue room. It held a huge iron bedstead, painted with blue flowers and covered with a crazy quilt of blue-and-gold fabric. A small washstand stood next to the bed, and in one corner there was a screen, painted with dragons and

11

stars. She shook her head and turned to plead with the woman standing next to her.

"It's all a dreadful mistake. I don't belong here."

Polly touched her elbow gently. "That's what we all say, honey. Don't none of us belong here, but we're sure as hell stuck here. Let me give you a little piece of advice; get on the good side of Hank. He treats us all pretty fair, doesn't hit us much, lets us keep half the money we make. It ain't all bad here, once you get the hang of it."

Sinclair gave her a shocked look, then felt the familiar comfort of her temper rising. "I have no intention of getting the hang of . . . it." Not that she was exactly clear yet on what, *it* was.

Walking to the window, she unpinned her small, prim hat with the lovely stuffed bird on top. "Furthermore, I think you should consider your role in this little drama. I am being held here against my will. That's kidnapping. If you help Mr. Borscht, you could also be convicted of a crime. My father is a very important man back in Philadelphia. He has very important friends all over the country."

She tilted her chin up and tried to put an arrogant, disdainful expression on her face. "If anyone hurts me . . . in any way . . . they will pay, and pay dearly." She allowed the threat to hang in the air, like the cheap perfume in the room below.

Polly looked nonplused. "The sheriff gets a good payment from this place every week, so I doubt he's going to be helping you. Your pa could be best friends with the President of the United States for all I know, or care. Hank pays me, puts a roof over my head and food in my belly. If he says for you to get undressed and stay in this room, then that's just what you're gonna do. Understand?" Her voice took a hard edge as her hand snaked out, jerking the bodice of the dark blue silk traveling outfit Sinclair wore. A button popped off.

"I am not getting undressed, most especially not in front of you, and not for that hideous man!" Sinclair folded her arms across her chest in a protective gesture.

Polly stepped closer and Sinclair found her back against the wall. She could see the small, cold pinpoints of the other woman's silver-gray eyes. She had a sense that Polly liked playing the oppressor.

"I could rip them clothes off you, but then none of us would get a chance to wear 'em. I could call in Old Hoss—that's the half-breed that does chores around here. He'd hold you down while I undressed you. Or, you could just take off that fine jacket and dress and give 'em to me. If you do what you're supposed to, you won't get hurt."

The two women stood staring at each other. Sinclair could hear a hurdy-gurdy playing in the background, the low murmur of men's voices and the occasional high-pitched sound of feminine laughter.

Staring at her captor in terror, Sinclair wondered how she could convince the woman to help her. Finally she decided compromise might be the best solution. At least it appeared to be the best temporary solution.

"You can have my gown, my hat and my jacket if you bring my bag in here with my other things." She stiffened her shoulders. "And I'll keep my undergarments on."

Polly considered the offer as she eyed the Glad-stone sitting in the hallway with interest. "I'll need to search your belongings, in case you got a knife or a gun." She scuttled over to the doorway, ignoring Sinclair, who began to unbutton her jacket with pains-taking slowness.

When Polly had dragged the alligator leather bag into the room, she held out her hand. "Give me the key."

Sinclair paused to consider, but realized that Polly would call in reinforcements if she didn't cooperate. Pulling a gold chain with a locket and key from the deep cleft between her breasts, she unfastened the clasp and handed the key to Polly.

Sinclair watched as Polly dumped out the contents of her traveling bag. She opened a bottle of lilac wa-ter, sniffed and then dabbed some behind each ear. Having been in close proximity to her, Sinclair was hopeful that the perfume might cover the woman's musky odor. Polly examined the pieces of jewelry spread on the quilt. She put the pearls back into the bag but pinned a small cameo to her corset.

Sinclair couldn't stand the pain as the familiar ache of loss gripped her. Tears flooded her eyes, and she blinked twice to keep from shedding them.

"That belonged to my mother. Those pieces of jew-elry are all I have to remember her by."

Polly glanced over her shoulder and grunted. "You have more than enough. I didn't take all of it. I just have a hankering to wear this for a bit. I'll borrow it and give it back when I'm done." She continued to sort through Sinclair's possessions. She fingered a nightgown of fine lawn with embroidery on it.

"A good friend would give this to another good friend, like a sort of get-acquainted present."

Sinclair understood. The woman didn't want to be accused of being a thief, she wanted the nightgown as a gift.

Sinclair stepped out of her traveling gown and handed it to Polly. "Why don't we make an agreement? You take this lovely silk. It came from New York, and it's the latest go. You may have it, like you said, a gift between . . . friends."

Polly's face brightened. "You're not just saying that now. You can't change your mind tomorrow. And you can't go telling Hank I stole it from you. Hank won't have no stealing between his girls."

"I'm sure the man has tremendous moral fortitude, not to mention a charming demeanor." Sinclair's sarcasm was lost on Polly, who was too busy dancing in front of the mirror to pay any attention to her.

Sinclair tried to think quickly. She refused to remove her undergarments. At least her pantalets, corset, chemise and petticoats provided her with some covering. She had no intention of waiting in this room, naked, for Hank to show up. Now, she needed to get rid of the rambling Polly.

". . . like to have whipped her skin right off her when he found out. Not that he does that, leastways not often. But she earned it, and he knew he had to make an example of her, 'cause the other girls, well . . . they would have taken advantage if they didn't see what stealing would get 'em."

Sinclair lost her train of thought as she tried to piece Polly's words into a conversation.

"Who are you talking about?"

15

"Annabelle, you know the blonde with the big . . . ?" Polly's hands formed large mounds in front of her chest.

Sinclair held up her hand. "Yes, I think I have an idea who you're talking about."

"Did it?"

Polly looked at her blankly. "Did it what?"

Sinclair nearly threw up her hands in exasperation. "Did making an example of Annabelle keep the other women here from stealing?"

Polly stuffed the remaining items back into the bag and shrugged. "Mostly keeps us from stealing from each other, but Hank don't care if we get extra money off the drunks. He says it's our bonus." She giggled. "Cowboys get so liquored up, they don't know where they spent their wages."

She turned to study Sinclair again. "What about all them fancy under things? Hank said you was s'posed to be naked." She pointed a finger, "so off with them too!"

Sinclair crossed her hands in front of her breasts, terrified that Polly was going to start ripping her underclothes from her body. She glanced toward the window.

Polly caught the glance and turned, then laughed. "In case you're figuring on going out that window, it's a good twenty-foot drop to the ground. You'll break your leg if you're lucky . . . kill yourself if you ain't."

Sinclair swore under her breath. "Damn, damn, double damn." Had her plan been so transparent?

She nibbled her lip again and remembered Hank's veiled threats. She was a woman with no weapons or protection. Suddenly she had a brilliant inspiration, but then thought better of it. No proper young lady would think of such a thing, much less discuss it. She glanced again at Polly, who appeared to be losing patience with her. It was a crisis, and she'd just have to do everything in her power to escape. Her virtue would be lost if she didn't, and she couldn't worry about respectability at this point.

Pushing out her breasts, she put a hand on her hip, in what she hoped looked like a seductive pose. *Heavens to Betsy,* she thought, *I have no experience with this sort of thing.* She fluttered her lashes and tried to make her voice breathless.

"I know how to drive a man wild with desire."

Polly made an unpleasant noise. "You don't even act like you know which end of a man to handle."

Sinclair felt her temper rising. How dare this, this . . . harlot question her expertise. Never mind that the woman was right, and that a few minutes ago she'd been worried about her reputation. She simply couldn't stand to be considered ignorant regarding any subject.

"I've traveled all over the world. With, my . . . patron. He's very rich, you see. And last year, we went to the Sandwich Islands. It's truly a paradise, with white sand beaches and turquoise blue water." Her words nearly tripped over each other in her eagerness to convince Polly. She leaned forward, as if she was going to share a deep, dark secret.

"The natives wear almost nothing, men and women. And at night, they light torches, drape themselves in exotic flowers and dance the hula-hula." Her voice was thick with mystery. Waving her hands in the air and shifting her weight from foot to foot, she could see that Polly was intrigued. "It's been called the dance of desire."

Polly studied her with real interest now. "So, you learned how to do this hula-hula dance, is that what you're telling me?"

Sinclair lifted her arms above her head and made a circle while moving her hips. "The dance of desire. It's been said to drive men insane with passion."

Sinclair said a small prayer, asking for forgiveness for the lies. It was just lucky that she'd found her father's personal journal from his trip last year. He would never have allowed her to read such risqué things, but now she was grateful for her snooping. She had to convince this woman that she was an experienced seductress.

Polly was watching her intently. "What does this hula-hula dance have to do with keeping your underclothes on?"

Sinclair gave Polly a small pout. "Taking your clothes off is part of the dance, that's what . . . excites men so much."

Polly seemed to ponder the subject carefully. Perhaps she considered this conversation to be some sort of research. Is this what such women did, traded secrets and advice? Sinclair hated to think what circumstances could drive a woman to sell her body in order to survive.

"If I let you keep them things on, can I have that nightgown? The one with all them pretty pink bows on it?"

Sinclair nodded. "Of course, and once I demonstrate my skills to Hank—" her mouth tasted foul just for saying the words—"I'm sure he's going to want me to teach everyone the secrets of the hula-hula." She winked at Polly, "But of course, you were my first friend here."

Polly grabbed the nightgown, the silk dress and several other baubles and hurried out of the room before Sinclair had time to change her mind.

Sinclair heard a key turn in the lock and she stood there, wanting to crumble to the floor and weep. Despite the obvious emotional release, she knew crying wasn't going to do anything to improve her circumstances.

Remain calm and think, she kept repeating to herself. It was her father's favorite advice when lecturing her about facing dire circumstances. Of course, what worked in the jungles of the Amazon might not be nearly so effective in the wilds of Montana.

She put her hand to her head. What did the princess do when the wicked witch locked her in the tower? Turn into a frog? She didn't think she could do that. Spread coal on the path? Well, that wouldn't help. Let her hair down . . . Sinclair glanced in the mirror, imagining her long blond locks twisted into Rapunzel's rope. She didn't think tying her hair to the windowsill would give her much length. And as much as she wanted to get free of this place, she didn't want to escape by yanking out all of her hair.

Glancing around the room, an idea seized her. Ripping the faded blue-and-gold quilt off the bed, she twisted it along its length. Pulling on the linen sheet, she tied it to the end of the quilt. Then she attached the makeshift rope to the bedstead and tugged on the material to test its strength. There was a thin cotton blanket folded on the bottom shelf of the washstand, and she added that to her creation. She tried to remember what her father had told her about the trick to a good, tight knot. She tested her handiwork once more, then tossed the bedding out the window. It hung about three quarters of the way to the ground. Sinclair hoped it would be enough to keep her from breaking her neck as she whispered a small prayer and eased out the window.

When she reached end of the rope Sinclair realized that she was still too far to drop to the ground safely. "Damn, damn, double damn," she swore again.

"Lookit that, Jefferson. It ain't every day you see a whore hanging out the window."

She looked down to see two dark shadows mounted on horseback beneath her.

"Howdy, ma'am. Are you trying to get in or get out?" The man's voice was deep and sounded friendly.

Her heart started to pound and her hands were getting damp as she felt fear crawl along her backbone. These men could be thieves, murderers or outlaws. She shouldn't say anything and hope they'd go away. Then again, perhaps she should consider her options.

"She don't appear to be friendly, Jefferson."

"Maybe we're scaring her, Ollie."

Sinclair could feel the fabric giving way, inch by inch. Still, she remained silent.

"Guess we'll be moving on, ma'am. Good evening to you." She could see the man directly beneath her tip his hat. Did outlaws have good manners? Before she could answer him there was a loud ripping sound and Sinclair dropped . . . to land squarely on the polite cowboy.

Sinclair grabbed frantically at the man as his horse reared back. He tried to collect his reins while Sinclair pulled at his coat and fought to stay mounted behind him.

"Great Galloping Gophers . . . now whores is dropping from the sky!" The other man sat watching the spectacle before him.

"Hang on, ma'am, if you can."

Sinclair had her arms firmly around the man's waist.

"Whoa," he had managed to shorten the reins again and the horse settled down. She could hear him talking in a sweet, soft voice.

"It'll be all right, sugar. Don't worry. Just stay calm. I got you."

"I'll be fine, now. Thank you for your concern." Sinclair wrapped her arms about him even more tightly as the horse made a quick sidestep.

"Meaning no offense, ma'am, but I was talking to the horse. And . . . well, if you don't mind, I think we should be introduced before we get so well-acquainted."

Sinclair didn't get his meaning until she realized what part of the man she was hanging on to. She jerked her hand back quickly and mumbled an apology.

"Jefferson, we don't have time for this kinda foolishness. Put her back and let's get going." The other man's voice was harsh.

Sinclair held on to the back of the man named Jefferson and pleaded with him. "Please don't send me

21

back there. I had to escape . . . if you help me, I can pay you."

"I'd be pleased to help you, ma'am, any other time, but we're in a bit of a hurry tonight. Maybe the next time I come into town." The man's voice was gentle, but he tried to loosen Sinclair's hands.

"You can't leave me here. My father is a very important man . . . they kidnapped me, they were going to force me into . . . I can't . . . there's no one . . . my aunt." The day's turmoil finally caught up to Sinclair and she started to sob quietly. She was quickly overtaken by her emotions and her shoulders began to heave as she found herself weeping, and then howling.

"She sure can make a powerful noise for such a little mite, can't she, Ollie?"

"Sounds like a mountain lion meeting up with a grizzly bear if you ask me." The man named Ollie answered.

Sinclair was beginning to calm down when she heard a commotion above her. Glancing up, she discovered Polly's head poking out the window.

"Take me with you, now," Sinclair demanded. Flinging her legs as wide as she could, she dug her heels into the sides of the horse who bolted forward at the unexpected and rough command.

The rider in front of her worked hard to keep his runaway mount on the dusty, well-worn trail gleaming in the light of the full moon. Turning her face against the man's back, Sinclair hoped that when they were finally introduced he wouldn't beat the living daylights out of her.

Chapter Two

Jefferson McCloud finally got his horse calmed down and under control a few miles outside of Ghost Horse Gulch. He tugged on the reins to bring them to a halt, then sat quietly for a moment to calm his nerves. He'd never plucked a woman from the side of a whorehouse before. It took some getting used to.

Ollie pulled up next to him, spit a wad of chewing tobacco out the side of his mouth, then sat in silence. He seemed to know a storm was brewing and sat patiently, waiting for Jefferson's next move. He didn't have long to wait.

Jefferson slid off his horse, pulling the young woman with him. He stood towering over her, removed his hat and slapped it against his thigh in disgust. He tried to say something, but his tongue couldn't seem to form the words. His hands were tightly balled into fists, and before he lost his temper completely, he turned, kicked the dirt and walked away. Ollie just sat watching him, then spat again.

A few minutes later he stomped back to stand in front of the woman.

"Damnation, lady, are you crazy? What in hell were you trying to do, get us killed?" Jefferson's voice thundered with anger as he glowered at the tiny blonde staring up at him in horror.

He watched as her trembling turned to shivers, and he realized she was clad only in her unmentionables. He could see she was a well-endowed, shapely female, and he started to admire the view, until he remembered he was mad as hell at her.

She regarded him silently as he paced in front of her. He ran a hand through his dark hair, then paused in front of her again. "You must be plumb loco."

"Are your questions rhetorical, or are you going to give me a chance to answer them?" She inquired in a wavering voice. Then she put a hand on her hip and stared him down.

Damn if she wasn't a fetching little thing, all long blond hair and soft white skin. He'd never seen her at the Blue Willow before, but he figured she'd earn a good living there. Men would fight each other for a chance to be with this vixen with hair like spun gold.

"I told you I was being kept there against my will. Polly took all of my clothes. And a horrible man named Hank was coming back later to, to . . ." she paused and looked down at the ground. She blushed so deeply, he could see it in the pale moonlight. He wondered what it would take to make a soiled dove blush? Hank must have had some pretty interesting plans to make her climb out a three-story window to escape.

"I need your help." Her voice became softer as she raised her eyes in appeal to him.

Leaning back on his heels, Jefferson stared down at her. "Usually, ma'am, I'm not the sort who'd refuse to assist a lady in trouble, but, as I tried to explain, we've got some urgent business tonight." He shrugged. "I guess we didn't exactly behave like gentlemen. My apologies, ma'am." He put his hat back on his head. "Have a good evening, now."

Sinclair watched him grab the reins of his horse and start to climb back into the saddle.

"You can't leave me here." She rushed forward, yanking on the edge of his dark coat. Gently at first, then firmly when he tried to get away from her.

He was halfway into the saddle, but Sinclair wasn't going to relinquish her hold. "I'll die out here alone," she wailed. Jefferson paused, then eased back down to the ground and put his hands gently on her shoulders.

"We won't let that happen. You got any kinfolk around here?"

Sinclair sniffed. "No."

"How about some friends or acquaintances. Someone your family knows?"

Sinclair rubbed at her nose and sniffed again. "No."

Jefferson untied the red silk bandanna from around his neck and handed it to her. She blew her nose loudly then handed it back to him.

He grinned at her. "You go ahead and keep it,

ma'am. I got a feeling maybe you're gonna need it."
He took a few steps toward the other man.

"We found us a stray, Ollie. What'd'ya think we should do with her?"

Ollie took off his hat and scratched his gray head in silence, as if pondering the question.

"Ask her if'n she knows anything 'bout little girls."

Jefferson nodded and turned back to the woman. "You know anything about little eight-year-old girls?"

Sinclair stopped crying. She swallowed. "I once was a little eight-year-old girl."

Jefferson glanced back over at Ollie. "That's good enough for me."

Spitting again, Ollie seemed to think for a moment. "Me too."

Jefferson held out his hand. "Miss . . . what did you say your name was?"

"I didn't, at least, not yet. Please allow me to introduce myself, my name is Sinclair Readford. My father is Professor William Readford, of Philadelphia. Perhaps you've heard of him?"

Jefferson shook his head. "I don't exactly keep up with folks back east."

Sinclair frowned. "Well, he's a professor of geography at the University of William Penn. He's known throughout the academic world."

"Well, Miss Readford, I guess we wouldn't travel in the same circles." He grinned at her as he shook her hand. "I'm Jefferson McCloud, owner of the Cripple Creek Ranch. And I've got an offer for you, Miss Readford. The fact that you seem educated works in your favor."

He appeared to have piqued her interest, because she stopped sniffling and rubbing her nose long enough to frown up at him.

"My favor?" she repeated, looking confused.

"For the position," he said, nodding.

"What position?" She put her other hand on her hip and gazed at him with a thoughtful expression on her face. "You're really not making any sense whatsoever."

The tone of her voice reminded Jefferson of one his former teachers. That old buzzard could still make him feel foolish when she wanted.

Jefferson grew irritated with the woman's attitude, after all, he was only trying to help. It hadn't been his idea for her to drop out of that window and onto him. He had better things to do that night than stand around and chew the fat with Little Miss High-and-Mighty. Maybe he should leave the runaway out here for a few hours, just to show her how lucky she was that he'd been the one below her when she fell. Then again, if he could convince her to come back to the Cripple Creek with him, it'd save him a lot of time and trouble.

Jefferson stepped closer to her. "You interested in some work?"

She looked up at him with suspicion, her eyes narrowing. "Doing what?"

"I have a little sister." He paused, as if considering what to say.

There was a disparaging noise from the man on the other horse. Jefferson scowled in his direction, then returned his gaze to Sinclair. "My stepmother passed on, leaving Maddie's care up to me and the

Judge." He paused again, as if searching for words. "The woman I hired to take care of her ran off a few days ago. Since it doesn't appear she's planning on coming back to the ranch, I was in town tonight looking for a replacement."

Sinclair blinked. "You're asking me, a perfect stranger, to come into your home and take care of your sister?" She paused, seeming to consider the offer. "Are you that trusting, or are you that desperate?"

Ollie gave a hoot of laughter. "She's smart enough to see right through you, boss."

Jefferson gave her another grin. "It would seem that we're both desperate, miss. I need a caretaker for Maddie, and you need a place to stay. Why don't you come out to the ranch for a few days? Then you can send a wire to your father and we'll sort this whole thing out."

"How do I know I can trust you, that you aren't just trying to lure me to your ranch? Or maybe you two are outlaws."

Jefferson shook his head in wonder. "You just fell out of a whorehouse window, frightened my horse nearly out of his skin, begged me to help you and told me you'd die if I left you here alone. Now you're telling me you don't trust my intentions. Do you have any choice?"

Sinclair twisted her fingers in her hair. "No. I guess you're right about that, it appears my circumstances are dire and my choices are limited." She gave a deep, dramatic sigh.

"How long does this job last?"

Jefferson felt a tremor of anticipation. The sooner

he settled the matter of his sister's care, the sooner he could get back out on the range with the boys.

"Just till fall roundup. You ever spend a summer in Montana?"

Sinclair shook her head. "This is my first visit here, and . . . well, I am without permanent lodging. Perhaps we can make an agreement. I'll come to your ranch and meet your sister. If it appears we'll get along, I'll give serious consideration to your offer." She strolled toward him, her chin lifting proudly in the air as she offered her hand. He stared at it for a moment, then took it firmly in his own and shook it.

"Deal," he said as he effortlessly lifted himself back into the saddle, then stretched out an arm toward her.

"Mount up," he ordered.

Sinclair shook her head sadly. "I'm not particularly fond of horses, but I suppose it's the only way to get to your ranch."

Ollie turned to stare at her openmouthed, as if she'd just uttered a terrible bit of blasphemy.

Jefferson nodded. "It's quite a ways on foot . . . so I guess you're just going to have to suffer riding with me."

He lifted her gently behind him, carefully placing her arms around his waist and taking a few extra moments to ensure she found the right handhold.

"Hang on tight," he said, as they took off at a gallop.

Sinclair didn't need the advice, as she leaned into the strong, firmly muscled back, closed her eyes and held on for dear life.

*　　*　　*

Jefferson never realized how far his ranch was from Ghost Horse Gulch until he rode the nearly twenty-five miles with Miss Sinclair Readford grasping him tightly about the waist. The sensation of the woman's soft, supple arms about him wasn't what disturbed him. He discovered she had a constantly wagging tongue that had given him a headache by the time they arrived at the ranch. Cowboys were a reticent lot by nature, and he figured she'd used up both his and Ollie's share of words for the whole damn year by the time they arrived at the Cripple Creek.

She had described in great, intricate detail the story of her abduction by Hank Borscht. She painted him as an ignorant, abusive buffoon who had threatened to hold her captive in his brothel. She expressed concern for her aunt Tilly, who obviously had been taken in by that weasel, Hank, and was traveling about someplace unaware that her respectable hotel for young ladies had been turned into a house of ill repute in her absence.

Ollie was heard to snort loudly, several times, and it took all of Jefferson's self-control not to inform the self-righteous Miss Readford that as far as he knew, the Blue Willow had always been a sporting house, and that he'd frequented the place himself on occasion. While he could agree that Hank Borscht was a lying, cheating son of a gun, a personal acquaintance with several of the young ladies of the establishment had convinced Jefferson that they were as accepting of their circumstances as could be expected.

Matilda Haynes was considered a fair and decent employer, and she had a reputation for "taking care of her girls." In fact, due to her generous gifts to the school and the Methodist church, she was viewed as something of a benefactor to the citizens of Ghost Horse Gulch.

Jefferson tried to put the pieces of Sinclair's story together, but the woman had a tendency to jump around like a bumblebee in a flower patch. She'd be going on about Hank, then suddenly relate some small incident she recalled from her home in Philadelphia. By the time she finished her story, Jefferson was so grateful for the peace and quiet he didn't ask any questions.

They came up over the ridge and looked down through the darkness at the ranch house and outbuildings. There wasn't much to see in the middle of the night, although a lantern had been left lit on the porch. They expected him to return tonight, but he doubted if anyone on the ranch could be prepared for the woman accompanying him.

To hell with them all, he thought. They'd sent him on a fool's mission, and he'd brought back a woman to take care of Maddie. He was sure to feel the sharp edge of Lettie Thorp's tongue in the morning, but he'd done the best he could.

Jefferson turned slightly in the saddle, and he felt a momentary surge of pity for the woman clinging to him. It was clear she was a tenderfoot, but whether she was the daughter of a professor, or a soiled dove who'd had a falling out with Hank and needed to escape, he couldn't say. It really didn't matter as far as he was concerned.

"That there's the Cripple Creek Ranch. Finest spread in Montana. I'll take you up to the house. See that you get settled in for the night. We can talk in the morning."

Sinclair mumbled something, but she was nodding, so he guessed she was agreeing with him. As the horse carefully picked his way down the rocky hillside, Jefferson could feel her grasp tighten. Under other circumstances, he would have enjoyed having a buxom blonde holding on tight to him. That night though, he'd been intent on completing a task. The woman's agreement to take care of Madison insured he could join his riders out on the range and get on with the spring roundup.

Miss Readford, if that was really her name, was available. It was her most attractive quality.

Sensing his feed and pasture nearby, the old sorrel picked up the pace as they continued down the wagon-pocked, dusty trail that passed for a road. It was only minutes before Jefferson turned back to Sinclair and tried to be gallant.

"Ollie can help you down, ma'am." His arm indicated his partner already dismounted and holding his hand up for Sinclair to grasp.

Sinclair didn't move. Sitting as though she was considering her options, she finally lifted one leg over the side of the horse and jumped down. Her grip on Jefferson slackened, but she never quite let go of him. By the time she touched the ground, he was leaning sideways.

Fearing the damn fool woman was going to yank him right out of the saddle, Jefferson jerked back. Sinclair's toes once again lifted off the ground. She gave a small squeak of surprise, but she still didn't release the edge of his coat, which she held balled up tightly in her fist.

"Ma'am, when a man's getting in and out of the saddle, it'd be good manners for you not to go yanking on him. If you let go, I'm going to be right down." His voice was as gentle as if he were talking to Maddie. Considering this woman's most recent behavior, she was more like his stepsister than he'd care to admit and he wondered exactly who'd be taking care of whom.

"Of course, I'm truly sorry for all of this inconvenience. I'm not usually such a bother." She released her hold and took a small step backward when she touched the ground. She made an odd noise, then her stumble was quickly intercepted by Ollie. Catching her easily he leaned her forward again. She finally seemed to find her balance and stood gazing up at Jefferson.

"I told you I really don't much care for horses. I believe that was the longest ride I've taken in my whole entire life." She seemed well-pleased with herself and lifted her nose in the air with pride.

Jefferson took his time dismounting, then stood with the reins in his hand, trying not to chuckle at the arrogant little Miss Readford.

"Well, in Montana that was hardly enough riding to go to the bother of catching a horse. If you're planning to stick around these parts, you'd best learn to like sitting in a saddle. Out here a horse is your best friend, and we'll hang a man for trying to steal one. A good horse'll save your life more'n once."

Sinclair shifted on her feet uncomfortably. "I suppose with enough practice, I could learn to tolerate the beasts."

Ollie snorted in the background and Jefferson was too shocked by her statement to form a response. By the time he opened his mouth to give her some much-needed advice regarding survival in the West, the overbearing Miss Readford was climbing the steps to the porch and giving them a description of the charming exterior of the ranch house.

"It's much larger than I expected, and not at all like the haciendas I pictured. Of course, that would be the southwest and California I suppose. I tend to bunch all of the West together, which aggravates my father to no end. 'They are different latitudes, Sinclair.' " Her voice took on a husky note, as if she were imitating her father. " 'And the topography and climate can vary significantly. One cannot make regional assumptions simply based on relative position to the Rocky Mountains or the Mississippi river.' "

Reaching the front door, she peered into the large circle of beveled glass.

Ollie stood next to Jefferson shaking his head sadly. "That woman is plumb loco. You understand anything she just said?"

Jefferson still hadn't moved from his horse's side. He was as confused as Ollie by this woman who yammered on about nothing at the drop of a pin. She sure was in love with the sound of her own voice.

Turning slowly to look at his friend, he tipped the edge of his Stetson back and grinned.

"I believe I might have found the one person on God's green earth who has a chance of understanding Maddie. Likely she is crazy, but I have to admit, she's also entertaining. If you're ever hard up for a word, Ollie, you just come right up here and see Miss Readford, because she's got enough of them for all of us."

Ollie shook his head and looked disgusted. "Whatever she's got, I hope you ain't gonna catch it." He grabbed the reins of the horses and headed toward the barn.

Jefferson followed Sinclair up the steps. He swept his hat off his head as he opened the door.

"Welcome to my home, Miss Readford. I guess you'd better come on in and get yourself settled."

Sinclair stepped into the vestibule as if she were a Philadelphia matron making a social call. Never mind that she was in the middle of the Montana wilderness with a man she'd met only hours before and clad only in her undergarments. Poise can take you anywhere, one of her more proper teachers had intoned, and tonight, Sinclair was putting that theory to the test.

She glanced about her, but the rooms were dimly lit and she could only make out large shapes cowering in the shadows. There was a dusty, unkempt smell about the place, as if these rooms were rarely used or aired out. She wondered about that briefly.

"I'll show you to your room, ma'am. After all your adventures today, you must be tired out."

Sinclair nodded and gave a deep sigh as she started up the stairs. The train ride and the excitement at the Blue Willow had been trial enough. Then she'd had to ride endless miles through half the night, bumping along on that bag of bones Mr. McCloud called a horse. Her entire body ached.

The hair on the back of her neck prickled as Mr. McCloud followed closely behind her. Perhaps too closely, as she felt his warm breath upon her neck. Likely that's what was causing the prickling sensation. That and the tremendous power emanating from the man.

She had felt it on the ride to the ranch, the subtle shifts in muscle as he directed the horse with just a click or a movement. The way he seemed to see the landscape, even though it was a dark night with only a bit of pale light from the moon to show the way. She recalled that Ollie had deferred to him and called him Boss the few times he addressed him. She could feel the controlled power of the man, and it excited her in ways she'd never experienced before. There was a white-hot, coiling heat within her that was new and terrifying. She had traveled to Montana in search of adventure, and so far the experience had far outstripped her expectations.

A thought suddenly struck her and she stopped abruptly, turning to nearly collide with Mr. McCloud. She tottered briefly on the step, stretching out an arm for balance. Catching hold of his shoulder she held on for dear life. When she lifted her eyes to his, she was captured by a dark, smoky look.

She shivered, but whether it was from fear or delight, she couldn't have said.

"My clothes," she murmured, still lost in the swirling, brown depths of his eyes.

His gaze traveled down her body and made her dizzy with the heat of his perusal, yet she wasn't offended, as she had been when Hank Borscht studied her earlier.

She swallowed as an unusual sensation whipped through her, a lazy, spine-tingling warmth that caught her by surprise. Snapping herself back to reality, she regarded him primly.

"I haven't any, at least none here. My trunk is locked in the station shed, and this is all I'm left with." She made a small movement with her hand, and McCloud's gaze once again moved slowly over her half-clad body, then returned to study her expression.

"Not to worry, ma'am. I'll send one of the hands for your things in the morning."

Sinclair hated to tear herself away from that hypnotic look, but she was beginning to feel foolish. Turning back to the stairs she muttered under her breath, "Of course you will."

The man was infuriating in his sureness. It never occurred to him that he would experience any difficulty in locating and retrieving her belongings. No one would question him. No one would accuse him of being someone he was not, or attempt to kidnap him. No one would force him to make up stories or to bargain for God knows what . . .

Sinclair reached the top of the stairs and shook her head. All the traveling and the terrible events of the day had likely caught up with her. She had no reason to be thinking ill of this man. He had saved her from a situation that could have ruined her forever. She should be eternally grateful to Mr. Jefferson McCloud.

She glanced his way as he opened a door for her. If only he wasn't so arrogant. Or so ruggedly handsome. And if he didn't have those deep, dark chocolate-colored eyes.

". . . be seeing you in the morning, Miss Read-ford."

Sinclair had lost track of the first part of the sentence in her musings. She simply nodded and watched him back out of the room. She could have sworn there was a small lift at the corners of his mouth as he made his exit, but she couldn't be sure. He'd lit a candle in the room, but that only cast a dim, shadowy light.

Sinclair fumbled to the small dressing table to splash water from the pitcher into the bowl. It was bone dry. Probably they hadn't been expecting a guest tonight. She brushed her hands against the soft fabric of her petticoat, then sat on the quilt-covered bed to remove her boots. She rubbed her aching feet, then crawled beneath the covers.

The mattress felt heavenly and Sinclair realized it had been too many days since she'd slept in a real bed. As fatigue claimed her, she closed her eyes and found herself recalling the handsome face of her new employer.

"Not exactly Prince Charming," she whispered, but he'd come to her rescue when she had most needed help. And despite the odd circumstances of their meeting she had an intuition that he trusted her. After all, wasn't he offering her a position in his home?

She felt herself drifting off to sleep, and she smiled as she considered that on her first day in Ghost Horse Gulch, she'd experienced more than living nearly twenty-two years in Philadelphia.

Exhausted from her escapades, she fell into a deep sleep almost immediately. The light of morning was still several hours away when she sat upright in the bed, shivering until her teeth chattered, as a thin, plaintive wail filled the air and echoed through the dark corners of the house.

Chapter Three

Sinclair tossed and turned until morning, sleeping fitfully. There were no more screams but that didn't help her settle in and rest peacefully. Finally, just as dawn was a faint orange light creeping across the eastern sky, she fell asleep.

She awoke to the smell of coffee and the sound of horses. And for a few minutes she couldn't quite remember where she was. She knew they didn't have any horses at their little house on Walnut Street. But she could hear them, the soft, deep whinnying echoing through the bright morning light. She opened her eyes, trying to rub the soreness and scratchy ache of too little sleep from them. In a rush of memory the previous day came back to her.

Sitting up in bed, the first thing she noticed was the amount of dark furniture that filled the room. The bright patchwork quilt covering her was the only touch of color in an otherwise drab interior. She gave a small wince as her bare feet touched the cold wooden floor. Crossing the room to peek out the window, she yanked open the heavy velvet draperies, then gave a gasp of delight at the view spread before her.

Mountains covered with snow stood at the edge of the horizon, like great mounds of frosted marzipan. The soft filtered light of early day warmed the room with its burnished glow, giving it a friendlier look.

She could see fields of deep, dark green grass spreading from the edges of the ranch to the hills beyond. The landscape stretched for miles before her, and she didn't see any buildings other than those directly beneath her.

There were horses in a wooden enclosure near one of the barns, and several men were standing about looking at them. She felt like a small bird, perched high in a tree, observing the world beneath her. The view of wide open space was both delightful and frightening at the same time.

Sniffing the delicious aroma of coffee again, Sinclair felt her stomach give a small groan. She realized she couldn't even remember the last time she'd sat down for a decent meal.

Walking to the commode, she gave a small sigh of disappointment when she remembered there wasn't any water in the pitcher. She frowned as she caught sight of her reflection in the small looking glass hung on the wall. Her hair was curling in a wild mess about her head, and she'd lost nearly all the pins that had held it in a small coil at the base of her neck. She tried to comb the mass of blond curls with her fingers, but found she couldn't really untangle the snarls or even begin to smooth it out.

Shrugging in resignation, she gave up. She truly regretted the loss of her Gladstone and its contents. She'd carefully packed that bag, so that she'd have a nightgown, and a nearly complete change of clothing. All of her toiletries were in it, too, including her beautiful silver brush and comb set. She couldn't possibly be expected to endure this wilderness without a single touch of civilization, could she?

She supposed she'd have to sit here in this room until Mr. McCloud managed to retrieve her trunk. She wished now that she'd also asked him to retrieve the Gladstone. After all, he was so arrogant, it would likely be a small task for such a great and powerful man.

She wandered about the room, inspecting the austere furnishings more closely. A small wool blanket folded at the foot of the bed gave her an idea. Shaking out the covering she draped it over her shoulders and, deciding it made a perfect shawl, she danced out of the room without bothering to put her boots on. She was too hungry and curious to bother.

Following her nose down the stairs and into the kitchen, Sinclair discovered a tall woman, with a back nearly as wide as the stove she stood in front of. Turning, the older lady gave Sinclair a cursory glance, then pursed her mouth.

"Guess you must be the new one. Come on in and get yourself some breakfast." Her tone was flat.

The woman inclined her head to indicate a table in the center of the room. Sinclair could see a small child seated there with her back to them. Dingy hair stringing down her back and the filthy pinafore she wore did little to inspire confidence in Sinclair.

"Is that my charge?"

The woman looked at her dumbfounded, frowned for a moment then silently returned to frying bacon in the cast-iron pan in front of her.

Sinclair thought the woman's manners were abominable, but since she didn't know if this was some relative or another employee, she decided to keep her opinions to herself. Walking cautiously toward the little girl at the table, she could hear loud slurping sounds. The child's head was leaning so closely toward the surface of the table, Sinclair couldn't see her face.

"Are you Madison?" Sinclair inquired in as sweet a voice as she could muster.

The slurping sound was her only answer. Sinclair moved closer, and wrinkled her nose at the unpleasant odor surrounding the child. She turned back to the woman at the cook stove.

"This can't be . . . this isn't . . ." but she had a sudden inspiration as to the reason for Jefferson McCloud's desperation the night before.

"Feebleminded," was the only response as the other woman turned the bacon sizzling in the pan.

Sinclair stepped around the table in order to see the child more clearly. She was shocked by the view of a very dirty, very unkempt little girl who was using her hands to scoop thick oatmeal from a wooden bowl and stuff it into her mouth as quickly as she could. She never lifted her gaze to look at Sinclair, and seemed to be totally absorbed with eating her breakfast.

43

Sinclair tapped her right foot as she considered the situation.

"Feebleminded and killed her own Ma. That's what you been hired to take care of," the woman at the stove cackled. "Guess the Boss didn't tell you 'bout that part. He don't mention it if'n he can avoid it, but it's just a waste of time to drag some fancy piece of baggage way out here, then have her up and leave once she catches sight of the girl." She cackled again.

Sinclair felt her temper rise, and she tried to stomp it down again. It was no use. The woman's bad manners and attitude had taken their toll. Sinclair was fighting mad.

Putting her hands on her hips, she marched over to the woman, who was nearly a foot taller but certainly didn't intimidate her.

"I beg your pardon. Did I hear you refer to me as a fancy piece of baggage?" Her tone was icy and the other woman's grin dissolved.

"If the shoe fits, wear it, missy!"

"You seem to make a number of assumptions, some of which are so grossly erroneous as to be insulting." Sinclair moved closer, her finger pointing toward the young girl. "Am I correct in assuming this child is Madison McCloud, the sister of Mr. Jefferson McCloud?"

The woman looked baffled but nodded slowly.

"It is certainly none of your affair what Mr. McCloud and I discussed regarding an arrangement for the care of his sister. In the future I expect you to refer to me as Miss Sinclair or Miss Readford." She puffed herself up as much as she could and took one more threatening step toward the woman at the stove. "And never, ever in my presence are you to refer to this child as feebleminded. That is a degrading, humiliating thing to call anyone, and I just won't have it."

Sinclair Readford had supervised servants all her life, and this rough woman was not going to destroy her confidence. "I believe I'll have my breakfast out on the veranda." She gave the woman one last cold glare, glanced at the child at the table who seemed oblivious to the proceedings and tossed her head as she marched out the door.

She was enraged. Why hadn't Jefferson McCloud told her that his sister was infirm? She wondered if it was because he didn't think she'd accept the position if she knew. Sinclair considered that for a moment, but still wasn't satisfied. After all, hadn't he pointed out how desperate her situation was, and that she had no choice but to accept any conditions he offered her for rescue?

She paced uneasily. Of course, he probably suspected her of being an impostor. Maybe he thought she was an escaped dove, desperate to leave a life of sin and debauchery. In that case he'd believe she'd go running back to town at the first indication of difficulty, most especially at the challenge of taking care of an infirm child.

Sinclair was startled from her reverie by the screen door screeching open. The tall woman appeared with a large plate, a steaming mug, some silverware and a dingy-looking linen napkin.

"Your breakfast is ready, miss." Her tone was cold but the mockery had disappeared.

"Thank you . . ." Sinclair looked uncomfortable, then shrugged. "I understand your frustration, if in fact many caretakers have been reluctant to undertake the challenge of teaching . . . a child, with . . . um, problems." She glanced out at the yard, and tried to gather her thoughts, despite the grumbling of her stomach as she caught the tantalizing smells from the plate.

"I want you to know I intend to give Mr. McCloud an opportunity to explain himself today." She gave the other woman a thin smile. "And perhaps we'll come to a mutual understanding regarding my duties here."

The woman set the plate, cup and napkin on a small pine table, wiped her hands on her apron and glowered down at Sinclair.

"I'm Lettie Thorp, the housekeeper here at the Cripple Creek. I didn't mean for you to take offense at what I said, but we've had a regular parade of ladies to take care of that young'n, and the Boss, he seems to forget to tell most of 'em that child ain't quite all there. Lives in a world of her own, that one. She can be a handful to take care of, and I got all the cooking, the laundry, the cleaning and near everything else that goes to keeping this place up. I ain't got no time for looking after a young'n, especially one that is feeb . . ." she swallowed the words as she caught Sinclair's expression. "That's tetched in the head."

The woman took a deep breath, as if all that talking had worn her out.

Sinclair nodded as she sat down and took a sip of the coffee. She nearly spit it out, but forced herself to

46

swallow instead. She wondered if the woman had used tar to brew it.

"I can understand why you might question my ability to cope, Miss Thorp."

The woman held up a large, callused hand. "Just call me Lettie. We don't go for fancy talk out here on the range."

"Of course, Lettie. And you must call me Sinclair."

"I reckon I'll call you Miss Sinclair, you being a well-spoke lady and all."

Sinclair nodded again. "Whatever you prefer. Now, let me assure you that despite the fact that Mr. McCloud did not fully apprise me of his sister's condition, I did make an agreement with the man. I expect to fulfill the terms of that bargain to the best of my ability. I will supervise Madison, try to teach her the things she needs to know and hope for the best."

Sinclair was starving and decided to signal the end of the conversation by eating her breakfast. She was enjoying the bacon, eggs and biscuits and didn't notice Lettie studying her carefully. When she finally looked up she was startled.

"Is something wrong?"

Lettie looked embarrassed. She wiped her hands on her faded calico apron, started to leave, then turned back from the doorway.

"Do you think that young'n could really learn anything?"

Sinclair chewed carefully, settled her napkin on her lap and smugly lifted her eyes to answer Lettie.

"I've observed the best methods of pedagogy for my entire life, and I believe with discipline, patience and the right attitude, anyone can learn. Even a child

47

with great . . . difficulties . . . can be trained. I intend to teach Madison, and I also intend that she shall learn."

Lettie Thorp shook her head as she closed the door behind her. "Well, God bless you both, because you're going to need it!"

Sinclair nearly laughed out loud, then considered Lettie's remark. Likely the woman was right, because despite Sinclair's boast, she had never been a teacher. Of course, she'd lived with one of the best teachers in the world, and if Professor Readford had instilled anything in his daughter, it was a love of learning. His position at the University of William Penn insured that she had access to a massive library, concerts and lectures of all kinds. She had attended the lyceums and she had even spent the previous summer at a Chautauqua, thoroughly engrossed in music, theater, literature and science.

She would simply review the basic things one needed to know to get along in the world, and develop ways to make the lessons interesting. She thought about the child sitting at the table, her hands filled with oatmeal. Perhaps she'd begin with table manners and the use of utensils. Madison would be a challenging pupil, but Sinclair relished a challenge.

Finishing her meal, Sinclair rose to get another cup of coffee. Once she had adjusted to the thick, dark taste she realized how bracing the liquid was on this rather cool spring morning. As she frowned down at her icy cold toes, she realized she should have taken the time to put her boots on. She heard a bright, tinkling sound as a shadow passed over her. Lifting her eyes, she nearly jumped back in surprise when she discovered Jefferson McCloud standing over her.

"I . . . I didn't hear you come up on the porch." She felt tongue-tied as she took in his western costume. A wide-brimmed dove gray felt hat she remembered from the night before covered black, too-long hair. A faded blue work shirt was stretched over broad shoulders, and a navy blue woolen vest was buttoned over top. Dark trousers were tucked into black leather boots that rose nearly to his knees. She could see small silver pieces attached to each boot heel, and she grinned up at him in delight.

Jefferson couldn't take his eyes off the vision before him. Sinclair Readford was enjoying her breakfast on the porch, wrapped in a blanket that couldn't hide the fact that she was a full-figured and shapely female. Hair the color of sunflower blossoms framed a heart-shaped face. He had seen her in the dark, and in dim candlelight, but he must have been a damn fool not to see how beautiful she was.

He felt a surge of liquid fire lunge through his veins, and he knew in an instant he'd better get this woman off the ranch. The last thing he needed was for his cowhands to be distracted by an attractive female. And if he didn't get rid of her for the sake of the men, he'd better do it for his own peace of mind. Because from the way his heart was thumping and the rush of heat traveling through his loins, she was going to serve as a major distraction to him. He needed to get her back to Ghost Horse Gulch. And even then he wasn't sure that'd be far enough away to keep his mind off her, now that he'd really taken a good look.

"Spurs, just like in all the stories. Real cowboys always wear spurs!"

Her face reflected wonder, and he couldn't help grinning at her.

"Keeps a man on a horse and helps the horse know who's boss," he responded.

Sinclair looked thoughtful for a moment, then smiled back at him.

"Perhaps that's where my riding instructor failed me. He told me I was a complete nincompoop when it came to riding, but perhaps if he'd given me silver spurs, I could have stayed on my horse."

Jefferson was drowning in two deep blue pools, and he didn't think he wanted anyone to pull him out. He could see a small dimple near the edge of Sinclair's soft pink mouth, and he had to resist the impulse to gently move one gloved finger along the edge of her face to explore it. He clenched his fist in order to curb the urge to touch her.

He took in her appearance, then remembered what he needed to tell her.

"I sent Ollie to town this morning with a buckboard to get your trunk. He should be back before noon, then you'll have something decent to cover yourself with." His gaze slowly traveled down her body, and he remembered the way she had leaned into him on the ride out to the ranch last night. He could have sworn the temperature rose at least ten degrees.

Sinclair prickled at the remark and pulled the blanket tighter about her.

"I explained my circumstances on the way out here last night, Mr. McCloud. I was accosted and threat-

ened, and I needed your help. I appreciate that
you . . ." she paused to frown, as if she couldn't quite
remember what he'd done for her, "assisted me, and
since you are fully aware that I had no choice but to
come to this ranch with you, I feel you deceived and
tricked me into taking this position." Her posture
was rigid and her voice prim and proper.

"Just how do you think I tricked you, Miss Readford?"

Her posture stiffened even more, and her mouth
formed a thin line, the dimple disappearing.

"You left a significant detail regarding your sister
unexplained. Of course, I did question your desperation, but since I was in equally desperate straits, I
had no choice. I couldn't stay out in the wilderness
by myself, and I certainly have no intention of returning to town and that awful Hank Borscht." She
pursed her lips at the man's name, her distaste obvious.

"So, I take it you've met Maddie, then." He held
his breath, waiting for her answer.

Brushing a curl from her eyes, Sinclair tossed her
head defiantly.

"I haven't actually met her, but I've seen her. Lettie
tells me that she suffers from an impairment, and it
was quite obvious that becoming her teacher will be
a significant challenge." She stiffened her shoulders
with pride. "And it just so happens it's a challenge I
feel confident to accept."

Jefferson could barely keep a straight face. The
proper little Miss Readford thought she could handle
Maddie. So far every woman he'd hired had given
up, taken off or mistreated the girl. Not one of them

had suggested they were up to the task of teaching her. This woman surprised him. Maybe she wouldn't run off like a jackrabbit sighting an eagle. He had to give her credit, she had spunk.

"I won't be holding you to that bargain, ma'am. I never intended to leave you out on the range in the middle of the night. And even if I'm not sure about your story, if you don't want to go back to the Blue Willow, it ought to be your decision. The sporting life isn't for everyone."

Sinclair's cheeks grew rosy with color at Jefferson's reference to the parlor house. "I *am* the daughter of Professor Readford of Philadelphia. Contacting my father is impossible, since he left for Egypt nearly two weeks ago. Until my aunt Tilly returns to Ghost Horse Gulch, I can't prove my identity, and you will simply have to trust me." She gave him a brilliant smile.

"I've never played any sports except lawn tennis and croquet, and I am who I say I am. But, more importantly Mr. McCloud, I consider my word to be a pledge of honor. I made a bargain with you, and I fully intend to honor my part. I agreed to remain here and teach your sister until the fall roundup."

She held out her hand anticipating a handshake. She got a nervous shake of the head instead.

"There's no reason for you to feel obligated, ma'am. Lettie can keep an eye on Maddie, just like she's been doing the past few days since Mrs. Tubbs left. I can't ask you to be held to a promise made without knowing all the facts, even if I'm desperate. When Ollie gets back with your things, you just let him know where you want to go, and he'll see you get there, safe and sound."

He tipped his hat and grinned down at her. She felt her mouth go dry and her heart flutter in response. His chocolate eyes became darker, more sultry.

"It's been a pure pleasure, Miss Sinclair Readford. Best of luck to you."

Before Sinclair could respond, he'd turned with a quiet jingle to disappear down the steps and around the corner. By the time she'd opened her mouth to inform him that she had no intention of going anywhere, he was galloping into the deep grasslands surrounding the ranch.

Sinclair picked up her, plate, cup, silverware and napkin. Lifting her head proudly, she smiled. She'd just have to prove to Mr. McCloud that she was made of sterner stuff than he thought. A Readford never backed down from a challenge. She'd just show him.

Chapter Four

Sinclair thought she'd seen wet, filthy, mongrel dogs that weren't as smelly as little Madison McCloud. Her clothes were too small, and the cloth so faded it was impossible to determine if there had ever been any pattern to the fabric at all. Long strings of dirty, dank hair hung about the girl's face, which was still smeared with the remains of her breakfast. She had an unkempt, abandoned air about her as she sat in the corner of her room, rocking and singing gibberish in a monotone.

Sinclair was still waiting for her trunk to arrive, but the morning was warming up, and it occurred to her that she should take advantage of the mild weather. Marching downstairs with determination, she put her hands on her hips and gave the house-keeper an uncompromising look.

"Lettie, could you put several large pans of water on the stove?"

Lettie stopped kneading her bread dough long enough to consider the question.

"You ain't needing a bath already, are you? I got more to do 'round here than I can handle, and if you're thinking 'bout taking a bath more'n once every week or so, you're gonna have to haul your own water."

Sinclair was becoming used to the woman's abrupt manner and complaints and she took this latest litany in stride.

"The bath isn't for me, although heaven knows after traveling several thousand miles across every kind of country you can imagine, I need a good soak in the tub."

Grabbing a bucket, she started out of the door to the pump she'd seen in the yard, midway between the barn and the house. She'd just get the water herself if Lettie was too busy. She jumped with surprise when the bucket was snatched out of her hand and Lettie gave her a hard shove back into the house.

"Land's sake, woman. You can't go traipsing 'round this ranch in your undies, or you'll have every lovesick and lonesome cowboy within fifty miles standing out here with posies in his hand, hopin' to court you. Let me get the water and when it's ready I'll bring the tin tub in here."

She raised an eyebrow at Sinclair as she slipped through the door. "You aiming to scrub that young'un?"

Sinclair twisted her hair, trying to hide her nervousness.

"She's a mess, and I believe it will require full-body immersion in order to remove the filth clinging to her. It appears to have been quite some time since she's had a bath."

Lettie shrugged. "That Tubbs woman washed her face and hands when she first got here, but Maddie put up such a fuss that she finally just gave up and let her be most of the time."

Sinclair wanted to inquire about the plight of the mysterious Mrs. Tubbs, and the circumstances surrounding her sudden departure from the Cripple Creek Ranch, but she was also impatient to get Madison cleaned up. She'd have to postpone her questions until later. She went back up to her room to gather the necessary equipment.

By the time Sinclair came downstairs again, Ollie was in the kitchen enjoying his breakfast. He stood to greet Sinclair with a polite nod.

"Morning, ma'am. Hope you're finding ever'thing at the Cripple Creek to your likin'."

Sinclair smiled, then gave Ollie a saucy wink. "Lettie finds me a terrible nuisance. I had no idea Madison was suffering from an impairment. Your boss seems to think I'm too incompetent to care for his sister and I believe he's summarily dismissed me this morning."

She tossed a blond curl back over her shoulder and gave Ollie a flirty smile. "But the view is magnificent, the air so fresh and clean, I wish I had a spoon to eat it with, and I am inspired by the adventure of finally arriving in the wild, untamed West." She spread her arms wide. "All in all, an interesting morning so far."

Ollie let out a loud laugh. "Ma'am, you got some of the best damn words I ever heared. If I knowed how to write, I'd put 'em in a book, so's when somebody needed taking down a peg or two, I could use one of them there fancy words."

Sinclair gave him an appalled look. She couldn't imagine a person managing to live without the beauty of books.

"If you ever decide you would like to learn to read and write, I'd be pleased to teach you, Ollie. After all, I believe it was your advice that influenced Mr. McCloud last night, otherwise he'd likely have left me to the wild beasts and Indians."

Ollie shook his head. "The boss wouldn't never leave no lady out on the range in the dark, even if he does seem a might hard. He's got his troubles, the boss does."

Lettie smiled with great affection as she refilled his cup. "That he does. More'n his share if you ask me."

Ollie seemed oblivious to the warmth in Lettie's eyes as he returned to his plate of biscuits, bacon and eggs.

"Brought that trunk of yours back from town. I'll have the boys unload it, if you're gonna stay. The boss said something 'bout you might decide to move on when you'd seen the lay of the land." He glanced at her over his coffee cup.

"Boss said I was to take you wherever you wanted to go and see to it you had fare to get you off."

Sinclair gave an exasperated moan and rolled her eyes. "You all seem to have the utmost confidence in my abilities, it's so inspiring. Well, *I* take the agreement we made last night seriously, even if Mr. McCloud doesn't. He expects me to go running back to Philadelphia with my tail between my legs. I plan to stay right here in Montana, on this ranch, and fulfill my duties to teach Madison." She folded her arms in front of her. "So, you can take my things up to the room at the top of the stairs." Straightening her shoulders, she tapped her foot impatiently on the smooth wooden floor.

Ollie grinned. "Don't give no mind to the boss. Sometimes he gets a little worked up over things. Just let him blow off some steam and ignore him. He'll be fine."

Sinclair gave him another flirty smile. "Ignoring him is exactly what I plan to do!"

She turned toward the stove. "Lettie, is that water warm enough for a bath?"

Dipping her fingers into one of the large pans, Lettie nodded.

Sinclair turned to march out of the room when she caught Lettie exchanging a look with Ollie. They both started to laugh at nearly the same moment.

"Boss thought he had troubles before, but he don't know how much calamity can come wrapped up in petticoats." Ollie shook his head, stood and was still grinning when he let the screen door slam behind him.

The screams brought several hands running to the house, worried that a wild animal had managed to get inside and terrify the women. Lettie assured them they didn't need to draw their guns.

Sinclair was soaked to the bone and as mad as the

proverbial wet hen. She had been forced to drag Madison down the stairs, with the child pulling and fighting her every inch of the way.

When they reached the kitchen and Madison spied the tub in the center of the room, she'd let out a wail and nearly scrambled halfway back up the stairs before Sinclair could catch her again. The child then proceeded to slump down heavily upon the steps and refuse to budge. It took both Lettie and Sinclair to carry her back into the kitchen.

Lettie held Madison's feet while Sinclair removed her dress and pantaloons. One look at the underwear and Sinclair ordered them tossed into the flames of the woodstove.

The two women lifted a kicking and screaming Madison to unceremoniously dump her into the tub, more for self-preservation than anything else. The water sloshed over the side and Madison came up spitting and fighting. Sinclair was ready for her.

With a bar of soap in one hand and a large flannel cloth in the other, she quickly grabbed one of the girl's arms to give it a good scrubbing. She managed to avoid Maddie's teeth, remove most of the dirt, then slide out of the way as Lettie dunked her under the water.

When Maddie came up again, Sinclair was on the other side, where she could repeat the procedure. With Lettie holding firmly to the girl's shoulders, Sinclair managed to rub the bar of soap into Maddie's hair. Another dunk beneath the water and Sinclair figured they had at least removed the first layer of dirt. She decided to conserve their energy to battle another day.

Sinclair and Lettie were thoroughly soaked, since most of the water from the tub was now on the floor. When Madison stood to escape, the women quickly wrapped a cotton blanket around her and they each grabbed a corner to carry the girl upstairs.

There was more twisting, screaming and kicking, but the blanket kept the writhing girl confined until they could deposit her on the small pallet in her room. She quickly kicked off the covering and returned to her favorite corner, rocking and sobbing softly.

Sinclair stood dripping water on the floor, biting her lip and trying to decide what to do. It upset her that she'd been forced to be so rough in order to execute the bath. She picked up the blanket to cover Madison, but her skin crawled with goosebumps at the child's reaction to her. Madison pulled away from her, putting her hands in front of her face, as if she anticipated an attack. As quietly and gently as she could, Sinclair wrapped the blanket around the girl's shoulders as she knelt down to the same level.

"Maddie, my name is Sinclair, and I'm going to take care of you. I'm going to make sure you have clean clothes to wear and decent food to eat." She made her voice as soothing as she could manage under the circumstances. "I want us to be friends."

Sinclair resisted the urge to touch the child, knowing it was too soon. "I know it's going to take time for us to get acquainted." There was no response from Madison McCloud.

"I'm sorry, Maddie. I promise I won't ever hurt you and I'll never let anyone else harm you." She stretched a hand up to smooth the girl's hair, but

Maddie yanked away from her, as if in fear.

Sinclair realized she would need to be patient. She didn't know this child's history, but there was sadness, loss and pain in the gray eyes that glared at her. If people thought she was feebleminded, treated her like an animal and ignored her most of the time, it was no wonder she chose to live in a world of her own.

Sinclair stood, shivered, then wrapped her arms around herself. "It appears we've both had a bath this morning, so I'm going to go change my clothes." Studying the furnishings in the room again, she noted the small pallet thrown on the floor and covered with a thin quilt. The only other piece of furniture was a scarred pine chest of drawers. The wallpaper in the room was faded, and dark velvet draperies obscured most of the light, filling the space with shadows.

"I'm going to do something about this room too. I thought mine was dreary, but this place is absolutely depressing."

Maddie had resumed her rocking and monotone song. Sinclair smiled at her and for one brief moment she could have sworn there was a flicker of interest in the silver eyes staring back at her. Then, as if a curtain had been suddenly drawn, the vacant stare returned.

It was enough to intrigue Sinclair. She sensed Madison McCloud was choosing to hide within herself. The sputtering, fighting child of the bath was no complacent imbecile. Sinclair had read about the Pennsylvania Training School for the Feebleminded and remembered such infirmities had different characteristics. She had a notion Maddie wasn't as profound as many of the students, and she'd read some of the residents there had been trained to become productive citizens.

Carefully closing the door behind her, Sinclair turned, only to smack into a hard, muscular chest attached to one very angry cowboy.

"What the hell have you been doing to my sister?" Jefferson McCloud demanded. His hands clenched her arms like a vise; there was granite in the line to his jaw and iron in his voice. The chocolate warmth she'd viewed earlier in his eyes had been replaced with a dark, malevolent iciness.

Sinclair tried to step back to gather her wits, but he refused to ease his hold on her. Tossing her head, she swallowed and tried to ignore the way his touch caused small ripples of awareness to dance up her arms.

"I was giving Madison a bath, trying to remove some of the filth you've allowed to accumulate on her." She stared up at him, her mouth hard and her voice filled with accusation. "That little girl is in need of a great deal more than simple caretaking." She swallowed again as his eyes narrowed and his hands seemed to pinch the skin of her upper arms. "What kind of man allows his own sister to be kept like an animal?"

With an angry growl, Jefferson McCloud released her, taking a step back and looking for an instant as if he wanted to strike out at her. Sinclair resisted the urge to cringe away from him, instinctively understanding he wouldn't hurt her, despite his anger at her words.

His glance took in her appearance and his complexion seemed to pale for a few moments.

"Woman, has your profession cured you of the notion of wearing clothes?"

When she looked down and realized how revealing her wet things were, Sinclair blushed a deep rose. She attempted to cover herself, then in desperation she flew across the hallway to her room. Snatching open the door, she slipped behind it. With only her head peeking out, she confronted Boss McCloud.

"As I said before, I was giving your sister a much-needed bath." She paused, giving a loud sneeze, then tried to wipe her nose as daintily as possible. "I was forced to do so in my underclothes since Ollie just got here with my trunk. And I assure you, sir, I have never indulged in the profession to which you refer. I am not . . . a . . ." She couldn't think of the proper thing to call it; and stammered as she searched for an appropriate, ladylike phrase.

His mood seemed to change from anger to mild amusement as he studied her discomfort. "Soiled dove, harlot, parlor girl, lady of the evening?"

"Whore," she snapped, then her hand covered her mouth as she realized what she had just said. She was humiliated by her outburst, and she could feel her face warm with an embarrassed blush.

"Well, we haven't exactly sorted out what you are, now have we, ma'am?" He took several long strides across the hall, his eyes danced with mischief and his lip curled into a sarcastic smile. "But if you've done anything to hurt my sister, I assure you I can be one ornery, ill-tempered son of a bitch when I want to be."

Sinclair forgot her wet clothes as she came around

the door with her fists held high. She knew her cheeks were now bright spots of red, and she suspected her blue eyes were flashing with anger. Her temper was in full bloom and she didn't give a tinker's damn. This arrogant cowboy had really made her mad this time.

"There's no doubt in my mind you're all of those things, sir, and likely much worse. In fact, it takes no stretch of the imagination to see you are an abusive, ignorant jackass who makes up his mind before he even has all of his facts in order." She inched closer to McCloud, giving him a hard-eyed glare.

"But, if I am to be in charge of your sister, I don't expect to be accosted in the hallway and threatened every time I attempt to improve her living conditions." She folded her arms firmly across her breasts, waiting for his response. She tapped her bare foot against the floor in agitation.

Her attack seemed to have left Jefferson McCloud speechless. For a brief moment, Sinclair thought he intended to grab her again, and she took a step away from him. He narrowed his eyes, but he didn't make any move to touch her.

Finally he seemed to find his voice again. "I told you this morning, I don't expect you to stay out here and take care of Maddie." He waved his arm indicating the doorway downstairs. "I figured you would have high-tailed it out of here by now. A fancy woman like you doesn't belong on a ranch."

Sinclair stared at him, hardly able to believe what she'd just heard. It seemed impossible to imagine, but she felt her temper grow even hotter as she considered the implications of his words. Her mouth drew itself into a hard, thin line.

"You don't know anything about me, *Boss* McCloud." Her voice became cold as ice as she glared up at him. "You don't know what kind of woman I am. You're just using the same silly arguments men always use to keep women in our place. You think I'm some weak, pathetic little thing." She punctuated her remarks by poking her finger sharply in his chest. "You think I can't take care of myself and shouldn't wander too far from the safety of my parlor. You think I'm just waiting for some man to come along to sweep me up into his arms and protect me." She wanted to wipe that insolent smirk off his face. She took a step back, tossed her head and gave him a furious glare. "Well, I don't need any man to take care of me. Not my father and certainly not you. I can take care of Maddie, and I can take care of myself."

"Miss Readford, I hardly think . . ."

She gave him another contemptuous look. "Precisely the problem with most men, they simply don't think."

She straightened her shoulders and lifted her head with pride. "Don't you dare try to tell me who I am, and don't ever presume to know what I can do." With that she spun on her heel, marched back into her room and slammed the door in his face.

Leaning back against the door, she felt tears prickle the back of her eyes. She shook her head, refusing to let Jefferson McCloud make her cry. He was an infuriating man, calling her wicked names, staring at her as if he could see right through her wet clothing.

She shivered at the memory of his eyes as they lingered on the swell of her breasts. There had been anger in his look, and something else she didn't understand, a longing that appeared for only an instant.

Angry with herself for displaying such a fit of temper, she paced across the room to grab a linen towel hanging on the washstand. She rubbed her arms and noticed there was still a spot of red on her upper arms where McCloud had gripped her. She felt a surge of self-pity. She would sport bruises the next day; her fair skin always marked easily. She considered showing them to Boss McCloud as proof of his savage tendencies. He couldn't know that if she only bumped against a piece of furniture she would be black and blue the next day.

Stripping off her wet clothes, she considered his words and her temper came back full force. He was just like her father, always lecturing about proper behavior and what women could and shouldn't do. She threw her corset on the floor, cursing all men who made rules for women.

Snatching her dressing gown from the pile of clothing in her trunk, she wrapped the soft white cambric about her and stood glaring into the mirror on the wall.

Yanking her brush through her hair, she tried to figure out a strategy for dealing with the difficult, opinionated cowboy. She grimaced as she worked the snarls out of her hair. Men were so complex, and she'd never excelled at managing them the way some of her friends did. It seemed her friends had only to snap their fingers and gentlemen bowed before them, eager to do their bidding.

Of course, Jefferson Cloudc was no gentleman by any stretch of the imagination. She had an idea he'd never bow before any man or woman. He appeared to be a man who was used to getting his own way, and he'd made it clear he intended to get rid of Sinclair, in any manner necessary.

Struggling with the emotions churning through her, Sinclair tried to forget that brief, hot, yearning look she'd seen on his face. It unnerved her. There was a hunger she didn't understand, and it created a dark, dangerous response deep within her. She gave herself a shake. She couldn't afford to develop any kind of sympathy for the man. He planned to send her away, and that made her furious.

She was tired of being dismissed as a weak and powerless female. Her father refused to take her to Egypt with him because he said she couldn't endure the heat or abysmal conditions. Now Boss McCloud insisted she was some kind of fragile, useless soiled . . . party lady. She gave a disgusted sigh. Men preferred women who swooned at the slightest provocation, giggled behind their fans and couldn't bother their pretty heads with a serious thought. Her own father had called her educated to a fault. She sniffed. As if any human being could be too well-read or too intelligent. She'd even overheard Professor Readford complaining to a colleague that he would be forced to arrange a marriage for Sinclair when he returned for the fall semester to insure she didn't become a bluestocking old maid left on the shelf.

She tossed her brush back into the depths of the trunk, then threw herself down on the bed to consider her alternatives. She had come to the West in search of her aunt Tilly, but also in search of herself. She was tired of being someone else's ideal. She wanted to explore her own talents, and taking care of Madison McCloud was a perfect opportunity to prove she could manage her own life. She stared at the ceiling in dismay. There was only one obstacle to achieving her goal, but it was tall, obstinate and unyielding. She would have to find a way to manage Jefferson McCloud, and the thought was both terrifying and exciting at the same time. Sinclair simply couldn't understand why she found the man so fascinating. Sitting up, she decided she could stew over the problem of dealing with Boss McCloud all day and never find a solution. She would simply take care of Maddie and prove him wrong.

Standing before the window and watching the long-legged McCloud cross the yard to the corral, she pondered her choices. She felt the corners of her mouth lift in a devilish smile. Proving that man wrong would be a delightful challenge.

Chapter Five

Sinclair yanked petticoats, dresses, assorted under-garments and accessories from her trunk in a flurry of distraction.

Tossing a powder-blue silk evening gown onto the bed, she gave a snort of annoyance and shook her head.

Where in heaven's name did she think she was going when she packed this trunk? Evening gowns, afternoon dresses for tea and even a dark burgundy velvet riding costume lay crumbled on the floor. She pushed a damp tendril of hair back from her face and scowled at the collection of clothing at her feet. There were few outfits fit for working on a cattle ranch, that was for sure. Plopping herself down on the hard wooden chair in one corner, she paused to consider her predicament.

Sinclair rarely indulged in self-pity, but she recognized that she was totally incompetent to deal with the circumstances of her employment. Despite all her blustering assurances to Boss McCloud, she knew next to nothing about taking care of children. She certainly wasn't qualified to care for a child like Madison. Yet she couldn't bring herself to admit defeat, agree with McCloud and return to Ghost Horse Gulch.

She also instinctively knew if she returned to town, she wouldn't be able to avoid another confrontation with Hank Borscht. She shivered at the thought. There was a hard, cold, darkness in that man's eyes that terrified her.

She lifted her head to examine the contents of the trunk again. Buried near the bottom of the pile of clothing were several day dresses she had packed to wrap some more fragile items. She shook out the faded blue-and-green calico house dresses and grinned. They weren't fashionable, but they were certainly serviceable. Smoothing the wrinkles from the blue floral-print outfit, she held it up against her. It would do nicely for daily wear.

Sinclair stripped off her wet undergarments and rubbed herself dry with a thick piece of linen she had discovered carefully folded beneath the washstand. Peering into the china pitcher, she noticed there was now tepid water filling it nearly to the brim. She whispered a brief word of thanks to Lettie. Despite the woman's complaints, she appeared to be a conscientious housekeeper.

Pulling on her corset, chemise and pantaloons, Sinclair had to laugh at the silkiness of the fabric and fine embroidery along the edges of each lace insert.

Considering the amount of time she'd spent prancing around in her underclothes lately, she should be grateful they were so finely made.

She decided to dispense with more than one petticoat and finished fastening the tiny glass buttons on the dress. Finally she pulled out a brush and tried to put the wild mane curling down her back into some kind of order. She found hairpins in one of the small bags tucked within the depths of her trunk. Gazing into the mirror before her, she finally managed to twist the mass of blond curls into a small, tight bun at the nape of her neck. Dipping one finger into the pitcher, she slicked several errant wisps of hair back into place. She straightened her spine, then turned back to face the mess she'd created in her room.

The bright sunshine of the day beckoned her. Glancing at the chaos, she decided to wait until later in the afternoon to put her gowns on the row of pegs hanging along one wall. She was in Montana, on a ranch . . . and her heart fluttered with the excitement of it. Sitting back down on the chair to don her stockings and boots, she found herself eager to begin investigating her new home. She bustled out of the room and down the stairs.

Sinclair took her time exploring the first floor. She found an abundance of velvet draperies, horsehair couches, overstuffed chairs, tasseled damask and mahogany furniture. Her fingers trailed along a marble-topped table, and she sniffed at the accumulation of dust. It appeared Lettie didn't take much interest in keeping these rooms in order. And somehow she couldn't picture the long-legged, rugged Boss

McCloudud perched on the edge of one of these over-stuffed chairs sipping tea.

She nearly let out a squeal of delight when she entered the library. At least there were books in the house, hundreds of them, displayed in several glass-fronted cabinets. A huge oak desk dominated the room and a faint odor of tobacco lingered in the air. Sinclair guessed this to be the McCloud lair. She could picture him seated in the huge leather chair, boots set comfortably on the center of the desk, a glass of whiskey before him and the bright ember of a cigarette clamped between his white teeth.

She blushed as she realized she conjured the image of her employer a bit more clearly than was ladylike or appropriate. He was a cowboy, for heaven's sake, one of those wild, untamed breeds she had read about in the Penny Dreadfuls. Although she had to admit, the real thing was a bit intimidating and certainly more exciting. She pushed his image out of her head and examined the books more carefully.

There were books on the law, which she presumed to be the property of Judge McCloud. There was a shelf of poetry and one filled with romantic novels. Cattlemen quarterly magazines were stacked on top of one cabinet.

She continued to wander through a dining room and into a small parlor. To her delight she found a harpsichord tucked in one corner. She couldn't resist the temptation to play a few notes, letting her fingers skip across the keys. Sighing as the music rolled out of the instrument she decided if she had books and music, she could survive anywhere.

"Miss, you back here?" Lettie's voice was hushed

and tentative. It surprised Sinclair. Her brief encounter with the woman that morning had led her to believe Lettie was a fearless, salt-of-the-earth type.

"I'm here . . . in the . . . music room, Lettie."

Lettie entered the dark room twisting her apron and looking apprehensive.

"Mayhap you shouldn't be in here playing the pianey. The Boss, well . . ." She glanced over her shoulder as if afraid McCloud might be standing behind her, "he wouldn't like it."

Sinclair let her fingers drift over the keys lightly, then gently closed the cover. She could see the obvious concern on Lettie's face. Why would Boss McCloud care about someone playing a very old, very out-of-tune instrument? There were so many questions in this house, and Sinclair was always intrigued by any mystery.

"I was just exploring, trying to get some idea of the layout of the house. It's quite interesting, isn't it?"

Lettie waved a hand in derision. "Damned tomb, if you ask me. I hope you don't intend to be sitting around and sipping tea someplace different every day. I ain't got the time to dust and fluff pillows for city folk."

"I don't expect you to wait on me, Lettie. As for these rooms, if I decide I'd like to sit in them, I'll just dust them myself." Sinclair lifted her chin as she shrugged past Lettie and headed toward the kitchen.

"I came back down to help you clean up the mess. I'm sorry the bath turned into such a disaster. That child reacts to water like a cat."

"Lordy, ain't that the truth." Lettie waved a hand. "I don't need no help with the mopping up, though, it was high time this floor had a good scrubbing anyhow."

Sinclair stood at the kitchen door. The tub was gone and the floor was still shiny from the water spilled during Maddie's bath.

"Well, if you don't need me, I'd best check in on Maddie. I probably frightened the poor child terribly, and I can honestly confess I don't relish the task of dressing her." Sinclair straightened her shoulders. "But as my father always says, the best way to tackle an unpleasant task is to get it over with."

Lettie nodded in agreement. "Don't let the girl fool you neither. She can take care of herself . . . just walk her out to the privy and give her some time. She ain't as feeble as she tries to let on."

Sinclair paused thoughtfully. "I think you're right about that, Lettie. It appears to me that child is lost inside of herself."

Lettie opened her mouth and looked as if she wanted to say something, then she abruptly snapped it shut again. "Best you speak with the boss about that."

Sinclair wandered back through the hallway to the stairs, taking her time climbing to the top, her hand brushing against the smooth wood of the banister. She had so many questions for Boss McCloud, if he ever stopped yelling at her long enough to carry on a conversation. What had made his sister a terrified, withdrawn waif? Who built this huge monstrosity of a house in the middle of cattle country? Why didn't he want anyone to play the harpsichord? And, furthermore, what had she done to offend him and make him dislike her so much?

Pausing at the top of the stairs, she stood staring at Maddie's door. How in the world was she going to convince this child she wasn't an evil witch, swooping down to inflict pain and suffering upon her? Sinclair tried to remember how she was comforted when she was a child. Closing her eyes, she could picture her mother sitting in a corner of her room, singing softly. She tried to recall the words, but could only hum the tune.

Opening the door, she continued to hum, letting the soft, gentle lullaby drift to fill the dark shadows of Maddie's room. The child sat huddled in a corner, rocking herself and making those sad, pitiful sounds. She gave no sign of recognition when Sinclair approached her, but she didn't withdraw or act terrified. Taking that as a good sign, Sinclair hummed a bit louder. She kept humming as she opened drawers in search of clothing for the girl.

Sinclair's hum turned into a whistle of derision when she pulled out several faded and worn dresses. They appeared to be too small for the girl seated behind her, but the other drawers revealed only a few sets of underclothes, some mismatched stockings with large holes in them and a moth-eaten sweater.

"Madison McCloud, is this your wardrobe?" Sinclair carried the pathetic items to the child and held them at arm's length.

"No wonder you want to stay in this room all the time. They dress you like a foundling. Why, I've seen street urchins in Philadelphia garbed better than this." She tossed the offending garments across the room in disgust.

Here was another question for Boss McCloud.

Why do you care more about your stupid cows than you do your own flesh and blood? Pacing the room, she leaned against the window frame, glancing up at the heavy draperies blocking the light.

"I can't understand why every window in this house has these dark, dreary coverings that block the beautiful sky and sunshine outside." With one yank she pulled the draperies down to the floor. Bright, clear light flooded the room. Sinclair gave a satisfied nod. She turned back to Maddie, who had stopped rocking and was looking up at her with surprise clearly reflected in her eyes.

"From now on, things are going to be different around here, Miss Maddie. Your room is definitely in need of redecorating, and I guess I'll tackle that first. Then we'll see about getting you more fashionably attired. And after that—" she brushed the dust from her hands and stood considering the little girl seated at her feet—"we'll find some interesting things to do."

Squatting down to meet Maddie's eyes directly, she was thrilled to see curiosity had momentarily displaced the lost, lonely look.

"Tell me, sweetie, what do folks around here do for fun?"

Maddie remained silent, but Sinclair would later swear that a small ghost of a smile flickered across the child's face.

By the time Jefferson McCloud returned to the ranch house, he felt as if he'd swallowed most of the dust in Montana. He and the ranch hands had trailed most of the herd up to the high country. He'd been reluctant to leave his men out on the range without him. Jefferson never asked a hand to do anything he himself wouldn't do, and it irked him to be riding back to the house that evening. But, he'd left a crazy woman in charge of his sister. Despite Miss Readford's low opinion of him and high opinion of herself, he needed to make sure she could handle the job.

He kept telling himself he was going home because of Maddie. Whenever the image of Miss Readford with her wet clothes plastered against her body, revealing all those soft curves and full, round feminine delights surfaced, he had pushed the memory from his mind. He told his horse they were making the long trek back to the ranch at twilight for his sister's sake, but Old Pete just looked skeptical.

When he finally reached the steps to the house, he sniffed. Something smelled awfully good. Scraping his boots before opening the screen door, he paused at the sound of soft, tinkling female laughter. A deep, baritone laugh joined it and Jefferson frowned.

He discovered Sinclair Readford seated at the kitchen table engaged in conversation with the handsome man across from her. They didn't notice Jefferson entering the room to stand in the shadows.

"Honestly, my lord, you can't believe how difficult it was for my father to convince the clan I wasn't a witch. They were sure I'd put a curse on them and wouldn't let us leave until it was lifted."

Lord Evan Billingsley laughed again, his brilliant, white smile beaming at Sinclair. "I've had a few encounters with the Scots myself, and I know how bloody tough they can be."

Jefferson coughed, and the couple seated at the table turned toward him as he stepped into the light and nodded imperceptibly.

"Billingsley. Didn't know you planned to make a social call tonight or I'd have come back sooner." Jefferson jerked the chair next to Sinclair and sat down, carelessly flinging his wide-brimmed felt hat toward a peg, where it caught easily.

"I just stopped by on my way back from Helena. Your father sent some papers to you." He gave Jefferson a quizzical look. "I gave them to your housekeeper." He paused to grin at Sinclair. "Your delightful Miss Readford invited me to dinner, and I must confess, in her company I've quite lost track of the time."

Usually Jefferson didn't find the company of Evan Billingsley irritating. In fact, the man was intelligent, a good cattleman and a reliable neighbor. His spread butted up against the Cripple Creek, and the two men had managed to forge a bond of friendship. Tonight Jefferson found himself being outright rude to his nearest neighbor.

"Well, it's almost dark, Billingsley, so maybe you'd better get going. Unless of course you'd be interested in bunking in with me and the boys, then you can stash your gear down at the bunkhouse."

Sinclair frowned at the ill-mannered dismissal. She leaned toward Evan Billingsley, her eyes sympathetic. "I simply don't understand these wild, barbaric westerners," she whispered, "but leave it to Boss McCloud to spoil a wonderful evening."

She was rewarded with a dark scowl from Jefferson. "And she's not *my* Miss Readford."

Lord Billingsley rose to take Sinclair's hand in his.

He bent slightly at the waist and kissed her fingers with reverence. Jefferson's chair scraped the floor as he pushed himself to a stand, towering over the English lord.

"McCloud."

"Billingsley."

The two men glowered at each other, then Lord Billingsley nodded at Sinclair. "Remember, my dear, my door is always open to you." He gave Jefferson a sidelong glance, grinned and left.

Sinclair poured herself another cup of tea and shook her head. "Imagine finding an English Lord living way out here in the wilderness? I knew many of the British aristocracy had invested in cattle ranches, but I never thought I'd actually meet one of them living in Montana."

Jefferson tried to ignore her as he crossed to the stove to open the warmer. Lettie always left an extra meal in there, just in case he or Ollie came back to the ranch during the night. His stomach groaned at the sight of ham, potatoes, biscuits and succotash piled high on the plate. He was too hungry to have a conversation with the woman seated at the table.

It didn't matter anyway. Sinclair Readford could talk enough for both of them.

She rattled on about his lordship for a while, mentioning some connection to someone. Seemed he was kin to some other kin who might be kin to the royal family. Jefferson couldn't have cared less, because he didn't hold with royalty. He was a democratic, freedom-loving American. As far as he was concerned, Evan Billingsley was just another cattleman.

She was talking about Madison now, and Jefferson

slowed down his chewing enough to try to catch the gist of her words.

"I took it upon myself to relocate some items from the rest of the house. Lettie warned me you might be angry, and I promised to assure you that she's not responsible for anything I do, which is just silly, because I'm sure you're not the kind of man who would begrudge his sister a few creature comforts."

There was a pinched look to her face that warned Jefferson something was wrong. Her blue eyes, as blue as the sky in the middle of summer, were staring at him. His mind raced. Had she asked him a question? He took refuge in a noncommital grunt, hoping to deflect her.

"Is that your answer?"

What the heck had she asked him? Exercising his only other option, he shrugged.

She threw her hands up in the air in disgust. "Men! You really are all alike. How can I be expected to do my job if we can't agree on this one, simple issue?"

Jefferson shoved a forkful of food into his mouth and mumbled. He figured if he waited long enough, she would enlighten him about the subject of their conversation. Well, her conversation, because so far, he'd hardly said a word.

"I think it's important for the comfort of your sister, don't you agree?"

It seemed like a safe enough question, so Jefferson swallowed then answered her. "I'm agreeable to making her comfortable if that's what you're asking."

A smile lit up Sinclair's face and Jefferson nearly choked. Damn, she was beautiful enough to be dangerous.

"Well, finally . . . something we can agree on. The quilts were from the linen closet, so I'm not concerned about them. But Lettie told me I was not to take anything from the master bedroom. I tried to make do, but I really needed that washstand, and since the pitcher and bowl were with it . . ." She gave him a thin smile and looked panicked when he didn't answer. "I suppose if you are really upset I could just put it all back."

McCloud scowled at her, then he carefully set his fork down, folded his hands and leaned forward.

"Do I understand you've helped yourself to anything in my house you felt like taking, using the excuse that you're making my sister more comfortable?"

Sinclair swallowed as she twisted her hands in her lap, dropping her eyes to avoid the anger he knew was reflected on his face.

"I didn't think you would mind. After all, I was led to believe Maddie's mother has been dead for quite some time. It doesn't seem fair the child should be without simple creature comforts and that room should be . . ." She paused and wet her lips, causing McCloud to wonder how one woman could turn his blood cold one moment, then hot the next.

On the verge of an angry outburst, he managed to pull himself back under control. Clenching his fists tightly, he sat back in his chair, silently considering the woman sitting next to him.

"You're a self-righteous, opinionated, stubborn woman, aren't you, Miss Readford?" His words were clipped and cold.

She looked confused. "I, yes . . . I suppose I am.

81

But you appointed me to take care of Maddie, and in my opinion that makes me responsible for keeping her neat and clean, for making sure she is well fed and for providing some type of education." Sinclair folded her hands primly in front of her and lifted her chin.

Jefferson looked thoughtful, then pulled a cigar from his pocket and nodded in her direction. "Mind if I smoke?"

She shook her head.

He held the thin cheroot in his fingers, taking his time as he searched for a match. He lit the end, took several puffs then settled his gaze back on the irritating Miss Sinclair Readford.

"If you're planning to stay, then I suppose it's only fair that I tell you the whole story. Likely you've seen and heard enough to make you wonder. I'd rather fill in the details myself than have you believing gossip."

Sinclair leaned forward expectantly, her eyes bright with curiosity. "I can hardly wait to hear this, Boss."

Chapter Six

"I want to make it clear, I don't begrudge my sister any of the simple comforts you've provided for her. Anything that can make her happier should be done, not that I believe she's aware of much going on around her, but, I've got my own reasons for keeping my stepmother's things as they were."

Setting the cigar on the edge of his plate, he rose to refill his coffee cup from the blue graniteware pot sitting on the stove. He paced for a few minutes, while Sinclair sat silent. Finally he cleared his throat and continued.

"Bess was the kindest, most loving woman I've ever known. When the judge brought her out here from back east, I thought she was an angel. She was a tiny little thing, with dark hair and even darker eyes. She was educated and refined and to a boy raised without much care from womenfolk, she was a wonder."

"She met the judge back east?"

McCloud started to pace again. "Yup. Her father had some kind of government job in Washington. Anyway, she'd been engaged during the war, but her fiancé was killed at Gettysburg. I guess she was just keeping house for her pa, until my father met her. I didn't even know he was considering marriage again, then one beautiful spring day he arrived home with Bess."

His face wore a lonesome, far-away look, and he paused, as if he could picture her climbing out of a carriage.

Sinclair rubbed the edge of her stoneware cup with her index finger. "How long had your mother been dead when Bess came here?"

"Nearly fifteen years. She died when I was four, giving birth to another baby boy. He didn't make it either."

Sinclair felt tears fill her eyes, and she wished she had the courage to reach out and touch McCloud's hand in sympathy.

"My own mother died last year, but she was ill for a long time before that, so I know how difficult it can be."

He paused to glance down at her. "At least you have a father who cares about you, I went for years without even seeing mine." There was bitterness in his voice.

"But after Bess came to the ranch, my father stayed around more. For the first few years, anyway. Then, after Madison was born, he accepted the post of Circuit Court Judge, and began to travel. Bess didn't like living way out here, without the company of other women. I heard her beg him to let her live in Helena, but he's a cold-hearted bastard. He'd just ride off and leave her crying."

Sinclair lifted her eyes to meet his. His face was angry, his lips pursed and his chin thrown out defensively.

"Was Maddie always the way she is now, so silent and alone?"

He considered her question carefully, then shook his head.

"She seemed to be a pretty content child. She never cried much, she talked some and she laughed back then. Bess doted on her. They were hardly ever apart, except when the judge came home. Then they'd put Maddie in her own room. I remember Maddie sitting outside their bedroom door just wailing." He gave Sinclair an odd look. "Pitiful little thing, she didn't understand, and the fact is, that's about the only time I heard Maddie cry, until after her mother died."

Sinclair rose to refill the teapot with hot water. She could feel McCloud's dark eyes on her back as she worked with careful precision. She refused to let the man intimidate her.

Moving back to the table, Sinclair brushed up against him. She felt that now-familiar shiver and tried to keep her hands from shaking.

He waited until she was seated again to continue.

"Bess got worse. She couldn't sleep, so the judge got Doc Pritchard to give her laudanum. It didn't do her much good, but she kept taking it and begging to leave."

Sinclair frowned. "You sound as if you blame your father for his wife's illness, but surely if he cared enough to consult a doctor, he must have been worried about her."

McCloud's hands came down so hard on the table the tea in her cup sloshed over the side and the plates jumped.

"He didn't give a damn for Bess, he just hoped she'd get well enough to give him another son. I heard him tell her so once." Now the bitterness was clearly evident. "He told her I'd never amount to anything, so he needed more sons."

Sinclair stood to gently touch his arm. "I'm sure it was just something he said in anger, or while drunk. Surely it's not the kind of thing a father would say and mean."

McCloud pushed her hand away and stepped away from her. His voice rose as he answered her.

"Oh, he meant it all right. It's something he's told me nearly every day of my life. I'm a big disappointment to the judge. I refused to leave the ranch to study law, and I want nothing to do with politics. He said I was just like my mother's people, tied to this land, like a horse to a plow. He never felt the way I do about the Cripple Creek."

Sinclair could see the anger burning brightly in his eyes. Her heart ached for the boy he'd been, left alone, with a hard, angry father who demanded too much and gave too little. She could begin to understand why the attention of his stepmother had been so important to him. At least Bess had noticed him.

"Still, he must realize now that you're running this

ranch how capable you are." She sat down again to pour herself tea.

McCloud ground his cigar in his plate and shrugged. "Since Bess died I haven't seen him. He just sends me official letters, and I send back an official reply." There was bitterness in his voice.

Sinclair could almost feel the dark shadow of sadness haunting Jefferson McCloud. Despite what he said, she thought he did crave his father's approval. After all, hadn't she worked hard all of her life for the love and esteem of her own father? She thought it must be a universal desire to be the pride of one's family. She felt a glimmer of dislike for this Judge McCloud who could be so cruel to his own blood.

McCloud's eyes searched hers. "I suppose you've heard the rumor that Maddie killed her own mother?"

Sinclair felt a chill sweep over her body with the question. She twisted her hands, uncomfortable with her choices: Answer, and he'd know she'd been talking about his family behind his back, or lie and pretend she didn't know anything about it. She paused to wet her lips, considered and decided the truth was the best option.

"Lettie mentioned it, but it seemed so farfetched, I thought she must be mistaken."

His body went rigid and his voice deeper. "No mistake. Bess never would have died if it hadn't been for Madison climbing out that bedroom window. She was only four years old, but she was a determined climber. One day, during a storm, she wanted to see the lightning and she went out onto the roof. Bess screamed for help, then went out after her."

Sinclair covered her mouth in horror. She was helpless to stop the story, but suddenly she didn't want to solve this mystery. It was too painful and ugly.

"Madison couldn't have known . . ." she whispered.

"No, she didn't even think about what she was doing, but that doesn't change anything. Bess slipped and fell. When we came running to the house, we found her near the rose garden, her neck broken." Emotion choked his voice.

"But, surely you don't think Madison was responsible. She was just a child, exploring."

Jefferson McCloud shook his head. "Maybe she wasn't directly responsible, but she seemed to know that something terrible had happened. She sat on the roof, crying for her mother." He glanced at Sinclair. "She screamed until she was hoarse. The day of the funeral we found her sitting and rocking." He shook his head. "You know how she does. The judge repeatedly ordered her to stop. When she didn't listen he grew more and more angry, until finally he slapped her. She's never said a word since Bess died, and most of the time she just sits and rocks, singing that gibberish." He gave Sinclair a sad smile.

"And you keep your stepmother's room as some sort of shrine?"

McCloud folded his arms in front of him. "I don't want people messing with her memory. Tomorrow you can replace the things you took, then stay out of there."

Sinclair stood so quickly the chair she'd been sitting on crashed to the floor. She ignored it. She waved her hands in the air in front of her and her voice snapped.

"That is the most ridiculous thing I've ever heard. Why should Maddie do without simply because you and your father cannot face reality? Bess McCloud is dead. That's the simple truth, and keeping her room intact won't bring her back."

McCloud stepped forward, and for just a moment she felt a flicker of fear crawl up her spine. His expression held a darkness, a hard anger that propelled her backward, away from him.

"You don't know a damned thing about it, so just keep to your own business of taking care of Maddie." His voice thundered in Sinclair's ears as he took another step toward her.

In an instant she reversed her course, matching his step forward, her fear dissolving in the face of anger. She found herself within inches of touching McCloud. Fury wafted off him like steam off a boiling kettle, but she had no intention of backing down.

"That's what I'm trying to do, but you make the job nearly impossible. Her room is a disgrace, she sleeps on a pallet on the floor like a dog, and until today she had one thin blanket to cover herself. Her clothes are rags and you feed her slop. In fact, I'm of the opinion you take better care of your cattle than you do your own flesh and blood."

Sinclair knew she'd gone too far. She could see a vein begin to throb in his throat and his eyes went completely dark, reminding her of midnight on a moonless night.

"You got no business telling me how to take care of my sister. You're hired help, Miss Readford. Despite your fancy ways I have every reason to believe you're nothing more than a common whore who thinks to better herself." His words poured over her like ice, making the blood in her veins run cold.

His hand suddenly jutted out and caught her by the shoulder, pulling her toward him and clamping her to his hard, unyielding length.

A metallic flavor filled her mouth, and she knew it was fear, fear so intense, her tongue felt thick with the taste of it.

His body was lean and the muscles of his arm bulged where he held her. His lips twisted into a mirthless smirk.

"In fact, maybe I should sample the goods. Just to see if I'm wasting your real talents using you to care for Maddie instead of taking you to my bed."

Before she could react, his lips came down hard on hers, shocking her with their harsh, demanding heat. She struggled against him, but he held her firmly, refusing to release her and increasing the pressure on her mouth.

After a moment she felt him relax. The tip of his tongue brushed against her lips, probing. She heard a small moan, then realized it had come from deep within her. Despite the violence of his attack, she was leaning into him, savoring his kiss. She snapped back to reality and gave him a defiant push.

He released her, a look of surprise on his face, his eyes now warm with that disturbing heat she'd witnessed earlier.

She slapped him hard against the cheek, her palm smarting with the contact. Her voice wavered as she stepped away from him.

"How dare you attack me. If you can't stand to hear the truth, I understand. But I refuse to be treated like a harlot. You, Mr. McCloud, are an uncivilized lout!"

She spun on her heel and marched out of the kitchen, ignoring his sputtering apology. Damn him to hell, she thought as she climbed the stairs. In the morning she'd have her trunk ready to go and she'd find Ollie to take her back to town. At this point she figured she'd take her chances with Hank Borscht rather than put up with that barbarian, Boss McCloud, one more day.

Boss, that was a fine title for the man since he thought he could order everyone around like a petty king demanding obedience from his subjects. Well, she'd just show him she didn't have to put up with his high-handed ways. She was a Readford, after all.

Sinclair paused at the top of the stairs. She brushed back a curl that had fallen across her forehead and took a deep breath. She could see the door to Maddie's room was open a crack, and she decided to peek in and check on the child. It was likely all that yelling downstairs had disturbed her.

Picking up the small kerosene lantern that lit the hallway, she held it up as she carefully slipped into Maddie's room. She could see the little girl curled up tightly on her small mattress. The warm quilt had been pushed to the side but the child slept soundly, her hair dark against the pillow beneath her head. Her thumb was stuck in her mouth, and she looked tiny and vulnerable.

Sinclair entered the room to kneel beside the sleeping child. She set the lamp down and straightened the

91

quilt, pulling it to cover Maddie more evenly. Her hand gently brushed the dark curls, and she whispered a small prayer she'd recited as a child.

How could she abandon this poor, lost creature? It made her want to weep when she recalled the way Maddie sat and rocked, shrouded in loneliness. Something in the way Maddie had glanced at her that day reminded her of the abandoned puppies she had dragged home time and again. How could Sinclair think of leaving her to Boss McCloud's care, when it was obvious he thought more of a dead woman's memory than her child living beneath his roof?

Sinclair leaned forward to softly kiss the child's cheek. Maddie stirred, but she didn't waken. Sinclair rose to her feet and turned.

She nearly jumped when she found herself facing Boss McCloud.

He started to speak, but Sinclair frowned and put her finger to her lips, indicating they shouldn't disturb the child. He nodded in agreement, then turned slightly and went into the hallway. She followed him, quietly closing the door to Maddie's room behind her.

"I'm not finished," he said.

Sinclair set the lamp on the table and put her hands on her hips, facing off with McCloud, yet again.

"Why, do you have more insults to hurl at me? More ridiculous reasons to excuse your behavior toward that child?" She pointed toward Maddie's door. "Don't bother to waste your breath, because I don't want to hear your pathetic defense. My mother died last year, and I've missed her every day since, but I've never thought that losing someone gives you an excuse to misuse someone else. I'm sorry about the accident that took Bess McCloud's life, but I'm more sorry for Madison. It seems to me that she's paid a bigger price than you or the judge ever will."

Sinclair turned to open the door to her room. She was shocked to feel a gentle hand on her shoulder, turning her back toward the hallway.

She couldn't see his expression clearly in the dim light, but she thought perhaps his eyes were softer, more apologetic.

"I won't give you excuses, Sinclair. Except to say that I was out of line down there, and you were right . . . I acted like an ass. You've got a way of making me see red sometimes, and I figure I just let my temper get away from me. But, I want you to know, I'm sorry about grabbing you like that."

Sinclair's foot tapped indignantly against the hard pine floor. "Let me get this straight, you're not sorry for blaming Madison for your stepmother's death, or for ignoring her and letting her be treated like an orphan. You're also not sorry for accusing me of being a liar and a lewd woman. You're only sorry for accosting me." She tossed her head. "If I were to accept that apology I'd be letting you off pretty easy, wouldn't I, McCloud?"

She could see his hands working themselves into fists again.

"See, you've got a way of twisting things around and then using them to make me mad."

Sinclair sniffed. "As if making you mad was any kind of challenge. You've spent more time angry with me than anything else. Maybe if you spent as much time kissing me as you spend yelling at me we'd get along better."

Jefferson McCloud stood staring at her in shock, his mouth open and his eyes wide. Then he threw back his head and laughed. The sound was musical, and Sinclair wished that she had more opportunities to enjoy it.

After a few moments he wrapped his arms around her and lifted her off the floor.

"Now there's a challenge to heat a man's blood. Should we start right now, Miss Readford, because I figure I must have a lot of catching up to do."

Sinclair slapped at his arms indignantly and demanded that he put her down.

"Mind your manners, McCloud, and don't wake up Maddie. As for kissing me, you're going to have to learn some manners before I ever let you do that again. A lady wants a gentleman to court her, and he should spoil her a bit before she allows him to kiss her."

"And exactly how does a man do that?" His arm was still about her waist, and Sinclair tried to ignore the warm trickle of pleasure that washed over her at his touch.

She looked up at him and turned her head slightly, realizing that she might be able to turn his sudden ardor to her advantage. "Why, I expect the gentleman could give the lady something she wants very badly."

Jefferson looked suspicious. "I expect so, especially if he wanted to make amends for being an uncivilized lout. What exactly do you want, Sinclair?"

She put her hand on his chest and rubbed, her fingers brushing the worn cotton gently. "Nothing too costly, just the furnishings for Maddie's room and some new clothes for her."

Jefferson's fingers found hers and he clasped her hand in his. "And what do I get in return for this favor?"

Sinclair's gaze lifted to his and she smiled faintly. "A good-night kiss perhaps? One that won't be followed by a slap."

Jefferson seemed to consider her terms. He glanced into her room, his gaze lingering on her bed, and she thought perhaps he wanted to suggest another sort of payment. She blushed at her own imagining, knowing it wasn't ladylike nor proper. But, the thought of inviting him into her room made her body tingle with anticipation.

He released her hand and one finger gently traced her cheekbone. "You can keep the things you've already put in Maddie's room."

Sinclair gave a squeal of delight.

He held up one hand. "But, from now on, just make a list of what you need and I'll arrange for you to go into town to get it."

He took a step back and frowned down at her. "Promise me you'll stay out of Bess's room."

Sinclair considered the request. She wanted to disagree, to point out how foolish it was to keep an entire room closed up and unused. Then she remembered how much she'd won already and decided to conserve her energy. There would be other battles to fight for Maddie.

"I can honestly admit I don't agree with you about

this, but in any case, I accept your apology and your terms."

She lifted her face and closed her eyes, her heart thumping as she waited for him to kiss her again. After a few moments she felt his lips brush her forehead, then he gently whispered good-night. She opened her eyes to see him descending the stairs.

She couldn't understand the wave of disappointment that washed through her.

Chapter Seven

"Look at me, Maddie."

The child kept her face down, as if the top of the worn pine table contained the most interesting pattern she'd ever seen. She avoided Sinclair's gaze and ignored her request.

Sinclair held the utensil out again. "It's a spoon, Maddie. And if you intend to eat your breakfast this morning, it will be with this."

Maddie lifted her head to look at Sinclair for a brief moment, then pounded on the table in frustration. She tried to slap the spoon away, but in the few days Sinclair had been caring for the child, her reflexes had improved. It was part of a survival instinct.

"I mean it, Miss Maddie. You will eat with a spoon or go hungry. Today the choice is yours!" Sinclair stood and set the utensil next to the girl.

"I'll know you're ready to eat when I see you pick up this spoon."

Sinclair turned to the stove to fill a tin plate with oatmeal. She heard the spoon hit the floor and sighed deeply. She had learned that every day was a series of battles with Madison McCloud. The child didn't want to be touched or held, or civilized in any way, shape or form. Since the war of the bath, the two of them had stood on opposite sides of every issue, from combing Maddie's hair to eating her meals. Today Sinclair had decided to dig in her heels and stand firm. She sighed again, disciplining a child was just so damned exhausting.

Returning to the table with the plate, she picked up the spoon, wiped it on her apron and sat down. Covering the mound of oatmeal with maple syrup, she moved the plate enticingly close to Maddie's nose. The girl's head lifted immediately and she reached for the plate.

Sinclair yanked the plate away and held out the spoon.

"With the spoon," she repeated.

Maddie's eyes studied the plate, the longing evident in her gaze. Then she looked at the spoon. Finally she seemed to consider Sinclair. They were in a stand-off and both of them knew it.

With aching slowness, Maddie reached for the spoon, then finally appeared to acknowledge surrender by grabbing it from Sinclair's hand. Sinclair felt her spirits soar, only to feel the pain of defeat a few moments later when Maddie sent the spoon sailing across the room to hit the stove and rattle to the floor.

Maddie's small, thin arms stretched toward the plate and she made a deep, guttural noise, as if demanding her food. Sinclair shook her head slowly, rose and returned the oatmeal to the warmer of the stove. Wiping her hands on her apron, she turned back to Maddie.

"I meant what I said, Madison McCloud. You will not continue to eat like a piglet with her nose in the trough while under my care. Civilized folks do not eat with their hands. I suppose we can begin our lessons for the day, since you have decided you don't want any breakfast."

Maddie slapped both hands on the table and screamed at Sinclair in a high-pitched, wailing tone. Sinclair had become used to this and simply pulled the girl's chair out to take her firmly by the arm.

"I believe we'll have lessons on the porch this morning. It's such a lovely spring day, don't you think?"

Maddie went limp and Sinclair uttered a small oath. She had become accustomed to this, too, as it was a frequent ploy when Maddie didn't want to do something. She simply became a rag doll.

Fortunately for Sinclair, Maddie possessed the bones of a bird. She was so light that it took little effort to simply lift and carry her wherever they were going. Lettie and Ollie had become familiar with the sight of Sinclair carrying Maddie about as if she were a small bundle.

Opening the door with her foot, she grasped Maddie about the waist and balanced her on one hip. With practiced ease they slipped through the door and onto the porch, where Lettie was scrubbing clothes in a tub filled with steaming water.

"Lands' sakes you haul that child more than a miner's mule headin' for a strike. Why don't you just let her be when she's actin' up?"

Sinclair set her screaming bundle gently on one of the rocking chairs and shook her head. "Because I believe that's the reason she misbehaves, so we will leave her alone. I want Miss Maddie to join the land of the living." Sinclair pursed her lips and put her hands on her hips. "She needs to understand I will not allow her to carry on with these tantrums and get her own way."

Maddie had slipped to the floor and was now rocking and repeating a series of nonsense words in a sing-song voice. Sinclair picked up a book and sat down next to her, adjusting her skirts.

"Let's begin with a review of yesterday's lesson. Do you know what these words are, Maddie?"

Sinclair held the primer out so the child could see the picture. "A rat, a cat, a cat, a rat, a cat and a rat, a rat and a cat."

"She wouldn't know the difference between a rat and a cat if her life depended on it." Lettie wrung the clothes and gave a derisive shake of her head. "Just foolishness if you ask me, tryin' to teach that child."

It had been a difficult morning and this judgment gave Sinclair the final push she needed to indulge in her own temper tantrum.

Standing, she stomped over to the woman bent over the laundry tub. With her hands on her hips and her blue eyes flashing, Sinclair let loose.

"Why does everyone simply assume Maddie can't be taught? Granted, she has some serious problems, but allowing her to grow up ignorant won't help matters. I don't tell you how to cook, or how to clean," she made a gesture toward the tub, "or how to do the laundry. Do you believe I'm so incompetent a teacher that I don't know what Madison might be capable of?"

Lettie looked embarrassed. "I'm sorry, miss. I sometimes just let my tongue go waggin' afore I give it somethin' worth sayin'."

Sinclair closed her eyes and took a deep breath, trying to regain control of her emotions, then opened her eyes again. "I didn't mean to jump on you like that, Lettie. I guess I'm just overwrought. I spend the days fighting with Maddie to get her to do things for herself and the evenings fighting with her brother, so he'll let me do things for her. I believe I'm just worn out."

Lettie nodded. "I see you're worryin' yourself sick about that child. Ain't none of them other ladies ever cared if she had a bath, how she ate her vittles, or nothin'. As for the boss, well . . . I gotta be honest, seems like the two of you fight like a couple of badgers. Neither one of you wants to give in."

Sinclair gazed off into the distance, looking at the snow-covered peaks. Lettie was right. After supper, when Maddie was finally settled into bed and Boss McCloud was ensconced in his office, Sinclair would often confront him with a series of requests. Requests that she considered quite reasonable, but that he found, "damned outrageous," as he was fond of saying.

The evening often resulted in a spirited debate, as she defended her petition and he gave her excuses.

She nearly smiled when she realized that despite his arguments, Boss McCloud had acceded to every one of her requests. Sometimes she had a fleeting intuition that the only reason he argued with her was to keep her in the study with him. More than once he ended the evening by pouring her a cordial while he sipped his whiskey and inquired about her life in Philadelphia.

That was the part that left Sinclair totally confused. The obstinate way Boss McCloud would disagree with her, only to fall into easy conversation with her later. Sinclair had been surprised when he asked her opinion on certain issues. Other than her father, no man had ever assumed she even held an opinion, much less cared to hear what it might be. And when Sinclair presented a passionate appeal for women's rights, McCloud didn't laugh the way the men in Philadelphia had laughed, or belittle her. He had nodded at her, agreeing that women did indeed suffer from the unfairness of the law.

"That man is an infuriating mix of contradictions." She didn't realize she'd said the words out loud until Lettie looked up at her in confusion.

"Who, the boss? Hell, takes no kind of brains a'tall to figure out a man. The way he's sniffin' 'round your skirts, I'd say you'd best watch out. A man takes an interest in a woman, she'd better be on her guard. No tellin' what kind of foolishness will get into their heads when they're thinkin' about courtin'." Lettie returned to her scrub board and shook her head.

Sinclair laughed. "I don't think you need worry about that, Lettie. Your boss isn't interested in courting me. I'm more inclined to think he'd like to tar and feather me, and if he wasn't so desperate for someone to take care of Maddie, he'd return me to the Blue Willow and let me take my chances with Hank Borscht."

Of course, there was the matter of the kiss. Since the night they'd argued in the kitchen, McCloud hadn't mentioned her challenge. Still, when she remembered the way his arms had felt around her, the hot, delicious feel of his lips on hers, and the way she felt heated from the inside out, she wondered if she could entice him to repeat the experience. She blushed in embarrassment at the lewdness of her thoughts. She had never imagined *doing things* with a man before she met McCloud.

That was the whispered designation the girls in her dormitory had given to the more intimate activities between a man and a woman. Although the piecing together of their combined knowledge of *doing things* had seemed somewhat sparse on details, they had all nearly swooned at the thought of seeing a man naked.

Sinclair felt herself jerked back to reality when Lettie repeated her question and gave her a shake. "Wake up, woman. You're wool-gathering, and I need to know if you want me to take Maddie up to her room."

Sinclair blinked, then cleared her throat to give herself a moment to clear her brain. Gazing out at the ranch yard, she had an inspiration.

"I don't think so. It's such a lovely day, I believe I'll take Miss Maddie for a walk."

Lettie lifted a gray eyebrow and her lips thinned

into what would have to suffice for a smile. "The two of you just gonna go for a little stroll?"

Sinclair looked down at Maddie, then back out into the yard.

"Yes. A walk might be just the thing on this lovely May morning. I believe more progressive doctors recommend a daily constitutional to keep one's blood flowing."

Lettie lifted a basket loaded with wet clothing and snorted. "In Montana, it ain't a good sign if there's blood flowin', but suit yourself. Walk right on back to Phillydellphia, for all I care."

Sinclair watched her climb down the steps carefully and waddle over to the clothesline. Despite the woman's harsh words, Sinclair knew they were developing a grudging respect for each other. But, just like everyone else she'd met in Montana, Lettie loved to argue.

Sinclair clapped her hands and was surprised to see Maddie lift her head to meet her gaze. Some success there, anyway.

"Let's go for a walk, Maddie."

The girl stared at her as if she had sprouted two heads. Sinclair tried to pull her to her feet, but Madison decided to once again play rag doll. It was a game that exhausted Sinclair in a very short period of time. She dropped Maddie gently to the floor and plopped down onto the porch swing.

It hadn't occurred to her that Maddie might resist taking a walk. She went to the privy out back with no problem, in fact, she needed no assistance in taking care of her needs. That was what had initially made Sinclair suspicious of the nature of Maddie's affliction. It had seemed too convenient for the child to be able to control her outbursts and behavior depending upon the circumstances. Sinclair was convinced that Maddie's feebleminded "fits" were engineered by her to avoid contact. Sinclair thought Maddie understood most of what what was happening around her, and used her supposed mental deficiency as an excuse to do exactly as she pleased.

Sinclair stayed up at night, writing her observations and theories in a journal. The chronicle of her daily life with Maddie supported her belief that the little girl would go to almost any lengths to avoid outside contact. Repeatedly she found herself recording instances in which Maddie had thrown a tantrum to keep people at a distance. It made Sinclair sad to think of Maddie in her own lonely little cocoon. How she wished she could find the key to setting this little butterfly free.

She pondered a few minutes more, then stood and decided they would have their walk that day, no matter what. She had conceded the spoon battle, but now it was a new fight!

Lifting the girl beneath the arms, Sinclair struggled to pull the child to her feet. Before Maddie could react, Sinclair tugged on her arm and nearly sent her flying off the steps. Capturing Maddie around the waist, Sinclair laughed and jumped down to the ground with her. *Keep things moving,* Sinclair thought. *Don't give her a chance to react.*

They were in the yard now, dodging the chickens as they pecked about, searching for grubs and bugs. Nearing the fenced enclosure that served as a corral, Sinclair suddenly swerved. There were several hands hanging about and Sinclair knew they would likely set Maddie off into a fit if they greeted them.

With quick steps they were nearly out of the yard and heading down a well-worn path when Maddie pulled Sinclair to a sudden stop and let out a blood-curdling scream. It was enough to make the two cow-hands turn and glare at Sinclair. She waved back with studied nonchalance.

Quickly, she lifted Maddie and balanced her on one hip.

"When I'm finished with this job I'm going to become a teamster, since hefting bags of grain about will be easier than this." She continued down the path, ignoring the screaming child and making small talk.

"The color of the sky is simply amazing today, don't you think? Look at that shade of blue. I swear, I wish I could find some silk that hue. It would make up into a divine evening gown. Or perhaps a walking dress. Yes, that would be perfect . . . a lovely walking dress, with white lace trim, just like those puffy white clouds. Don't you think that would be just the thing for strolling about in the Montana wilderness, Miss Maddie?"

The child was still screaming, but the tone had dropped from ear piercing to droning. She was re-peating her nonsense again, something that sounded like *Mammm, Mammm, Myyyy, Meeee.* Sinclair found herself matching her pace to the sound.

They came around a small copse of blackberry bushes and Sinclair halted at the sight of Jefferson McCloud watering his horse at a spring. He stared at them as if he couldn't quite believe what he was seeing. It seemed to Sinclair that Maddie was suddenly as heavy as a hundred-pound sack filled with stones, and she shifted her to the other side.

It didn't interrupt the drone whatsoever.

"Miss Sinclair, may I ask what you're doing to my sister?"

Sinclair felt the muscles in her arms beginning to ache, and she flinched as she tried to adjust the weight of the child she carried.

"Maddie and I are going for a walk."

Jefferson McCloud studied her for a moment. "It appears only one of you is walking."

Sinclair smiled at him. "Yes, I suppose that's true. I was the one who wanted to walk. Maddie just wanted to play rag doll. Being rather tired of that game today, I decided we'd walk. I'm really not sure which of us won the argument."

Seeing her discomfort, Jefferson looped the reins over his horse's neck and approached her. "Perhaps I should carry her for a while, it appears you're getting tired."

Before she could protest she felt him lift the child's weight from her arms and she watched him try to drape Maddie across his shoulder. Sinclair was forming the words to warn him how much Maddie hated to be touched, when she was shocked to see the child wrap her thin arms around Jefferson's neck. The little girl settled in, perfectly quiet and obviously content.

Sinclair stared at the brother and sister in surprise. Maddie *always* flinched or screamed and tried to pull away when she was touched. Lettie had told her it had been that way since Bess had fallen to her death. Yet, here the child was, held in her brother's strong arms with no resistance, no tantrums. In fact, she seemed perfectly happy, or at least what passed for happy with Madison McCloud.

Jefferson looked as astonished as Sinclair and a bit in awe of the small, trusting child in his arms. He looked down at his sister with amazement and something else. Sinclair thought perhaps a glimmer of affection. Maybe the little girl could win him over.

"Would you like to walk for a bit? I believe the fresh air and sunshine will do Madison good. The one thing mothers back home went on and on about when they had those endless discussions about their children was the importance of fresh air and sunshine." Sinclair felt like she was babbling. An unfortunate habit when she was in the presence of this handsome cowboy.

He nodded and carried Maddie as if she was a precious and very fragile package. Which, come to think of it, she was. It encouraged Sinclair to see Maddie looking at Jefferson, almost studying him.

"Were you close before Bess died?"

Jefferson frowned and Maddie made a small noise of discomfort. He smoothed out his features with a smile, and she settled back against him.

"There was the difference in our ages. I was a young man, interested in wild times and riding the range when she was born. But, when I was home I found her charming, she was so small and so . . . incapable of doing anything."

Sinclair laughed. "Babies do not come fully equipped for life. That's what parents are for."

Jefferson glanced down at his sister sadly. "And I'm afraid Maddie didn't get the luck of the draw on that one. One died too soon and the other one doesn't seem to be capable of loving his own children."

Sinclair was sorry she had mentioned it. She could hear the despair in Jefferson's voice.

"But she has you, McCloud, and the two of you are family. And you have Ollie and Lettie. They're your family because they love you. That's what my father used to tell me, your family is composed of all the people who love you best of all. So my aunt Tilly and our housekeeper, Old Meg, and her husband, Shep, they're all my family."

Jefferson stopped suddenly to pause and look down at her. "Do you think that's all there is to it, a bunch of people living together? My father lived with us, but I never felt we were part of a family, or that he ever wanted to be with us. He left Maddie here like she was a stray calf, not worth thinking about. He can't even bear to face me, he sends missives with my neighbors when he wants me to do something." His eyes were full of pain and loss. "Family? I don't have a family . . . and I'm not sure I'd even know how to be part of one."

Sinclair had never heard such bitterness, and his words left her feeling bereft. Here was a man who didn't think he had a family, even worse, who apparently didn't even want one. It was the saddest thing she'd ever heard and tears filled her eyes.

"I'm sorry for you, McCloud, if you can't see what's right in front of your face. I suppose it's easier to pretend you don't have something than to acknowledge you might be responsible for losing it in the first place. Give me the child. I think I'm tired of walking now and I'll head back to the house."

McCloud shook his head. "I'm not going to argue with you about it, Sinclair, I'm just telling you the truth, the best I know it. As for Maddie, I'll take her on back. Why don't you finish your walk? I'll have Lettie put her up in her room. She looks a mite tuckered out from all this fresh air."

Sinclair was going to protest, then realized it had been a long time since she'd enjoyed a brisk walk in the sunshine. She shielded her eyes with her hand to look up at the sun, slowly climbing in the soft, blue sky.

"I forgot my bonnet and parasol, so I can't stay out very long." She wrinkled her nose, "I'll be covered with freckles. If you wouldn't mind though, I would enjoy a few more minutes out here."

Jefferson McCloud gave her a lopsided grin. "I don't mind, but be careful, Miss Sinclair. Don't step on any rattlesnakes."

Sinclair felt her eyes go wide in horror, then she quickly looked down to reassure herself a snake wasn't curled up at her feet, ready to strike. When she looked up, McCloud was already nearly to his horse, and she watched him mount easily, then settle Maddie gently in front of him.

Despite what Boss McCloud thought, it was obvious to her that he did indeed have a family. He spent a great deal of his time worrying about how to take care of them, but maybe it was time he learned to let them take care of him right back.

Chapter Eight

"I ain't too sure about this, Miss Sinclair. The boss won't like it." Ollie held the reins of the dark brown sorrel tightly, the expression on his face reminding her of a schoolboy caught in some mischief and afraid of the consequences.

Sinclair lifted her chin slightly, caught Ollie's eye, and winked. "Let me handle Boss McCloud. If everything goes as planned today, there's no reason he need ever know about our little exercise."

Ollie shook his head sadly, his expression growing even darker. "Boss seems to hear 'bout ever'thing that goes on here at the Cripple Creek. Sometimes I think he's got the Injun medicine for the sight. They call it the Eagle Eye."

Sinclair brushed past him to take a closer look at the horse. "He just makes it his business to snoop. No special power to that. I have friends in Philadelphia who have the same gift." She put her hand out tentatively to touch the smooth side of the mare. The horse flicked her tail, glancing back to take a measured look at Sinclair. Their eyes met briefly, and Sinclair was somewhat reassured that this was the calm, easygoing ride Ollie had promised her. She swallowed her fear.

"Besides," peeking around the horse's neck, she sent Ollie a concerned look, "you told me he was riding up in the high country, and Lettie said with the stock scattered about the way they are, he's not expected back for a few days."

Ollie paused to spit, making Sinclair wince. It was the hardest thing for her to get used to with these rough men—their penchant for chewing tobacco, then spitting whenever the mood struck them. At least Boss McCloud didn't seem to have acquired the habit, or he kept it well hidden from her.

She had been relieved when she noticed this, although why the personal habits of the man should interest her was confusing. She tried to pretend she didn't care about Boss McCloud, then found herself pumping Ollie and Lettie for information when he disappeared for days at a time.

Ollie grunted. "Lettie don't know ever'thing she thinks she does 'bout ranching," he mumbled, glancing sideways, as if he wanted to make sure the maligned housekeeper wasn't within earshot.

Stepping back, Sinclair straightened the skirt of her dark burgundy velvet riding costume. It was the height of fashion in Philadelphia, ordered from Strawbridge and Clothier especially for her equestrian jaunts through Fairmont Park. Jaunts that never materialized because her riding instructor had declared her a nincompoop and a danger to horses, broke her riding crop over his knee and ordered her out of his stables. She had never fully recovered from the humiliation.

"Does this horse have a name?"

"Brown Sugar," Ollie replied.

Sinclair studied the horse carefully. "That's a lovely name for a horse." And certainly any steed with such a sweet name would possess a similar disposition. Ollie had promised to teach her to ride if she would teach him to write his name. After several weeks of tutoring, not only could he write the words *Oliver James Wheaton,* but he had progressed halfway through the *McGuffey's Eclectic Reader* that she used to teach Maddie. Or at least that she shoved in front of Maddie each day. So far, Ollie had shown ten times the aptitude and interest of her small charge, and Sinclair appreciated his efforts. It made her feel like less of a failure.

"I got your riggin', ma'am, but I got to say it," he paused and shook his head, "Boss ain't gonna like you usin' that fancy saddle that belonged to Bess."

Sinclair swallowed her smart retort, knowing it might be repeated to Boss McCloud, and smiled serenely. "I would simply have to explain to him that learning to ride is a survival skill for a woman in the West, and I couldn't be expected to don trousers and ride like a man, now could I? Besides, if you're as good at this as you claim, we'll have that saddle back in the barn before sunset."

Ollie spit again and shook his head. "Seems like a simple plan, ma'am. But I learned me a few things livin' out here, one of 'em is there ain't nothin' as simple as it looks."

Sinclair waved her gloved hand at him grandly. "Just come over and hold my parasol and help me up. I've been looking forward to this for days."

She had spent long hours imagining this ride. She had continued her daily walks with Maddie, who now accompanied her without tantrums or screaming, but with no sign that she recognized or enjoyed the beauty of the landscape surrounding her.

This land had captured Sinclair's imagination. The sharp green of the new grass, the changing colors of the sky from sunrise to sunset, and the mountains standing like icy stone sentinels off in the distance stirred her as no city view could.

She felt like part of the country here and knew a person could put down roots that would go deep and last for generations. She was beginning to understand what kept men like Boss McCloud anchored to this place, not like a slave forced to labor, but as a partner, working with the land to unlock its potential. It took strong men like McCloud to commit their lives to staying in this challenging, but rewarding territory. She realized the tie wasn't forged from obligation or inheritance. McCloud worked hard and loved it. This was the place he wanted to be; he belonged to Montana.

She sighed deeply, grasped the saddlehorn and gave Ollie, who was now standing next to her, a nod. "I'm ready, give me a boost up, would you?"

She felt his large, meaty hand grasp her boot heel, and with his push she found herself nearly propelled clear over the other side of the horse. She swallowed a squeal, afraid it might frighten the animal. Somehow she looped her leg over the horn and found herself sitting upright. It was an immense relief.

As Ollie handed up her parasol and the reins, she gave him a smile of confidence. "That wasn't too bad, was it?"

"You ain't ridin' yet, ma'am. Yer just sittin'."

Sinclair adjusted her hat covered with the large pink velvet roses and shrugged. "All the men around here seem capable of riding with little or no effort. How difficult can it be, with the right horse?" She shifted her seat a bit, and as Brown Sugar took a step forward, her courage faltered.

"Stay put, horsey."

Ollie gave her another odd look as he stepped to his own pinto named Storm. "Tell her 'whoa' and pull back a bit on the reins, gentle like though, don't go spoilin' her mouth by yankin' too hard."

Sinclair put her shoulders back in an attempt to straighten her posture. She felt the warmth of the sun on her cheeks as she gazed up at the sky and remembered her parasol. It wouldn't be worth the ride if she sported a whole new crop of brown freckles for the effort. She raised the pink silk parasol, with the small embroidered roses to match her hat, over her head. How she wished Boss McCloud could see her. She imagined she was quite a vision.

With a loud *furumph* she folded out the parasol, the fabric creating a pool of shade to surround her.

The sudden movement of Brown Sugar took her unawares, and she bounced hard on the saddle as the horse reared back on her hind legs and gave a long, terrified shriek. Sinclair held on to the reins and the horn tightly with one hand, trying to balance her parasol in the other.

She felt the horse put both feet back on the ground, but she didn't have time to think about climbing down. Brown Sugar took off in a run that sent Sinclair's parasol flying and convinced her to hold on with both hands. She heard a loud oath from behind her and wanted to turn to apologize to whoever had been there. She thought perhaps they had been struck by her parasol, but she couldn't turn around; she was too terrified.

She tried pulling lightly on the reins and yelling, "Stop!" in her most authoritative voice. It had no effect on the runaway horse.

Sinclair realized the landscape was flying past her at an alarming rate. She could hear voices behind her and she fervently prayed that Storm was a faster horse than Brown Sugar. She would never have guessed the small, brown sorrel was capable of such speed. Back at the ranch she had appeared docile enough. And slow. She'd never imagined the horse could be this quick.

The sound of hoofbeats echoed the pounding of blood in her own ears, drowning out the voices behind her. She was afraid that any small movement would unseat her, and she considered closing her eyes, but then she'd be even more terrified.

"Pull . . . tight . . . on reins." Were those the words she was hearing? What had Ollie said about yanking? Something about spoiling a horse's mouth. She wondered what that could mean?

At least she could be grateful that Boss McCloud wasn't around to witness her total humiliation. She was cheered by that thought for a few brief seconds before she caught sight of the river in front of her.

She didn't know if a horse would run into water. She knew virtually nothing about horses, and found herself listing more reasons to dislike the animals. It was possible the horse would stop, but what would she do if Brown Sugar decided to go for a swim? Sinclair knew the heavy skirt and petticoats she wore would pull her down beneath the water, possibly drowning her in minutes.

The water was growing closer and Sinclair began to panic. Riding was one thing, swimming quite another. It was not at all reassuring to realize she had even less of an idea how to stay afloat than to sit a horse.

Closing her eyes, she pulled back sharply on the reins and yelled in her strongest voice.

"Whoa, you damned flea-bitten, bandy-legged son of a bitch." It was an epithet she had overheard when one of the hands was breaking a horse. She should have been embarrassed to say the words, but found that swearing gave her a jubilant sense of freedom. And Brown Sugar came to an abrupt halt.

Sinclair didn't have time to feel any satisfaction, as she found herself sailing through the air. Terror coursed through her as she felt herself plummeting . . . right into the waters of the Cripple Creek.

She swallowed a mouthful of water as she sank into the depths of the creek. Despite its name, the stream seemed as deep and wide as the Schuykill back home. Struggling to pull herself to the surface, her face momentarily came out of the water, and she coughed in an attempt to breathe deeply. She swallowed more water as the weight of the velvet and two petticoats pulled her back down again.

She wondered if she would see her life flash before her eyes, as she'd heard that's what happened just before one died. As her body grew heavy, she had one sad thought: She wished McCloud would have kissed her again.

She was in a soft, floating world as she recalled that kiss, and she struggled as arms grasped her tightly around the waist to pull her toward the surface. She wanted to succumb to the darkness swirling about her, but found the tug of those strong, sure arms alluring. She continued to fight briefly, then allowed them to capture her.

She felt a sharp slap on the cheek and heard her name. "Damn it, Sinclair. Wake up!"

The tone was familiar and she realized she was in the arms of Boss McCloud. Of course, she reasoned, angels must look like the last person you remember in life. Her dying thoughts had been of McCloud, so a vision of him had appeared to shepherd her to the next world. It made sense, it would make the crossing over to heaven much simpler that way.

She could feel herself being carried through the water, but that made sense too. The hereafter wouldn't be at the bottom of a creek. She wanted to open her eyes, but was afraid of what she might see. She wondered if she had made it to the pearly gates, or would she spend an eternity cast into hell for swearing only moments before she died?

Her bottom settled on the hard, smooth rocks of the creek bank, and she marveled that the physical experiences of life could be present in death. It was so interesting. . . .

Her shoulders were grasped tightly as she was pulled roughly to a sitting position and her back pummeled by a hard, angry fist.

"Wake up, woman. I'll be damned if I'll let you die before I can kill you myself!"

The words echoed through her head and her eyes snapped open in surprise. She found herself in the arms of Boss McCloud. Not an angelic version, judging from his expression.

Water dripped from his hair and Sinclair could see that his clothes were soaking wet. She blinked in confusion.

"What happened to you, Jefferson?"

Despite his angry expression, there was a note of relief in his voice. "I had to jump into the creek to pull out a crazy woman who spooks horses, steals property and doesn't have enough sense to stay out of trouble."

Sinclair was too happy to be alive to pay any attention to his words. "You saved me? Why, that makes you my hero, doesn't it?"

Jefferson McCloud wished he could throw the annoying Miss Sinclair Readford back into Cripple Creek. She was certainly more trouble that she was worth, giving a sweet horse like Brown Sugar a scare and taking off on a wild ride. Didn't even a green tenderfoot like Sinclair know that all you had to do to stop a well-trained horse was pull back on the reins and say, "whoa"? What kind of education did eastern women get if even this small knowledge was withheld from them?

Despite his rough words, he settled Sinclair back down gently, then moved to kneel beside her. He could see the confusion in her eyes and he realized what a close call she'd had. If he hadn't been riding in from the range a few days early, it was possible he'd have arrived only to see the beautiful Miss Readford laid out in a pine box. The image of her slipping beneath the water would haunt him for a long time, and he couldn't bring himself to lecture her.

"You should have asked me to take you riding." His voice was gentle, as he smoothed a damp, golden curl away from her eyes. Her hair had fallen from its usual tight bun and the thick, blond tendrils dripped water. He grinned as she tried to brush it over her shoulder, then gave up.

Sinclair struggled to sit up, coughed, then went pale. She pulled herself to her knees, threw him a look of horror, then vomited. He held her head as her shoulders heaved and she cleared her body of the water she'd swallowed. When she appeared to be finished, he handed her his faded blue bandanna and she wiped her mouth daintily. She attempted to hand it back to him, but he declined with a lazy grin.

"You go ahead and keep it, ma'am. You might need it."

"I meant what I said. You are a hero, Jefferson." Her eyes were full of adoration and Jefferson felt about ten feet tall.

"Just doing what needed to be done, Sinclair. I'm a rancher. There's nothing heroic about that. Just ask my father. He'd be glad to tell you how I've wasted my life."

Her sudden brush with death seemed to have given

Sinclair courage. "Your father might be an educated man, but that doesn't mean he understands what's important. I've spent my entire life listening to so-called educated men talk about books and philosophy and what's important. It seems like they spend years trying to figure out what they should care about, and most of the time all they're really concerned with is what others think of them." She waved a sodden arm toward the horizon.

"Out here, a man is the measure of his courage and tenacity. I think you're more of a hero than you'll ever know, Jefferson." Her blue eyes were full of adoration and it made him blush, then swallow.

Jefferson hoped he'd never forget that look in Sinclair's eyes. It warmed him to his bones and he felt something . . . some small piece of himself, shift within. The fact that this beautiful, intelligent woman could see something worthwhile about him gave him hope. He grinned at her.

"Maybe you'll write one of those dime novels about me, Miss Sinclair."

Sinclair rose to her feet and began to squeeze the water from her dress. "I certainly made a fool of myself today, I don't know what possessed me to think I could actually learn to ride a horse."

She noticed her hat lying on the creek bank and moved toward it. He could hear the squish of each step. Picking up the hat, she shook her head at its bedraggled state.

"What happened to Brown Sugar? Did I ruin her mouth?"

Jefferson frowned, then nodded in understanding.

"I bet she's already back at the ranch, giving everyone a fit about our whereabouts. We'd best return. I told Ollie to get some water boiling, in case you broke your fool neck." He glanced at her wet, dripping clothes.

"Likely you'll need a bath to warm you up." He took a few steps to grab the reins of Old Pete, then turned back to her.

"Come on over here. I guess you'd better get used to riding with me. It seems like the only way I can protect my horses." He swung into the saddle, then held out his hand. She prepared to climb up behind him, as she had on the night he'd rescued her from the Blue Willow and brought her out to the ranch.

As he easily pulled her onto the horse, Sinclair seemed shocked to find herself seated in front of him. She blushed at the intimacy of the position, their bodies pressed so close to each other.

"I thought you'd be more comfortable up here, with my arms around you," he whispered into her ear.

Sinclair blushed an even deeper red, and she remained silent as the horse slowly wandered back toward the ranch. Every step of the stallion made him more aware of the woman sitting in front of him. His arms wrapped around her gently, and she relaxed and leaned back into him. He felt a heat begin to rise within him, a heat that had more to do with Sinclair than the sun in the sky. He was beginning to wonder if he would be able to resist her closeness, the temptation to kiss her.

She seemed lost in a daydream, and didn't answer him the first time he murmured his question. He gently touched her cheek and drew her gaze back to look into his eyes.

"What made you go racing off like that on Brown Sugar? Didn't you know you could have been hurt, maybe even killed?"

She gave him an odd look. Almost as if she didn't understand the question. Perhaps she was still over-wrought from falling into the Cripple Creek. He tried not to get lost in the swirling blue depths of her eyes, or to let his gaze stray to her lips. For the more he thought about kissing her, the more he was tempted to taste the sweet pleasures her mouth could elicit. He struggled to keep his train of thought on the question.

"I didn't know the horse would run away. All I did was put up my parasol, and she took off like I'd slapped her with a whip. I was terrified." She hung her head in shame. "And I didn't want you to know what an awful rider I am."

His finger gently lifted her chin back up, forcing her to meet his eyes again. "When I realized it was you taking off from the yard, I nearly went crazy. You scared the hell out of me, Sinclair. If anything should happen to you . . ." His voice trailed off, lost in the sounds of the chirping birds and the soft rustle of the wind.

Sinclair licked her lips and waited. She leaned against him, and put her hand gently against his chest, waiting for him to say more. He swallowed and tried to avoid her gaze. What had he been about to say? That he cared for her? What a damn fool thing that would be, letting her know that he'd rushed back to the ranch because he'd wanted to see her again.

She was a temporary solution to his problem with Madison, but there was nothing permanent about Miss Sinclair Redford and Montana territory. Staying at the ranch was a lark, and a city woman like her viewed the experience as an exciting adventure. She didn't belong there.

He continued to avoid her eyes, then cleared his throat.

"What if something should happen to me?" she asked in a soft, plaintive voice.

Jefferson tried to straighten himself and put a few inches between their two bodies. "Why, it'd be a damn nuisance, that's what. I'd have to find somebody else to take care of Maddie. And despite all the trouble you cause, she seems better since you got here."

He heard her breath come out in a rush, and she stiffened beside him. "Well, maybe you'd find a less troublesome female, one who could ride a horse and keep her mouth shut. I suspect that kind of woman might suit you better than me."

"Yup. A less bothersome woman would be a nice change."

He could see her color turning more rosy and her lips thin to very straight line. "I'm sure I know your type. The Shady Lawn School for Ladies of Quality was filled with them. Meek, little things who couldn't imagine having a thought a man didn't put into their silly little heads. All they cared about was getting married and raising children as stupid as they were."

Jefferson frowned. "You make the state of marriage sound pretty distasteful. Don't you ever plan to get married, Sinclair?"

"Not likely," she responded, the sadness evident in her voice. "Because I'll only marry a man who wants me exactly the way I am. And as you've so accurately pointed out, I'm a great deal of trouble. I don't believe there are any men who want an opinionated, headstrong woman. At least my father tells me there are none, and that's why I should learn to be more reticent in expressing my views."

Jefferson grinned. "Does that mean less inclined to think you're right all the time."

She swung her head to face him, narrowed her eyes and seemed about to say something, then gave him a small smile and tossed her head. "It's not that I'm inclined to think I'm right, I simply know I am."

Jefferson gave a great howl of laughter.

He finally recovered and shook his head sadly. "Of course, out here, there are lots of opportunities to meet men. Why, a woman like you, so smart and refined, well, you shouldn't give up." He felt the corners of his mouth twitch. "It doesn't hurt that women are in short supply either. Men can get pretty desperate for female companionship. You'll likely find yourself a husband before the summer's over."

He prepared himself to be soundly smacked. Instead she studied him for a moment, then seemed to consider his words.

"Would you help me?"

Jefferson frowned at her words. "Find a husband?"

She blinked at him in confusion then shook her head sadly. "Do you think it's hopeless?" He could see tears well up in her eyes and he cursed himself for being such a fool. He'd only been teasing her, but she thought he was serious about a man needing to be desperate in order to marry her. The little fool didn't even realize what a treasure she was.

"I guess I might as well give up." There was a note of despair in her voice.

Jefferson pulled on the reins to bring Old Pete to a halt, and he looked down at her. She turned away in embarrassment.

"There are some things I'm good at, ma'am, and some things I'd be hopeless doing. An honest man realizes his own shortcomings and admits to them."

Sinclair dismissed his words with a wave of her hand. "I'd rather have you help me find a husband than anyone else. I've heard you're a man who can be trusted. I've certainly trusted you with my life on several occasions. If you believe I'm that hopeless, I'll just give up. I guess it's simply not meant to be."

Jefferson sat in silence for a few moments, unsure of what to say to make her feel better. He didn't want to hurt her feelings, but he didn't plan on encouraging other men to court Sinclair. He'd be damned to burn in hell before he'd let any other man put his hands on her, and that thought startled him. When did he start feeling so proprietary toward Miss Sinclair Readford?

"Well, I'm mighty humbled by your confidence in me, but matchmaking isn't exactly my area of expertise. Besides, you don't want a rancher for a husband. You need a businessman or a professor like your father."

Sinclair shook her head emphatically. "I've never been so serious about anything in my life. And if I must marry, I'd prefer a man as different from my father as possible." She gazed off into space for a few moments. "I want a man who loves his home so much, he never wants to leave it." Her voice was tinged with sadness.

"Besides, in this wild country, you're free to be yourself. I'm beginning to think that's the most valuable thing you can ever possess." Her voice fell to a whisper. "Freedom."

Jefferson gave her a measured look. He honestly didn't know if she was playing a game with him, or if she really wanted him to help her search for a husband.

"Are you sure about this, Sinclair?"

"It could be advantageous for both of us, don't you think?" she asked, her voice husky. Their eyes met, and he felt a surge of heat rush through him. She was so beguiling, so innocent of her own power. He pulled her closer, losing himself in her warmth and softness.

Before he even realized what was happening he found his lips on hers. Kissing Sinclair was better than he remembered. Her arms crept around his neck, her fingers tangling in the short hair at his nape. Moaning in pleasure, he deepened the kiss. In response, she pressed her body against him and the intense longing that was beginning to possess him exploded into uncontrolled desire.

He lifted his mouth from hers momentarily, to look down at her, then reclaimed her lips, realizing the few seconds they were apart were more than he could bear. He plundered her mouth as if it were a soft, erotic treasure.

When he finally pulled away from her, she gave a

small whimper of pain, like a child forced to give up her favorite toy.

"We can't . . . not here." His words were slurred with emotion. He battled with himself as he removed his hat to wipe his brow with his shirtsleeve.

She looked stunned. "I'm, I . . ."

Jefferson touched her lips gently with one finger. "Let's not discuss this to death, Sinclair. Let's just wait and see what happens.

"But just so you understand, I have no intention of helping you find a husband. You're on your own with that little project." As if he'd let another man take his place. She'd be lucky if any of the eligible bachelors in the area were allowed within fifty yards of her after that day.

Sinclair laughed. "That's fine, Boss McCloud, as long as you understand that simply because you won't become my ally doesn't mean you won't be a candidate yourself." Tossing her head she gazed up at the sky. "After all, you're the one who said there are some pretty desperate men out here."

He nodded and nudged Old Pete in the ribs to get him moving again. "I'll let you know when I'm that desperate, Sinclair."

The funny thing was, considering how much he wanted to kiss her again, he might be a whole heck of a lot closer to desperation than he wanted to admit.

Chapter Nine

Jefferson McCloud paced across the worn surface of the porch and paused to glare down at his watch for the third time in less than fifteen minutes. It was nearly seven-thirty in the morning and the woman wasn't ready to leave yet. He swore under his breath and suppressed the urge to open the screen door to yell up the oak staircase at Miss Sinclair Readford. Not that he believed bellowing at her would make any difference. In the few weeks she'd been on his ranch he'd learned that despite all of his efforts, Sinclair wouldn't do a damn thing unless she really and truly wanted to.

Flipping the watch case closed, he slid it back into his pants pocket as he studied the bright morning sky. He was on a fool's mission in the first place. A damn fool, if the truth be told. When Sinclair had approached him about going to Ghost Horse Gulch to purchase some things for Maddie, he'd been agreeable. But every hand on the place knew he didn't have to escort her there himself.

Jefferson knew he was going to waste a full day of spring roundup on a shopping trip, and he'd been ready to turn the task over to Ollie on several occasions. Then he'd see Sinclair walking with Maddie, or hear her reading to Lettie and Ollie, and he'd remember how precious little time he had to spend with her. Time he was starting to crave like a man in the desert thirsting for a cool drink of water.

"I believe I'm ready, Mr. McCloud, if you are?" Sinclair's voice was filled with excitement and Jefferson decided he'd try to be courteous, even if she had kept him standing outside for nearly an hour.

When she appeared on the porch, he instantly decided the wait was worth it. She wore a pink dress that dipped in all the right places, wrapping her like a package bedecked with lace and ribbons. The color brought out the blue of her eyes and he noticed she was wearing another one of those silly hats with too many roses and a stuffed bird on top. On most women they looked foolish, but the slight tilt of the hat and the soft veil shading her eyes made her look exotic and way too appealing.

She brushed past him quickly, down the steps to the rig, suddenly in a hurry to be on their way. She stood patiently waiting for him to help her up. He fought the urge to put his hands around her tiny waist and lift her onto the soft, brushed velvet seat. Instead he tucked her small, gloved hand in his, as she smoothly stepped up into the buggy, settling her skirts around her. When his father had purchased the

Corning buggy, Jefferson had considered it a waste of money. Especially since it was rarely used after Bess died. Today he was grateful he could escort Sinclair in style.

He snapped the reins and the dark black gelding took off. Glancing sideways at Sinclair, he could see she was delighted at the smooth gait and fast pace. Despite her claim of ignorance regarding horseflesh, he had discovered Sinclair possessed an intuition about the animals. She insisted she would ride Brown Sugar again, despite her last unfortunate experience, because in her own words: "She's the horse I've managed to stay on the longest, so I guess she trusts me."

Jefferson was learning Miss Sinclair Readford had her own kind of logic, and it was useless to argue with her. Not that it stopped him. He admitted to himself he searched for ways to irritate and ignite her, mostly just to see the rich color flood her cheeks and her eyes grow bright with enthusiasm. Arguing with Sinclair was better than making love to most women. Not that he didn't entertain the thought of doing that with her on a regular basis.

In fact, he hoped the ride into town would provide him with an opportunity to question Sinclair about their conversation on the way home after her fall into Cripple Creek. A conversation that had haunted his nights as he tossed and turned and imagined the voluptuous Sinclair beneath him in his bedroll. She had challenged him, but he still didn't know if she was playing a game with him or if she'd been serious about indulging in a husband hunt while she visited Montana that summer.

"What's that called?" Her finger pointed to a deep green plant growing near the dirt path.

"Buffalo berry, a kind of elderberry. Makes good wine, if you know how to do it. Bess had a wonderful family recipe, but Lettie has never had the knack for it. It was sweet, but had a kick like white lightning." He realized for the first time he could talk about his memories of Bess without the familiar tightening of his chest. He could recall the good parts without the sense of guilt that usually overwhelmed him.

The horse settled into a gentle gait and Jefferson leaned back in the seat, holding the reins loosely and feeling more at ease than he had in years.

"You never talk much about your family. Do you have sisters and brothers?"

Sinclair smoothed the silky fabric of her dress and shook her head. The bird on her hat bobbed gently, as if getting ready to take flight.

"I'm afraid not. I'm the spoiled child of rather indulgent parents. My mother was frail for most of my life, and my father was . . ." she paused to glance off into the distance, as if searching the soft green fields for the word. "Busy."

"But you were happy?"

Sinclair looked at him in surprise, as if this question was totally unexpected.

"Happy?" she repeated, her hands twisting the ribbons of her reticule in absentminded consternation. "I suppose I was. My parents were never mean to me, and I lived in a beautiful house with servants and books. I had lessons and all the right opportunities."

He nodded. Her words didn't match her tone of voice. There was a lingering sadness there. It wasn't any of his business, but for some reason it bothered him that something in her past could make her sound so dejected. He was used to the bubbly, effervescent Sinclair, who faced the world with verve and high spirits. It had never occurred to him that she held deep pockets of sadness.

"Why do I suppose being given all the advantages didn't add up to happiness?" He kept his eyes on the back of the horse, afraid that such a nosy question might offend her.

There was silence for a few minutes and Jefferson started to regret his statement. After all, he didn't have any right to question her. People came to the West to forget their past, not to have folks dredge up bad memories by reminding them of where they came from, or what they might be running away from. Sinclair Readford might have left another life behind her and created a new identify for herself, but it was really none of his business. He almost voiced this sentiment, but she spoke first.

"I don't think all the material advantages I had made up for the lack of love and attention I felt. My parents were always so concerned with appearances and propriety. Every decision seemed to be predicated upon what other people would think. When they chose my school, it was based on who I could make connections with, instead of academic merit." She pulled a fan out of her bag and started to wave it languidly.

"But . . . you're well-educated."

"Despite my attendance at the Shady Lawn School for Ladies of Quality." She snapped the fan in agitation. "They considered etiquette and deportment the most important curriculum for young ladies. Heaven knows, I can pour tea for royalty, but what sense is there in that if I cannot debate the important issues of the day?"

He could see the familiar rise in color as her cheeks turned rosy and he settled in for a long, drawn-out discussion. "Isn't it important for ladies to know how to make a home comfortable for their husbands? And folks put a lot of credence in fancy ways. That's how they know a place is civilized, when the ladies put up lace curtains and have tea parties."

"Tea parties?" Her voice rose an octave. "We are denied the right to vote, given no voice in this democracy and told we should settle for tea parties? Why, it makes my blood boil when my father tells me to just settle down and get married, like a proper daughter should. When he finds out that I'm . . ." Her voice trailed off as if she realized she'd said too much.

Jefferson was intrigued. "When he finds out that you're what?"

Sinclair stiffened primly on the seat. Jefferson waited, and the silence hung heavy in the carriage. He turned to raise an eyebrow in her direction and she nervously pointed at the landscape.

"What are those mountains called?" She shifted uncomfortably in her seat again.

"The Rockies." He gave her another perplexed look. "What exactly are you doing that your father wouldn't approve of Sinclair?"

She adjusted her hat, settled her hands in her lap and gave him a resigned smile. "I'm working for you. My father would have a fit if he found out I was employed on a ranch in Montana. It would be even worse if someone at the university should discover it. He would be humiliated if someone knew I was a . . . servant."

"I don't understand. You're a teacher. And that's a respectable profession for any woman, certainly better than . . ." He stopped as he realized what he'd been about to say. Better than being a whore. He didn't think that'd be a comparison Sinclair would appreciate. Especially considering he was still just as suspicious of her history as the day she'd fallen out of the window at the Blue Willow. Women just didn't end up in places like that by mistake.

Now it was Sinclair who looked at him expectantly. "Better than working in a parlor house?" Her voice dripped with sarcasm. "What kind of alternatives do the women there have? Do you think they want to work for a man like Hank Borscht? A woman doesn't have many options in today's world, get married and suffer the consequences if you've made a bad choice or become a woman who uses her body to make a living." There was disgust in her tone. "And we have men to thank for this state of affairs."

Jefferson rubbed the back of his neck. Damn it all. He didn't want Sinclair blaming him for everything that was wrong with the world. If he intended to get anywhere with her this afternoon, he'd have to soften her up, not make her madder'n a wet hen.

"You're a damn fine teacher, that's for sure." He hoped a change of subject might work.

Sinclair stared at him in disbelief. "Really? Maddie doesn't show any interest in reading or writing. She still ignores most of the things I tell her to do and I have to prepare for her bath on Saturday night as if it was a prize fight. Just how did I manage to go from troublesome female to damn fine teacher, Mr. McCloud?"

Jefferson considered her question carefully. "I believe that happened about the time you rode Brown Sugar down to the creek and had yourself a little swim." He gave her a lazy grin.

Sinclair nearly snorted in anger,

"So, you kissed me and that makes me a better teacher. How does that make me any different from the women at the Blue Willow?"

Damn the woman. How was it that she could take anything he said and twist it around? Kissing her wasn't the same as the things he'd done with the girls in the parlor house. Not that he couldn't picture her stretched out on a bed, naked. But that was just his imagination, not something he'd ever mention. She was different than the other women he knew. He felt things for her, but hell, how could he explain that?

Jefferson pulled back on the reins to bring the buggy to a halt. He wrapped the leather leads around the brake, then hauled Sinclair roughly into his arms.

She struggled against him briefly, then gave in with a resigned sigh. Grasping her chin in his hand, he forced her to look at him.

"You're a good teacher because you care about Maddie. You make her do things she hates, like eating with a fork and taking a bath. Things she's gotta learn to do if she's going to have a regular life. You badgered me into taking you into town today because you want what's best for her. A whore does what she does for the money, but you stay at the ranch and look out for Maddie because you care about her. Isn't that right?"

Sinclair looked shocked at the rough, demanding tone of his voice, and she seemed torn by his question. Her eyes were wide as they stared back at him and he thought for a moment he detected fear in them, then they grew hard with resolve.

She lifted her chin proudly. "That's true, Boss McCloud, and I force you to care about that little girl, even when you want to pretend she doesn't even exist. I persist and I make you see her, because I will not allow her to be invisible." Tears filled her eyes as she continued.

"The most terrible thing you can do to a child is to make her feel invisible. Maddie is real and alive! Yes, I want to teach her because I do care, now that I've seen all that she's capable of becoming. I won't let you destroy her spirit and abandon her again."

Jefferson released her as if he'd been scalded. He resisted the urge to slap her for the insult she'd hurled at him. His voice was hard and terse when he finally grabbed the reins.

"Do me the favor of keeping your damned opinions to yourself, Miss Readford. I pay you to teach my sister, not to pass judgment on me."

Sinclair realized that she'd gone too far. She wished she could take back the cruel words she'd just flung at him, but it was her fate it seemed, to often regret the quick tongue and fiery temper she possessed. To her detriment, both were often unleashed, only to be lamented when she had time to calm down and reflect. Or when she faced the consequences of her undisciplined remarks or crazy schemes. Boss McCloud was truly angry with her, and an apology would do little to soothe his hurt feelings. She twirled a loose curl and tried to think of a way to repair the damage.

They traveled in silence for nearly an hour, Sinclair afraid to breach the wall that had grown between them, McCloud sitting and managing the buggy with a dark scowl on his face.

The road was dusty and Sinclair began to hope that they might stop and have a drink. Dirt gathered like grit in her mouth, but she pursed her lips, determined that her first conversation with Boss McCloud after their argument wouldn't be a plea for water. The buggy continued to bump along on the rough trail.

"I don't suppose that was a very polite way to attempt to make my point." Her voice sounded harsh to her ears, as if parched from disuse, like a pump that couldn't be primed because it had sat dry too long.

He didn't look at her. He didn't even give any sign that he'd heard her speak. The silent treatment, a favorite tool of her father. When Professor Readford really wanted to punish her, he'd simply pretend she wasn't there. Invisible Sinclair. She wouldn't let McCloud do this to Maddie, and she'd be damned if he'd do it to her.

"Lovely weather we're having, don't you think? There doesn't appear to be any sign of rain and look at that sky. Spring has certainly sprung, hasn't it?" She paused to glance at him. His lips were drawn in a thin line, and he didn't even acknowledge that she'd spoken.

"Well, yes, Miss Sinclair. This is quite lovely

weather for Montana in the springtime. No blizzards on the horizon. And might I say, that is a fetching gown you have on today. The color puts roses in your cheeks, that's for sure." She made her voice low-pitched and gruff.

His scowl deepened, but he remained silent.

She giggled. "Why, sir . . . you say the most outrageous things. You could make a lady swoon with compliments like that. But, don't you suppose you can turn my head with such talk. No, sir. It will take a gentleman of pure heart and immense courage to win a lady like me." She had made her voice a high-pitched imitation of Miss Amy Lehigh, the most annoying girl at the Shady Lawn School for Ladies of Quality.

She could see him stiffen and his ears were turning a little pink. It was a good sign, it meant that he was getting irritated, just like her father.

"Why, Miss Readford, I am the man you've been waiting for all your life. I have the utmost regard for your womanly sensibilities. You are that rare creature, a sublime combination of gracious kindness, gentility and intelligence." She nearly laughed when she saw his expression go from anger to outrage.

"What the hell are you doing?" He glared at her.

She tossed her head and gave him an indignant glance, then fixed her eyes on the horizon. "Keeping myself company, because the present company is boring me. I'm having a pleasant conversation, thank you."

"With yourself?" He gave her a look that clearly said he thought she was insane.

"At least it's better than sitting here and being ignored while you have a temper tantrum." She heard him suck in a breath at her words, and she smothered a smile. She was getting under his skin and she was enjoying it.

"The devil take you, Sinclair Readford, because you are the most exasperating, ornery, unruly female who ever walked the face of God's green earth. You make Eve look like a Sunday school child. You could tempt a man to do a great deal of damage, just with that ever-flapping tongue of yours." His eyes snapped at her, and he yanked his hat down to cover his ears, as if he could block out her voice.

Sinclair considered his words for a few moments. "Well, that might be true, because I know I cannot be easy to live with, so I won't be offended by that description. There's just one thing . . ."

He flicked the reins and shook his head. "I'm afraid you're going to tell me that one thing, whether I care to hear it or not."

She smiled. "I suppose so, for I wouldn't be so exasperating if I just sat quietly and kept my mouth shut, would I? Or is it troublesome?" She gave him a challenging look. "No, wait, it's ornery."

"We'd enjoy the ride more if you just sat there quietly and kept your mind on your own business. I've heard enough from you this morning to last me well into next week." He gave her a dark look, which she supposed would have sent any one his cowpunchers off to ride the edge of the herd for a day or so. But, she was getting used to his moods and just ignored him.

Turning her head slightly, she gave him a beguiling smile. "If your prophecy should come true, we'll be traveling to hell together, sir. For you can be a devil to deal with and a trial to my patience."

He couldn't seem to form a response, and they sat silently as the dusty landscape flew past them. Finally he turned to her, an angry scowl on his face, but she'd pretended to drift off to sleep. He sat looking perturbed for the rest of the way to Ghost Horse Gulch.

When he yanked the buggy to a halt outside the Golden Hammer saloon, Sinclair woke with a small stretch and a yawn. He couldn't tell if she'd really been sleeping or just pretending to nap in order to make him mad. Either way, he *was* mad. She'd spent part of the trip giving him hell about the way he took care of his sister, then the rest simply ignoring him as if he didn't exist. Well, he'd show her that he was the boss, and he called the shots on his spread and with women. No matter how smart and educated they were.

Jumping down from the buggy, he hooked the reins around the hitching post, then took the two steps up the boardwalk with one long stride. As if he were suddenly reminded of her presence, he glanced back.

"My name is all the credit you'll need in Ghost Horse Gulch. Get what you need, then get back here. I'll be in the saloon." He made his tone clipped and harsh to show Sinclair he was all business and in charge. With two more long strides he was entering the cool confines of the saloon, with the familiar sawdust floor and smell of old beer, tobacco and unwashed men. It was comforting after the trials of dealing with a woman. When one of the girls rubbed

141

up against him enticingly, he pulled her toward him and kissed her roughly.

"I'll buy you drinks all afternoon if you just sit here and don't say one damned word!"

The woman stared at him in surprise, then nodded silently. Jefferson grabbed a tall, cool mug of beer and caught the bartender's eye. "Keep 'em coming till I tell you to stop."

The woman followed him to a table and Jefferson sat down, then ignored her. Sipping his beer, he marveled that a silent woman could be such good company.

Sinclair sat and stared at the swinging doors of the saloon in disbelief. She knew Boss McCloud was angry with her, and she'd intentionally irritated him even more when he silently ignored her. But, she simply couldn't accept that he'd left her all alone and unescorted in town. He had turned his back and walked into the saloon without a backward glance or modicum of concern for her comfort or safety.

She wished she had the temerity to follow him into the saloon and give him a piece of her mind. She could let everyone in this town know what an uncouth lout he really was. But, it was likely they already knew that. She sat and fumed, but realized that if she intended to get her errands done, she'd just have to do them by herself.

Gathering up her skirts, she stepped down out of the carriage. At least McCloud could have helped her from the buggy. She straightened her back and studied her surroundings. On her previous visit to town, she'd been distracted and in a hurry. Now she had time to study the false-front facades of a variety of businesses that made up the commercial core of Ghost Horse Gulch. There was a mercantile, a pharmacy, at least half a dozen saloons, a hotel with an attached restaurant, and only a few doors down from there, a sign that said Dressmaker and Millinery. Exactly what she was looking for.

Sinclair adjusted her hat and climbed the wooden steps of the boardwalk that led to the saloon. Then she marched past the double doors without a glance, trying to ignore the harsh sound of female laughter and the tinny music of the hurdy-gurdy coming from within. Sniffing in indignation, she imagined Boss McCloud seated inside, with a plump, barely clad woman perched on his knee. The man could be such a barbarian.

She paused at the door of the dressmaker, then pushed it open and entered a small room piled high with fabric, feathers, ribbons and trim. Sinclair closed the door and sighed deeply, happy to once again be in a familiar place that reminded her she was a woman. She'd had enough of cows, horses, dirty trails and arrogant cowboys. Sinclair grinned as a small woman came out of the back room and inquired if she could be of service.

"Perhaps you could tell me one thing, is Mr. Jefferson McCloud known as a wealthy man in these parts?" Sinclair let her eyes roam over the lovely velvets and satins laid out on one table.

"Oh yes. He owns the Cripple Creek Ranch and it's one of the biggest spreads in Montana. I'd say he's a man of excellent means."

The woman studied Sinclair with a critical eye. "Is there anything I can help you with?"

Sinclair nodded emphatically. "Mr. McCloud is my employer, and I'm here to place an order for clothing for his sister, Miss Madison McCloud. You do make children's clothing, don't you?"

The woman smiled back. "Of course, and it would be a pleasure to provide a service for Mr. McCloud, everyone knows what a terrible burden that child has been." Her voice dropped to a stage whisper, "Not right in the head, that one."

Sinclair wanted to form a sharp retort and tell her Maddie wasn't nearly as much of a trial as her overbearing, bossy brother. But she didn't want to alienate the woman, who might be the only seamstress in Ghost Horse Gulch. Sinclair could sew, but she didn't really enjoy it and she was too busy caring for Maddie to make her a new wardrobe. She swallowed her response and put on her best "lady of the house" expression.

Fingering some of the finer cloth, she sniffed. "I'm Madison's teacher and I'm in charge of ordering a new wardrobe for her. I can see that your goods are not up to the quality I usually demand." She gave a haughty toss of her head. "But of course, this is Montana, not Philadelphia, so I'll have to make do."

The two women stood facing each other. For a moment it appeared that the dressmaker was going to take offense, then she seemed to calculate the cost of a new wardrobe for Miss Madison McCloud, and gave Sinclair a polite nod.

"I don't have much demand for ball gowns or evening wear. Simple calicos and durable cottons are more to the liking of Montana women. But, I do have some lovely yard goods over here." She pointed to a table with several rolls of fine lawn, batiste and eyelet. "I believe I can make some charming things for a little girl."

She stretched a small, delicate hand towards Sinclair. "My name is Abby-Rose Clement and I'm the dressmaker. I don't have much call to make children's clothing, but I have some lovely patterns for little girls." She looked a bit wistful. "I had always hoped for a child of my own, to make little dresses for."

Sinclair melted at the despondent tone in Abby-Rose's voice. Abby-Rose Clement wasn't that much older than she was and there was an air of loss about her. Despite her awful morning ride with Boss McCloud, Sinclair didn't intend to spend the whole day in a bad mood.

"Calico and cotton will be perfect, and you're right of course, more suitable for a child on a ranch. Why don't we have some tea?" She winced when she remembered McCloud's earlier reference to ladies and tea parties. She pushed his arrogant, handsome face from her mind's eye. "Then I'd like to see your pattern books. I'm sure you'll have some enchanting ideas for my little Miss Maddie."

Abby-Rose cheered up at the suggestion of tea and conversation. "Let me put the water on to boil, then I'll get my books. Why don't we sit over here, near the window? The light's better there."

Sinclair moved to the small table covered with a delicate lace tablecloth. There were two deep chairs upholstered with a pale rose fabric and Sinclair sank into one of them gratefully, admiring the color and comfort. The lurching of the carriage on the way into town had made her back stiff. She settled in for a pleasant afternoon of tea and female conversation. And it was her plan to have a grand time spending as much of Boss McCloud's money as she could. It was poor revenge, but it would simply have to do.

Chapter Ten

Sinclair left the dressmaker's shop feeling smug and content. The hour spent with Abigail Clement had lifted her spirits, as only conversation about fashion and style could. Sinclair had even ordered a new riding habit and discovered she preferred the simple, elegant design Abigail offered over the heavy, velvet costume she had ruined with her fall into the creek.

With eager steps Sinclair swept into the mercantile, pausing to allow her eyes to adjust to the dim interior. There were men clustered about a checkerboard and several women in gingham dresses and simple bonnets standing at the counter conversing with a tall, distinguished-looking man who appeared to be the owner. They all stopped talking to stare at her.

Sinclair smiled like a dowager queen bidding good-day to her subjects and began to peruse the merchandise. The store was filled with so many wares, it was difficult for her to take it all in at once. There was a wall filled with canned goods, kitchenware, tin pans and washtubs, scrub boards, brooms and every household item she could imagine. On the opposite wall she could see tack, bridles, rope, spurs, even hats and dusters. All along the back wall were tins of coffee in colorful cans, tobacco, rolls of fabric, and an assortment of items placed to entice the customer.

There was hardly an empty space on the counter, with baskets of eggs, rounds of cheese, glass containers filled with penny candy and a display of revolvers and ammunition placed strategically under glass. Sinclair delighted in the bright confusion of the scene.

The man behind the counter gave her the measuring grin of a born salesman. "I'll be right with you, ma'am. Would you like to browse around a bit?" There was a soft cadence to his words, and Sinclair thought she could detect a drawl.

Sinclair nodded. "Could you please direct me to the children's things . . . shoes and such?"

The women didn't bother to stop staring at her, and Sinclair had a momentary inclination to wrinkle her nose or stick out her tongue. Didn't people in Montana know it was impolite to stare? Instead she just lifted her head and moved as regally as she could toward the table piled high with children's clothes.

She sorted through the shoes carefully, then used her hand to measure the bottom of a boot. The tip of her middle finger to the center of her palm. Perfect. She tucked the boots under her arm and wandered toward a display of bisque dolls, a miniature iron stove and several sets of tiny china dishes. She suddenly realized Maddie didn't have a single toy to play with. No small rag doll or stuffed animal to pretend with, and no jacks, marbles, or top . . . in fact nothing. Sinclair shook her head sadly. Every child needed toys.

She moved on to a display of ladies hats, which she quickly dismissed as poorly made and ugly, then turned as the man with the soft voice beckoned her. "Anything I could help you find, ma'am?"

Sinclair was relieved to see that the two busybodies had left the store, and she carefully stepped around barrels of flour, sugar, pickles and nails to stop at the smooth oak counter.

"My name is Miss Readford, I'm employed at the Cripple Creek ranch by Mr. McCloud." She paused at his name, thinking she'd like to add, that arrogant know-it-all who has the manners of an aborigine.

The man nodded at her. "How do you do, Miss Readford. Does Lettie need supplies?"

Sinclair pulled a folded piece of paper from her reticule. She smiled when she recalled the way Lettie had insisted she write down each item, as if she suspected Sinclair was too stupid to remember. After completing the list, Sinclair was inclined to agree with her. There were items Sinclair didn't recognize on the list, but she'd be darned if she'd give Lettie the satisfaction of knowing that. She caught the words *extra fancy cotton web girth* and frowned. She didn't have a clue what that could be, but Lettie had insisted Ollie needed one. Considering the rather substantial size of the man, perhaps it was some kind of belt.

Sinclair held out the list. "Here are the supplies Lettie wanted, and I'd like to add these to Mr. McCloud's account." She set the small pair of boots on the counter, then glanced over her shoulder. "And the items in your window display, the little stove, dishes and the doll. I would like to take the toys with me, if you don't mind. Lettie said one of the hands will be in on Tuesday to pick up the rest of the supplies."

The businessman was all affable charm now, as he realized that he had a customer of quality in the store. "Could I interest you in some yard goods? We just got a nice shipment in from St. Louis."

"No, I think not." Sinclair's eyes went to the large glass jars of penny candy, and she had a sudden, brilliant inspiration. "But I would like some of these, in fact . . ." She remembered something she had seen on the back shelf, and she turned to point it out. "If I could have that small glass dish, the one shaped like a heart. And some of these"—she indicated a jar of peppermint sticks—"and some of those butterscotch candies, and some of those." Her small gloved hand notioned to the row of glass candy containers as she picked out a handful of each type of candy displayed. She only hoped Maddie had a sweet tooth.

The storekeeper was ebullient. "I'll wrap these up for you right away. And Miss, if there's anything else, you just send word by one of the hands, and I'll get it right out to you."

Sinclair turned to wait for the man to wrap all of her items, when she had another inspiration. She turned back to the shopkeeper. "School supplies?"

"Slates, primers, chalk, pens, ink and chapbooks. I got 'em all." He pointed across the room, just beyond the wooden case filled with a rainbow of embroidery thread. Sinclair gave him a brilliant smile and headed to the shelf, gathering the supplies eagerly. She could almost smell the chalk dust and ink that brought back memories of her own school days. She had everything she needed when her eyes fell upon a small container that read ARTISTS' CRAYON PENCILS. Sinclair remembered her own joy as a child, as she sat and drew pictures of the far-away places to which her father traveled. Drawing had filled many long, lonely hours of her childhood and on impulse she picked up the small wooden box, adding it to her pile.

Dumping her treasures on the counter, Sinclair pondered her purchases carefully. "I suppose this should do it, at least for today. I'll send word if I discover there are any items I'm missing." She watched with a small measure of trepidation when she realized the amount of money she had spent. McCloud had only mumbled that his name was sufficient credit and hadn't given her any specific guidelines. It would serve him right if she bankrupted him. Although she rather doubted a man with as many cows as he had and land that stretched across the horizon could be poor. Still, she should give him an accurate accounting.

"Could you tally a bill for the items I've purchased today? I'll need to give it to Mr. McCloud." She made her voice sound as matter-of-fact as possible. Well, if she'd spent too much money, it would just give him something more to complain about. And the man certainly seemed to enjoy doing that.

When all of her items were gathered into several bundles of brown paper and secured with string, the shopkeeper handed her a neatly printed invoice. She felt a small ripple of relief when she saw that she had only spent ten dollars. She had all of these wonderful things for Maddie, and all for only ten dollars. The clothing she'd ordered from the dressmaker had totaled nearly twenty dollars, which Sinclair felt was a magnificent bargain considering the quality. All in all, a most productive day.

Sinclair stepped outside into the bright afternoon sunlight and glanced across the street at the buggy, still standing in front of the saloon. She gave a thin smile when she noticed McCloud was nowhere to be seen. Likely he was having too much fun with the dancing girls in the Golden Hammer to give a thought to her. Her heels clicked firmly against the boardwalk as she advanced on the buggy. She'd just put her packages in the boot, then she'd go to the restaurant and enjoy a lovely lunch. If he decided to come looking for her, fine. But she was darned if she would just sit out in the hot sun all afternoon waiting for him to stop sucking down beer long enough to remember he'd brought her to town with him.

Sinclair was so busy working herself into a temper that she failed to notice a quick movement in the alley as she prepared to cross the street. She was too surprised to even scream when an arm snaked out to grab her, pulling her into the shadows.

"Well, well . . . if it isn't my little runaway. I figured if I waited long enough, you'd turn up."

Sinclair stood facing Hank Borscht. His cold eyes moved down her body and she shivered. She wanted to scream, to pull away, but she was frozen in his grip, too terrified to make a sound. She could see the small corners of his lips turn up into a grimace of a smile.

"I've been thinking about you, sweet thing, and missing you. Have you been missing me?"

Jefferson sat down with a plateful of sausages, bread, boiled cabbage and potatoes. His stomach grumbled in anticipation and he decided that as soon as he finished his lunch, he'd go and find Sinclair. He'd resolved as he sat and mused into his beer that perhaps he'd been a bit gruff with her that morning. The woman could be a burr under his saddle, but he had to admit, she was fine to look at and once in a while she even had a point. While he didn't think he ignored Maddie, he certainly didn't make much effort to spend time with the girl. When the spring roundup was over, he'd take more of an interest in her. It wouldn't be much of a chore to spend time with his sister if the shapely little blonde was around to keep things interesting.

He heard a commotion at the front of the saloon as Ole Bowlegs from the Triple X came running in, whispered to several patrons and they all rushed out through the swinging doors. Maybe there was going to be a showdown out in the street, he thought, although most of the time it just consisted of two drunk cowboys who needed someone to disarm them. Stories of gunfights were highly exaggerated.

There was more whispering and several of the saloon girls went to look out the front window, then laughed and headed out the door. Jefferson was curious, but he was reluctant to leave his lunch to see what was going on. He kept eating as he watched the bar clear, but put down his fork when the poker players scooped up their winnings, threw down their cards and headed out the door. If the game was breaking up, there must be a real show out in the street.

Jefferson wiped his mouth on his shirtsleeve and decided to join everyone else out in the street. Pushing his shoulders through the swinging doors of the saloon he could hear one of the crowd commenting.

"I'll bet it's that runaway, hula-hula whore everybody's been talking about. The one Hank lost. He mighta found her, but that's one Calico Queen who ain't gonna go easy!"

Jefferson shoved his way through the people on the boardwalk and stopped when he finally caught sight of the commotion that had drawn everyone outside.

Sinclair was brandishing her parasol in the air, aiming for Hank Borscht, who wasn't doing a very good job of avoiding her. She smacked him several times on the side of the head, but it appeared her efforts only served to make Borscht more determined as he advanced upon her.

Jefferson felt his temper surge as Sinclair stepped backward, trying to escape from Borscht, then tripped over some brown packages that were strewn behind her. Her legs flew up into the air as she sat down hard and Borscht grabbed the parasol, tossing it aside.

Jefferson's long legs couldn't carry him across the dry, dusty street fast enough. He felt his hand on his revolver as Borscht raised his arm to slap Sinclair.

"If you want to live to see another sunrise, Hank, I'd advise you to drop your hand."

Jefferson's voice sounded calm and cold, considering how flaming mad he was. He crossed to stand in front of Hank and stare down at him, the revolver pointed at the bastard's heart.

"In Montana, we don't care much for men who beat ladies in public. In fact, we're not too fond of those who beat 'em in private neither."

Hank stared at Jefferson in shock, then stepped back to brush his starched white shirt carefully, as if Sinclair's attack had mussed him. He pointed his thumb at Sinclair.

"You're right, McCloud. She's a bit of a handful, if you know what I mean. I'll get her back to the house and deal with her there." He leaned down to grab Sinclair, and Jefferson shoved the muzzle of the gun into Hank's belly. Hank stopped to stare up at Jefferson, his face showing his confusion.

"She's stubborn and smart and a man needs a firm hand with a woman like her. Just let me get her to the Blue Willow. I'll straighten her out, that's for sure." His hand stretched out again to grab Sinclair.

"I can't let you take Miss Readford anyplace she doesn't want to go, Hank. As for handling her, I have an inkling it's gonna take a better man than you to do that. Now, you'd best step away. You touch her again, I'll be obliged to shoot you."

Sinclair sat silently watching the two men engaged in a cold, angry battle of wills.

Hank glanced down at her, seemed to consider his options, then forced a smile at Jefferson. "It's none of your business, McCloud. This whore owes me some money or some service. Either way, I need to get paid."

Jefferson never took his eyes off Hank Borscht, as he stepped back to lean down and offer a hand to help Sinclair up. She moaned softly and he felt her lean against him as she came to her feet. He could see her wince out of the corner of his eye. She'd been hurt and it was all his fault. He was supposed to be protecting her, but he'd been too busy nursing his wounded pride to make sure she was safe. He should just shoot Borscht.

Jefferson wanted blood, but it occurred to him a city woman like Sinclair wouldn't think shooting a man too heroic. In fact, she was the type who'd likely hold such a thing against him, so he'd have to reconsider. He enjoyed playing her hero too much to jeopardize it over a man like Hank Borscht.

"The one thing you need to keep straight, Hank, is Miss Readford works for me at the Cripple Creek. You know how I am about the ranch and the folks who work there. I'll discuss this matter of money with her, and see you get paid, if there is a debt."

Hank looked like he wanted to argue, but glanced at Jefferson's face, then the gun, and shrugged.

"You'll get tired of her, McCloud. She's not one of those biddable females you like. This one's more thorns than roses, and you'll get worn out from being scratched. I'll wait for her."

Hank gave Sinclair a dark scowl, then nodded in the direction of Jefferson. "Let me know when she's more trouble than she's worth, McCloud, and I'll take her off your hands."

Jefferson watched as Hank finished dusting off his shirt and climbed the steps to the boardwalk, heading back toward the parlor house. When he was sure the man wasn't coming back, he put his gun back into his holster and turned toward Sinclair.

She was hobbling about, gathering up the packages strewn on the ground and tucking her bedraggled hat with the stuffed bird on it under her arm. In the scuffle with Hank it had fallen to the ground, then she had apparently sat on it. She held the packages out toward him and gave him a disgusted look.

"Would it be too much trouble to ask you to carry these to the carriage for me? I appear to have hurt my ankle and I'll need to lean on my parasol in order to get across the street." Her tone was chilly and aloof and Jefferson felt the familiar rise of his temper. He'd almost killed a man to protect her and she acted as if the whole incident was his fault. Then he realized he'd been blaming himself just a few moments earlier. Still, she could say something nice to him. He liked it when she said that hero stuff.

Instead she shoved the packages toward him and glared. Then her eyes filled with tears as she leaned forward to take a step. He forgot about being angry with her as he grew concerned over her injury. Without a word he dropped the packages and swept her up into his arms, carrying her across the street.

"This is not necessary, McCloud. You're making a spectacle of me in front of the whole town." Her lower lip trembled and he could see the anger in her eyes.

McCloud gave her a sideways grin. "As if attacking Hank with your parasol in the middle of the street and being called the runaway hula-hula whore wasn't enough of a spectacle? Sugar, you're the whole damn circus come to town."

Sinclair stared at him silently. She glanced over at the people gathered in front of the saloon and her face turned a rosy pink that matched her dress as she heard them laughing and making lewd remarks.

As McCloud settled her into the buggy and went back for her parcels, she tried to ignore the people pointing at her. She sat in glum silence as Jefferson climbed onto the seat and yanked on the reins to get the horse moving.

"I have never in my life been so humiliated. How could you leave me all alone and unprotected? Why, I could be back at the Blue Willow right now, with that awful Hank Borscht, doing God only knows what." She tossed her head defiantly.

"I'm going to have to learn to shoot in order to protect myself on these excursions, as I can see that once you're distracted, it takes a battle to pull you away from your beer and your chippies."

Jefferson sat silently as Sinclair droned on about all of his faults, from ignoring her and guzzling beer, to neglecting to put a bullet in Hank Borscht's evil heart and ridding the earth of such a vile, despicable lowlife. Jefferson slowed down finally and pulled the horse and buggy to a stop in the shade of an enormous pine tree.

Sinclair was trying to adjust the bird on her hat. "I swear, I had no idea Montana would be so hard on millinery, I'd have brought more hats."

She glanced up as the buggy stopped. "Why have we stopped here? Is there something wrong?"

Jefferson climbed out of the buggy, went to her side and without a word lifted her down to the ground. Removing his hat, he threw it down on the seat, then turned to face her.

"What the hell is a hula-hula?"

Sinclair swallowed. She could see the dark flare of anger in his eyes, and she didn't know how to explain the situation to him without sounding offensive.

"I only told Polly that so she wouldn't take all of my clothes." Sinclair brushed back a wisp of hair that was falling over her forehead and into her eyes.

"And what is it, Sinclair?" His voice was hard as he pronounced her name and advanced toward her. She tried to step back but winced at the pain in her ankle. Glancing up at him, she gave him a smile, but his expression didn't change.

"I only know it's a primitive dance, performed by the natives of the Sandwich Islands. I read about it in my father's journal once." She tried to make her voice plaintive. "I was rather desperate at the time I told Polly I knew how to do it. It distracted her."

"So, you told Polly that you knew how to do this dance, in order to keep her from taking all your clothes?" Now he seemed intrigued. "And do you know how?"

Sinclair straightened her shoulders. "I hardly see how that relates to our agreement, McCloud. I doubt that performing a dance will be part of my duties at your ranch."

Jefferson looked thoughtful. "I don't know, things can get pretty dull around the Cripple Creek, maybe I'd like to see this, um . . . hula-hula dance." His voice deepened over the words, and Sinclair felt as if he'd caressed her. She was staring up at him, as he gently reached down to curl a strand of her hair around one finger.

Her heart was beating fast again, and she felt a strange lightheaded glimmer flow through her. She

159

liked the way he was watching her, it made her feel full of womanly charm.

"I really can't perform the hula-hula, I only read about it once." Her voice sounded breathless to her own ears and she couldn't seem to turn away from the heated look in his eyes.

"You've got a pretty good imagination, Sinclair. I bet you could do it, if you really put your mind to it."

Sinclair shook her head violently. "I really couldn't. It sounded so . . . primitive and sensuous."

She could feel his gaze fixed on her lips and she wanted to run her tongue across them, but he was too close, nearly suffocating her with his presence.

His finger traced an imaginary pattern down the side of her cheek to rest at the lace edge of her gown. "Sensuous?"

She closed her eyes as his arm encircled her waist and pulled her toward him. She finally did run the tip of her tongue across her lips, in anticipation of his kiss.

"The women perform it nearly naked." Her breath was coming in small bursts now and her blood felt heated. "The men dance with them." She was swaying on her feet as his warmth enveloped her and she inhaled the combination of leather and pine that she associated with him.

He tightened his hold, pulling her hard against him. "If that's the truth, I'll be thinking about taking a trip to those islands, because that must be a sight to see."

His mouth claimed hers. There was tender ferocity in his kiss, as if he barely held himself in check. Her arms snaked around his neck as she pulled him down to her, the taste of him making her shiver in delight. Her limbs melted easily into his. His hand cupped her bottom to pull her closer to his hips, their bodies melding as if they were designed for each other. They clung to each other, until Jefferson finally lifted his head to study her.

"I've been thinking about doing that since the last time I kissed you. Been trying to work up the courage," he said.

Sinclair felt warm and docile, she didn't want his lips torn from hers, all she wanted was more. There was an inexplicable humming in her veins that told her there was so much more to experience. She was hungry for the pleasure that he seemed on the verge of offering. She didn't want to talk, she wanted to be held and kissed.

"Stop talking, cowboy," she whispered as she pulled him back toward her and her lips found his again. She reveled in the delightful feelings coursing through her. And she felt powerful as she heard him moan softly as she stroked his chest.

He pulled away from her, a thin sheen of moisture appearing on his forehead. Pushing her gently from him, he wiped his face with his bandanna. "God, Sinclair. You can't do that to a man."

She looked at him innocently, her lips felt bruised and swollen from his kisses. "Do what?"

He started to reach for her again, then turned aside and took a few steps away from the buggy. Glancing back at her, he took a few more steps. She started to follow him but he held out his hand, as if to warn her.

"Stay back there, or I can't be responsible for anything I do. Woman, you push a man way beyond the limits."

Sinclair was baffled. "Are you angry again? I suppose you're going to turn around and take me back to Hank because I'm so much trouble. I'm surprised you didn't just hand me over when he said that. I've heard you express that same opinion more than once."

She had her hands on her hips and stood glaring at him. He looked at her and chuckled, then began to laugh in a great rollicking roar. He stood and laughed while Sinclair fumed. After a few minutes he finally gained control.

"Hank's wrong, you know, I'm beginning to think the rose is worth the thorns. Honey is all the sweeter for the trouble it takes to get it, just ask any grizzly." There was a catch to his voice and dark knowledge shining in his eyes.

He was still grinning as he helped her back up into the buggy. She gave him a disparaging look.

"I never know what to expect from you, McCloud. You rage at me, then kiss me as if you mean it, but end up laughing at me. How can I tell from one moment to the next how you really feel?"

Jefferson put his hat back on and grabbed the reins. The dimple appeared again as he leaned forward, stopping only inches from her face and giving her a wide smile. "If I'm kissing you, sugar, I mean it."

They rode in silence for a few minutes, then Sinclair shifted in her seat and looked at him. He was still grinning.

162

"I suppose you enjoy this sort of thing, making a woman crazy."

Jefferson raised an eyebrow at her. "I can't say I have much experience doing that, but if kissing makes you crazy, I'm all for it."

Sinclair stared out at the landscape and tried to ignore him. She heard him chuckling again and turned to study him. In the weeks she'd been at the ranch she had rarely seen him even smile, but today the man was in such high spirits he couldn't seem to control himself. She wondered what had happened to cause such a change. Then she considered the morning and realized that she had happened. She had made Boss McCloud happy. Or at least she'd made him laugh. She smiled at the thought.

"You have dimples, you know."

Jefferson frowned. "I didn't know that."

"And a really nice laugh, it's just too bad you don't use it more often." She gave him an impertinent look.

He grew serious for a moment. "I can't say there's been much to laugh about in my life until lately. Maybe I just got out of practice, but I reckon with you around, well . . ." He started laughing again.

Sinclair wrinkled her nose at him. "I don't think that being attacked and called the runaway hula-hula whore by the whole town is really a laughing matter. But, please, enjoy yourself at my expense." She waved a gloved hand in his direction.

"Folks will talk about nearly anything, from the weather to each other. Gossip isn't worth paying attention to. As for Hank, you let me worry about him."

Sinclair tried to reassure herself and she almost told

Jefferson about Hank's threat. She swallowed when she recalled his words, flung at her as he dragged her into the dark alleyway. "You'd better come along with me, missy, if you ever want to meet that Aunt Tilly of yours."

Hank knew something about her aunt's disappearance, and she wanted to share that information with Jefferson. He had protected her and she felt sure if it had been necessary, he'd have killed Hank Borscht to prevent her from being taken back to the Blue Willow. She watched the man riding next to her, handling the reins with ease.

Jefferson shook his head at her. "I was just trying to picture Hank managing you. Now, don't take offense, because I mean this in the best way, but you're a handful. Hank isn't enough man for you by any means. You'd outthink and outmaneuver him without even trying."

Sinclair lifted her nose in the air. "That man is a stupid pig. It wouldn't even be a challenge to manipulate him."

Jefferson laughed again and Sinclair narrowed her eyes at him. "I suppose you think you're the kind of man who can manage me?"

Jefferson gave her a side-long glance, clicked at the horse, then gave a deep sigh.

"I'm beginning to think I might like to try, and God knows even if it killed me, it could be worth it."

Sinclair smiled wickedly and decided that providing entertainment for Boss McCloud was proving to be a pleasure. She fidgeted in the seat for a few moments, then leaned into the hard, muscular side of the man riding next to her. He held the reins with one hand while he put the other around her shoulders protectively. Savoring the sweetness of the moment, she enjoyed the warmth of his body next to hers and decided not to mention Hank's threat.

Chapter Eleven

"You plannin' on ridin' drag today, Boss?"

Jefferson jerked on the reins of his horse and pulled Old Pete to a halt. Damn, he thought in irritation, if he didn't start paying attention, he would end up at the tail end of the herd, eating dust all day.

Ollie spit on the ground as he rode his horse up next to Jefferson. "Guess you must be all tuckered out from that tossin' and turnin' you were doin' last night. Musta put your roll on a pile of rocks."

Jefferson tried to ignore the old man. Ollie had been with him for a long time and he felt he could speak his mind whenever he had an inclination. Right now Jefferson was in no mood for jokes or sly remarks.

He had tossed and turned all night. Every time he managed to finally fall asleep, he dreamed of Sinclair. He could feel the softness of her lips and the way she pressed against him, every warm, womanly curve of her body fitting against him perfectly. Then he'd suddenly realize it was just a dream and he'd wake up, his body rock-hard with desire and aching for release.

Ollie started to roll a cigarette and motioned toward the herd. "We almost got 'em up to pasture. Why don't you head back in? Seems to me like you been eager to get back to the ranch ever since we left. Maybe yer worried 'bout Maddie."

Jefferson gave his best friend a dark scowl. Ollie never pried into his business and he was the best cowhand Jefferson had ever known. Years ago, when he'd seen the way Jefferson had wanted to learn and prove himself, Ollie had taken him under his wing. Everything Jefferson McCloud knew about cattle and ranching was because Ollie had the patience to teach him.

"Seems like I can't think straight these past few days. Maybe I will head back in, the men know what they're about."

Ollie nodded in agreement. "Best hands this side of the Mississippi. And when you get back, why don't you invite Miss Sinclair to the dance over at the Circle B? Bet she'd like to see Lord what's his name again. Seems like she took a real shine to him when he come by."

Jefferson felt his grip tighten on the reins. He tried not to let his irritation show, but the mention of Evan Billingsley's name made him see red. He was jealous of the Englishman, with his smooth ways and fancy education. He remembered the way Sinclair had talked about him and how she admired his knowledge of books and his fancy pedigree. Hell, what did a cowboy from Montana have to offer a woman like Sinclair Readford?

Jefferson shook himself. "You know I don't bother with the roundup dances, Ollie. Waste of time if you ask me."

Ollie nodded in agreement. "I know that, Boss. But, if I had me a fine-lookin' filly, I'd saddle her up and take her to town, just to show her off and make the other fellers jealous."

Jefferson gave the suggestion some consideration. All the ranchers from the area would be at the dance and most of the folks from Ghost Horse Gulch. It was a tradition to gather at the spring and fall roundup, visit, dance and exchange stories. There was always too much work on a cattle ranch and most folks took advantage of any chance to have a good time. He hadn't been to one of the gatherings since Bess died, but maybe Ollie was right.

"Might be worth it to see their faces when she shows up in one of those fancy dresses with all the fixin's. She sure is easy on the eyes."

Jefferson might have challenged another man for noticing Sinclair, but he trusted Ollie. And he knew the old man admired Sinclair Readford above most other women, because she'd taught him to write his name and to read. Some days he'd gone on about her so much Jefferson had wondered if Ollie wasn't just a little bit in love with her himself. Not that he'd blame the man, but it might be an inconvenience for both of them to have a hankering for the same lady.

Jefferson nodded. "Might be worth it, to see their faces." He tried to make his voice noncommittal.

"Bet she can dance. City girls go to schools fer lear-

Join the Historical Romance Book Club and GET 4 FREE* BOOKS NOW!

A $23.96 Value!

Yes! I want to subscribe to the Historical Romance Book Club.

Please send me my **4 FREE* BOOKS.** I have enclosed $2.00 for shipping/handling. Each month I'll receive the four newest Historical Romance selections to preview for 10 days. If I decide to keep them, I will pay the Special Members Only discounted price of just $4.24 each, a total of $16.96, plus $2.00 shipping/handling ($23.55 US in Canada). This is a **SAVINGS OF AT LEAST $5.00** off the bookstore price. There is no minimum number of books I must buy, and I may cancel the program at any time. In any case, the **4 FREE* BOOKS** are mine to keep.

*In Canada, add $5.00 shipping/handling per order for the first shipment. For all future shipments to Canada, the cost of membership is $23.55 US, which includes shipping and handling. (All payments must be made in US dollars.)

NAME: _____

ADDRESS: _____

CITY: _____ **STATE:** _____

COUNTRY: _____ **ZIP:** _____

TELEPHONE: _____

E-MAIL: _____

SIGNATURE: _____

If under 18, Parent or Guardian must sign. Terms, prices, and conditions subject to change. Subscription subject to acceptance. Dorchester Publishing reserves the right to reject any order or cancel any subscription.

nin' such things. I bet she'd be the prettiest girl and the best dancer." Ollie flicked the cigarette away. "Man'd have to be a damned fool not to take a woman like Miss Sinclair to a dance."

Jefferson gave his friend a grin. "I been accused of being that more'n once, but I get your drift. I think Miss Readford deserves a night out, and seeing her in her fancy duds at the Circle B would be something. Like you said, it would make the other men greener than new grass in the springtime."

Ollie slapped his knee. "That's the spirit, Boss. But you make sure you hang onto that little gal real tight. I don't want none of them other fellers puttin' their arms 'round her and holdin' her real close. She smells so good, one of them boys is apt to sneak off with her."

Jefferson turned his horse toward the Cripple Creek and leaned forward in the saddle. He gave Ollie a hard look.

"You ever know me to let loose of what's mine?"

Ollie leaned back and gave Jefferson a measured look. "I ain't sure that gal is your'n. Better make up yer mind."

Jefferson shook his fist at Ollie. "You old buffalo fart, you'd better mind your own business." As Jefferson kicked his horse and rode off he could hear Ollie laughing.

Jefferson let the screen door slam shut behind him as he paused to inhale the warm, yeasty smell of bread baking. Now this was a welcome home. He set the buckets of water on the floor and paused at the scarred pine table long enough to rip off a chunk of bread and stuff it into his mouth. Its warm, airy texture melted on his tongue and he looked over his shoulder sheepishly to make sure Lettie wouldn't catch him as he ripped off another piece.

When he heard her steps on the porch he quickly ducked into the pantry and felt like a schoolboy once again. He heard the door slam and then steps come to a halt at the table.

"Now, what kinda varmint has been inta my bread? I swear, I cain't get one thing done around here without another thing appearin' in its place. Looks to me like I'd best get my razor strap out 'cause someone in this house needs a lickin'."

Jefferson came out of the pantry licking his lips. "In more'n one way, Lettie. That's the best bread I ever ate."

Lettie put her hands on her hips and glowered at him. "I should have figgered it was you. None of the other men 'round here have the guts to mess with me. 'Cept that broken down old man you travel with and Lord knows he just ain't got no sense at all."

He could see that despite her words, her eyes were quickly scanning the room to see if Ollie was with him.

"No need to worry about him, I left him out on the range."

Lettie rubbed her hands on her apron and tried to look unconcerned. "Good enough place for that old fool." She glanced up sharply at Jefferson.

"And what are you doin' back so soon? Did ya get that herd up to the new grass already?"

Jefferson leaned back against the wall and nodded. "Close enough, so I figured I'd come back and clean up, then maybe take you and Miss Sinclair over to the dance at the Circle B."

Lettie stared at him dumbfounded. She went to the basket of clothes she'd brought in with her and started to fold linen towels.

"Don't recall the last time you went to one of them shindigs." She paused in her folding to purse her lips. "Seems like I remember last year you called it a bunch of foolishness."

Jefferson was slightly embarrassed.

"Lettie, don't start on me. I need a bath, so I'm going to bring in the kettle and put it on the stove. Could you find me some of that store-bought soap the judge uses and bring it down?"

Lettie sniffed, threw a large towel at him and tucked the basket under her arm.

"Next thing I know you'll be gettin' all cut and curried proper, just like that fancy Englishman over at the Circle B."

Jefferson frowned. Why was it today everyone had to remind him that Evan Billingsley was a perfect gentleman? He was beginning to really dislike the man, which was a shame, because up until now he'd considered him a friend.

"Is Miss Sinclair around, I thought I'd invite her to go with us this evening."

Lettie gave a snort of derision. "I ain't goin' to no fancy doin's. My feet hurt and my back aches from haulin' this wash all day. You take Miss Phillydelphia and go on. Make a fool of yerself but leave me be. I'd rather stay here and keep an eye on Maddie."

Jefferson could hear her muttering under her breath as she went up the stairs. He grinned as he went out to the woodshed and hauled in the big iron kettle, poured the buckets of water into it and put it on the stove to heat. He couldn't help thinking that he'd be spending the whole evening with Sinclair. Alone.

Climbing the stairs two at a time, he paused in front of Maddie's door to watch Sinclair reading a story to his sister, who was nestled in her lap. Funny thing, he couldn't remember any of the other hired caretakers holding Maddie. In fact, the only thing he could remember was a parade of women who told him the girl should be locked away so she couldn't harm anyone.

Maddie was hugging a doll and if he didn't know better he could imagine she was just a child listening to a story. She wasn't screaming or rocking. In fact, she appeared to be studying the book Sinclair held in front of them with intense concentration.

As he stood in the doorway he realized the room seemed different. Had it always been yellow? He didn't think so. And there were lace curtains at the window. The afternoon sun was shining through them to reveal patterns of light and shadow on the polished floor. It was warm and cozy and it smelled like Sinclair. Like riding through wildflowers in the middle of summer.

He realized the voice had stopped. When he glanced across the room he found Sinclair giving him a warm smile as she gently set Maddie aside to hurry over to him.

"Jefferson," there was delight in her voice, "you're back. I'm so glad to see you."

Jefferson swallowed. It had been a long time since

he'd been welcomed home like that and he held out his hands as she moved toward him. She grabbed them easily, lifting her glowing face to laugh up at him.

"I thought you'd be gone at least another day, that's what Lettie said."

Inhaling her scent, he closed his eyes to treasure this moment. He wanted to keep this memory safe with all the other small pleasures that came too few and far between.

"I wanted to surprise you," he said.

Sinclair gave him an impish grin and pulled him toward Maddie.

"We have a surprise for you too. It's so exciting, Jefferson. Maddie is getting better." The excitement in her voice was contagious and Jefferson found himself grinning back at her.

Standing proudly in front of Maddie she put her finger to her lips to signal Jefferson should remain quiet.

"Maddie?"

The girl lifted her head to look at Sinclair. "Would you like to go for a walk?"

Maddie stood, gave Jefferson a glance and then nodded at Sinclair.

Jefferson felt a thick lump in his throat. Madison had responded. He gave Sinclair a fleeting look, then found himself moving slowly toward his sister, staring at her in wonder.

Sinclair gave him a small shove and whispered under her breath. "Kneel down and talk to her, please."

Jefferson felt lightheaded as he stared at Sinclair in amazement, but he found himself falling to his knees as she'd requested and gently putting his hands on Maddie's shoulders.

"Sweetie, do you know who I am?"

The girl looked like she was going to cry and Jefferson was afraid he'd frightened her, then she tilted her head slightly, as if to study him. Finally, she gave a small nod.

Jefferson felt like a star had burst inside his heart. His sister recognized him. Without even thinking he pulled her into his arms to hug her. "Maddie, baby, sweetie." His voice was thick with emotion.

He felt a small hand on his face and he leaned back to see Maddie smile. He felt a lump in his throat, so thick he couldn't say anything as he hugged his sister again. He finally pulled himself to his feet. He needed some air, some time to think about this. He started out of the room before he remembered the reason he'd come in search of Sinclair in the first place.

He cleared his throat. "I was . . . thinking."

Sinclair looked at him expectantly.

"Do you like to dance?"

She frowned, as though trying to figure out what he was talking about, then her eyes narrowed suspiciously. "Is this about the hula-hula again, Jefferson, because if it is, I fail to see the humor in . . ."

He held up a hand and she paused. He shook his head.

"There's a dance at the Circle B, tonight. Would you like to go, with me?" He found it difficult to spit the words out and he wished she'd answer him quickly. He really needed that air.

She looked surprised, then nodded. "Yes. I like to dance."

He started out the door and paused only long enough to glance over his shoulder. "Good."

Sinclair stood staring after Jefferson, then turned back to Maddie. She smiled as she swooped the child up in her arms to spin her around the room, finally settling her onto the thick Ohio star quilt.

"I'm going dancing, Miss Maddie. What do you think about that?"

Sinclair spun around the room again as she picked up toys, books and clothing. She was humming as she cleaned.

Maddie watched Sinclair twirl around the room, humming and laughing and she thought that Claire was the funniest person she'd ever seen. And Jeffie liked her. He liked her enough to smell her hair and Maddie figured that must be good. She wanted Jeffie to like Claire a lot, because Claire made everything nice.

Maddie hugged her doll and closed her eyes and made a wish that Claire would stay with her and Jeffie forever. The only time everything felt really good and safe was when they were all together. She would wish this every night on the twinkle star and then maybe her wish would come true.

When Maddie opened her eyes Sinclair was pulling out the rainbow pencils and paper. Maddie stood quickly. The rainbow pencils were her favorite. Sometimes she could pretend the pictures she made in her head were real. The rainbow pictures could make the bad dreams go away sometimes.

"Here you go, Maddie. You can draw while I'm getting ready."

Sinclair paused to gently kiss Maddie on top of the head.

"I promise I'll come in and show you my gown when I've finished dressing."

Madison was stretched across the floor, already engrossed in making patterns on the paper. She heard the door close as Sinclair left. Maddie put a bright yellow streak on one corner of her picture. She'd make the wishing star, so she could keep wishing for Claire to like Jeffie. She could wish it lots of times every day. And maybe, once in a while, she'd make a different wish. She'd wish that she could talk again.

Chapter Twelve

Jefferson settled himself into the steaming-hot water and felt his muscles begin to relax. Leaning back, he tried to sort out the thoughts that had been churning inside his head since he'd come downstairs.

He still couldn't believe what he'd seen in Maddie's room. Not only had she responded to Sinclair's question, but she'd recognized him. They had all given up on Maddie so long ago, and they'd all been wrong.

Jefferson felt a tightness in his chest. It also meant he'd wasted years of his sister's life. She'd been lost in that lonely world of her own, and he hadn't done enough to bring her back. The old guilt washed over him again, as he tried to shut out the memories, but failed.

He could still see the wild look in Bess's eyes, the way she'd held his shirt in her clawlike hands, urging him to help her escape. And he remembered the way he'd pulled away from her, unable to give her the only thing she really wanted. Freedom from the Montana wilderness that frightened and depressed her.

He had pleaded with her to just stick it out, assured her that she'd feel differently in the spring, when the weather cleared up. But that spring he'd watched them lower her coffin into the ground and he knew he'd failed the only mother he'd ever known.

Sitting up he rubbed the soap across his chest, trying to ease the ache in his heart. If Maddie got better, maybe he'd finally be able to come to terms with his stepmother's death. Helping his sister could ease the sense of responsibility he felt for Bess's accident. Ducking his head beneath the water, he tried to wash away the painful memories.

Sitting up again, he shook himself and scrubbed at the dirt embedded beneath his fingernails. He wondered if Sinclair would notice his hands were rough and callused. She'd certainly notice if he managed to slide them down her bare skin, and he felt himself grow thick and heavy at the thought. He swore at the way his body betrayed him. It simply proved that when it came to Sinclair Readford he was beginning to possess no self-control whatsoever.

He'd better finish his bath and get dressed, or the better part of the evening would be wasted trying to settle himself down long enough to be around her. He just hoped he wouldn't make a complete fool of himself, especially in the company of every rancher within a hundred miles.

He finished scrubbing his feet and ducked under the now tepid water once more. Grabbing the towel

Lettie had thrown at him, he stood, rubbing his head roughly to dry his hair.

He froze when he heard a startled gasp, then quickly dropped the towel to cover his lower body. He twisted his head and found himself staring back at two very wide, bright blue eyes.

Sinclair's gaze was frozen on his backside, and he didn't dare move, or he'd give her an even more interesting view.

"I . . ." Her voice trailed off and her cheeks were bright red spots of color, but her eyes never left their target. He waited for what seemed like an eternity, but she didn't move.

He had a moment's inspiration to drop the towel and turn around. He thought that would likely shake up the proper Miss Readford plenty, but then again, she'd probably be so embarrassed that she'd refuse to be alone with him that night.

He gave her an impish grin. "Enjoying the scenery, Sinclair?"

Her blush seemed to deepen, but she didn't give a maidenly squeal and rush out the door. Instead her smile grew seductive as her gaze moved boldly up and down his body again.

"Jefferson, I had no idea. You are magnificent."

And with that she backed out of the door.

Jefferson dropped back down into the tin tub with a groan. He put his head in his hands as he realized how totally and absolutely lost he was with a woman like Sinclair.

Sinclair stood at the top of the stairs and nibbled her lower lip. She knew she looked very presentable, but she wondered if Jefferson McCloud would think she was beautiful? It was suddenly so important that he admire her, and she was startled at the realization. She had thought the compliments men showered on her were silly when she'd been back in Philadelphia. But none of those men had mattered, and certainly none of them had been as virile and attractive as Jefferson.

She remembered opening the door to the kitchen and seeing him standing there, naked. The muscles of his body had gleamed in the late-afternoon light, and she had found herself recalling the marble statutes of male perfection in the museums of Italy. A coil of heat had curled inside of her and kept her rooted to the spot. Even when he discovered she was staring at him, she couldn't tear herself away from the view. And when he finally challenged her, she had been embarrassed, but, she had also certainly been impressed.

She took a deep breath to calm her thoughts, then draped the silk shawl around her shoulders and regally floated down the stairs.

Jefferson was nowhere to be seen and Sinclair was irritated she'd wasted her efforts. Glancing into the kitchen she discovered the tub was gone and there was no sign of Lettie or Jefferson.

She started to call his name, then thought that might be too bold, to roam about the house bellowing for him as if she was one of his lost cows. She considered sitting in the parlor and waiting for him to appear, but she was too agitated to perch on a horsehair sofa and look composed.

Finally she wandered toward his study and stood at the oak door, poised to knock, when it was sud-

denly yanked open. Sinclair stepped back in surprise
as she found herself facing, Jefferson McCloud? But,
was it Jefferson? He looked so different she could
hardly make sense of his appearance.

His face was clean-shaven and his hair trimmed
and neatly combed back. There was a natural part in
the center and waves framed the high cheekbones and
strong planes of his face.

His broad shoulders were still evident, but he was
garbed in a fine broadcloth frock coat that hugged
his frame perfectly. A silk vest peeked out from beneath the coat and she could see a fine white linen
shirt with a neatly buttoned collar tucked beneath the
vest. Gold cufflinks gleamed at each sleeve.

His dark pants matched the coat perfectly, yet she
noticed the tips of polished boots peeking out from
beneath the trim hem of his trousers. She wondered
if he still wore his spurs, even in dress garb.

She gave him a seductive smile. "As I said before,
Jefferson McCloud, you are magnificent."

She saw a hot, golden flicker in his eyes and she
nearly drew back from the heat she suddenly felt rising from him. With a simple gesture he drew her into
the room, then leaned her back against the door as
he slammed it shut.

He towered over her, but she didn't experience
even a moment of fear. Instead, she was wickedly
excited. His hands moved up her bare arms and she
moaned as his lips found the soft, delicate place just
beneath the pulse of her neck. His tongue trailed a
path of fire to her collarbone, then he nipped her
gently.

"God, you look good enough to eat," he murmured.

His words brought the spiraling heat back to her center.

"Kiss me," she whispered, urgent in her demand.

He didn't need much encouragement. His mouth moved over hers, gently tasting at first, but hard and eager as the kiss deepened and he leaned his long, muscular body against her. When he finally lifted his head to search her expression, there was no doubt in her mind he desired her. She felt powerful with the knowledge.

"Kiss me again," she urged, her voice husky.

Jefferson took a step back, his hand still lingering on the bare flesh of her arm.

"If I do, we might as well stay here tonight."

She felt bold from the kiss and tilted her head. "Then let's stay here."

Jefferson stood bolted to the floor, wondering if she really understood the invitation in her voice. He could feel the blood rushing through his body, and he had no illusions about how the evening would end if they stayed here, in this mood. But he suspected Sinclair didn't know and he wanted to protect her innocence.

"Then I couldn't enjoy showing you off, sugar. You're every cowboy's dream, and I plan to give them all a treat tonight."

She blushed beneath his compliment. "I wanted to look special for you, Jefferson. I don't give a fig about anyone else."

He swallowed hard. He wondered if he'd ever be able to thank God enough for her. Would there be enough hours, enough minutes tonight to truly appreciate this woman? He didn't think so, but he was going to start right this moment.

He traced his finger gently over her lips. "A man doesn't get this chance often, Sinclair. Let me enjoy it."

She put one hand against his vest, and he knew she could feel the heavy beating of his heart beneath the fabric.

"Promise me," she demanded.

His dark eyes searched her face. "The sun, the moon, the stars. You name it and it's yours."

She laughed. The sound was like a soft breeze tickling the leaves of the Aspen trees.

"That you'll kiss me again." Her lips formed a soft pout, and he was tempted to demonstrate that he'd be hell-bent to keep from kissing her throughout the rest of the evening and into the night. He reined in his self-control.

"I promise I won't stop kissing you until you beg for mercy." His imagination quickly reviewed all the things he wanted to do to her. He pushed the images away.

She laughed again and stroked his cheek. "Good."

He laughed with her, allowing his arms to fall back to his sides, then offering her his elbow. "Then it's settled, you're only going to be content when I'm kissing you, and since I have no intention of stopping, you're going to be one contented lady."

She sighed deeply as they went out the door to the buggy.

"That sounds wonderful."

Jefferson thought he was probably dreaming, but

he'd kill the man who woke him up. He wanted to stay in this magical place, where dreams really did come true, for as long as possible.

Sinclair settled her dark rose silk skirts around her and he could hear the rustle of petticoats. It brought to mind the first night he'd met her, dangling from the side of the Blue Willow in her unmentionables. He remembered the way he'd clenched his jaw as she rode behind him, painfully aware of the softness of her woman's body as she leaned into him.

She slid closer to him as he held the reins, her thigh brushing his, then settling against him. He briefly wondered if he could manage this buggy ride to the Circle B without tearing her clothes off and making tender, passionate love to her. Tonight was certainly going to be a battle between desire and propriety. He could hardly wait to see which emotion was going to win.

"Do you think the people at the party will have heard the rumors of the runaway hula-hula whore?" Sinclair didn't look upset, just interested. He wondered if he should lie to her, convince her the gossip would have died down and that nobody would associate her with the now legendary shady lady on the run. It wouldn't be fair to her though.

"Oh, I'm sure they've all heard about your escapades. Likely since we've been to town, the legend has grown."

Sinclair looked thoroughly interested now. "Do you really think I'm a legend?"

Jefferson slid an arm around her to pull her closer. "After attacking Hank with your parasol, I'm sure of it."

Sinclair put her head on his shoulder and seemed to ponder his words. Then she gave him a disparaging glance.

"I still don't understand why you won't teach me to shoot. Then I'd feel safe from Hank."

Jefferson realized his hand was itching to trail over her shoulder and down the front of her dress and he withdrew it in order to avoid temptation.

"Because, sugar, you can do enough damage with that parasol. I'm not prepared to see what kind of havoc you could create with a gun."

Sinclair didn't appear to be satisfied with his answer. Leaning forward, she gave him a view of her creamy white breasts that made him feel as if someone had put a hot branding iron to his manhood. He nearly jumped out of the buggy seat.

"I could be a very good shot for all you know." There was a note of challenge in her voice. She certainly knew how to wound a man, that was for sure.

"The West isn't ready for a gun-toting, runaway hula-hula whore. Believe me." He tried to keep his eyes on the road.

Sinclair sat silently, pondering his words for a few minutes. "What about a rifle?"

Jefferson wiped the thin film of sweat from his forehead. "It's still a gun."

That seemed to satisfy her, at least for the moment. Jefferson tried to think of a topic of conversation that wouldn't involve the words *gun* or *whore*.

"I was wondering how you managed to make Maddie so agreeable. She's been like a wildcat with every woman I hired, spitting mad, screaming that nonsense and rocking. How'd you tame her?"

Sinclair gave him a self-satisfied grin. "I just went back to my original qualifications for the job. Remember, when you asked me if I knew anything about little eight-year-old girls that first night we met?"

Jefferson nodded. "I believe you said you'd once been eight years old. I was so desperate, that seemed like a reasonable qualification for the job."

Sinclair thumped him soundly on the shoulder.

"Yes, the only thing you cared about was that I was willing to come out to the ranch with you. As if I had many choices."

Jefferson gently rubbed her cheek. "So, are you regretting that decision now?"

"On the contrary, Mr. McCloud, I'm well satisfied with the bargain we made. I've never felt so . . . confident about myself."

Her words surprised him, because since the moment he'd met her he'd been astounded by her self-confidence and strength. He wondered if she just didn't recognize those qualities in herself.

"When I was eight years old, Miss Klotz, that year's governess, discovered I had a weakness and she exploited it to make me behave."

"A wise woman, she knew how to manage you."

"A lazy and stupid woman, she didn't know anything worth learning, but she did manage to make me sit in the schoolroom and study. She perceived I had a fondness for sweets and she kept bags of candy hidden in her room. When I was well behaved, she gave me some." Sinclair licked her lips and rolled her eyes.

Jefferson laughed. "I'm surprised you didn't turn into a chubby little girl."

Sinclair gave him a devilish smile. "I was never that good."

Jefferson roared, imagining that she was indeed a devilish imp as a child.

"So, you figured you'd try the same thing with Maddie. And it appears to have worked."

Sinclair looked thoughtful for a moment.

"I think many things worked for her. She craves attention and I give it to her, but I refuse to succumb to her tantrums. I try to make things better for her. I'm inclined to think any child would respond to someone who genuinely cares about her."

Jefferson sat quietly for a few moments. The guilt washed over him again. How many times had he promised himself he'd take more of an interest in his sister? And how many times had he found excuses to avoid doing just that? He wished he could make things up to her, but at least Maddie had Sinclair now. It gave him a jolt to realize that both he and Maddie had Sinclair. But, how was he going to keep her with them after the fall roundup?

"If I'm going to make the right impression, I'll need information about everyone who will be attending this dance."

Jefferson frowned. He'd been lost in his own musings. Information? What was she talking about?

"For example, who are the ladies with the most influence? I suppose they might be the wives of the richest men in town, or the owners of the largest ranches. It's difficult to tell in the West though, so many things are exactly the opposite of what one would expect." She patted her hair gently, adjusting the two large ostrich feathers she'd tucked into her chignon.

Jefferson thought for a moment. He wondered who would have the most influence? Drew Jacobs was the banker and his wife, Harriet, was a force to be reckoned with, he'd heard that more than once. Of course it was a well-known fact that Evan Billingsley was the richest man in town. But since he wasn't married she wouldn't have to worry about making a good impression on his wife. Instead Jefferson had to worry about Billingsley trying to impress Sinclair with his English title and fancy ways.

His mood darkened at that thought. "Ask me which woman has the sharpest tongue or is the biggest gossip, I could likely tell you that. But, since I don't belong to the Ladies Aid Society, I can't say who's the biggest fish in the pond."

He could see that Sinclair wasn't really satisfied with his answer. He had to think harder and his head ached from all the talk about ladies and gossip.

"I guess I'd be the most influential man, because my father is the territorial judge and nobody wants to piss off—" He paused as he noted her raised eyebrows and took a deep breath as he nodded at her. "Um . . . sorry, make the judge angry."

Sinclair perked up immediately. "Really? That would make things so much simpler. Why, just appearing with you could ease the awkwardness. Perhaps we need to concoct a story. Could I be your long-lost cousin visiting from back east?"

Jefferson stared at her mutely. She seemed to reconsider. "No, I don't suppose that would do if we want to indulge in more kissing."

Jefferson settled one long leg against the front of the buggy and grinned. "I promised to indulge in more kissing and I'm a man who believes in keeping a promise to a lady."

Sinclair snuggled against him. "How chivalrous of you."

Jefferson nodded in agreement. "A man has to keep a promise like that."

They rode in silence, then spoke in unison. They laughed, then he urged her to go ahead. She blushed, offering to let him suggest the topic of conversation. They both laughed again but there was an uneasiness between them.

"It's just that . . ."

He waited patiently for her to finish the sentence, then asked. "What?"

"It would appear proper and all, what with me staying at the ranch."

He felt the horse stumble a bit and he yanked back on the reins, concentrating more on handling the buggy than her words. "I'm sure that would be a good idea, to appear proper and all."

"But, it might prove embarrassing, you know . . . when we finally tell people, the truth." Her voice faded.

"The truth can be embarrassing, that's for sure." Once again, he had no idea what she was talking about. Was it just the way of women to talk around something when going straight through would be the fastest trail?

"So it's a ridiculous idea, is that what you're saying?" she asked.

He considered her question for a moment, then answered slowly, as if weighing the words.

"It depends. Explain it to me as clearly as you can, Sinclair, then we'll decide." He was proud of himself for digging his way out of that gopher hole.

"We could say we've been corresponding, you know, letters in the mail. Then I decided to visit Montana and, of course, that's when we made it official." She was talking fast and toying with the ruffles on her gown, as if she were unsure of herself.

Jefferson gave her a long, questioning look. "Officially what, Sinclair?"

"Engaged." The word came out in one short, deliberate breath, then she stared down at her hands folded primly in her lap.

His head jerked to attention so quickly, he thought it must have made a noise. Or perhaps that was his heart plunging to his feet.

"To be married?"

Somehow all of the passion flowed out of him as the terror flooded in. Marriage? It was something he figured he'd get around to, eventually. But, after he visited Seattle and bought a new wagon. And lately he'd added a trip to the Sandwich Islands to that list of things to do before he got married.

"Us?" He knew there was a note of astonishment in his voice, but he couldn't help it. This was an idea that took a little getting used to.

Sinclair watched him carefully.

"No, the horses." Her voice indicated her irritation with him. "Of course us. That would be the whole idea . . . that we plan to be married. That explains what I'm doing in this metropolis of the West, Ghost Horse Gulch. Instead of plying my trade at the local parlor house and gaining a reputation as the famous parasol-wielding, runaway hula-hula whore."

"Married?" He coughed and had some difficulty catching his breath.

"Do you need to loosen the buttons on your collar? Or are you choking on the word *marriage*?" Her eyes were narrow and her voice sharp. "I'm not proposing, McCloud. I'm suggesting. We could pretend that we're getting married and that would explain why I'm visiting your ranch. I don't think it would be prudent to mention my association with Aunt Tilly, do you?"

"So it would be a fake marriage?" His voice still sounded a bit strained and high-pitched, even to his own ears.

Sinclair clenched her hands into fists and seemed to be resisting the urge to slap him.

"Pay attention, McCloud." Her voice was as soft and patient as if she were speaking to Maddie. "We would *pretend* to be engaged. Not real, pretend. It would give me an opportunity to get to know some of the local women, without them thinking I'm a scarlet woman of loose morals."

He coughed again.

"Pretend?"

Sinclair nodded, "No one would suspect it's pretend, because we'd act as if it were real. Then, when I find out what happened to Aunt Tilly, we'll just act as if we changed our minds."

Jefferson rubbed his chin with one hand, carefully considering her words.

"Pretend? But, won't that make it difficult for you to find yourself a real husband, if all the men think you're getting hitched to me?"

Sinclair punched him in the arm.

"You certainly know how to make a woman feel attractive. I was just teasing you that day about wanting to find a husband." She rolled her eyes. "A woman needs a man like one of your cows needs a parasol. Just forget it. Let them call me whatever they want. I don't care!" Her chin lifted in defiance as she sat back and pouted.

Jefferson was quiet for a few minutes, contemplating her idea.

"It's worth considering."

Sinclair folded her arms and gave him a disparaging glance.

"Oh, really."

"Yup," he responded.

She sat patiently waiting, but he just kept his eyes on the horizon spread out before them. She tapped her fingers on her lap, agitated. Still, he remained quiet.

"Is that your answer, cowboy? Yup. Like it's the only reasonable answer in the universe. Because civilized people usually manage to link several words together to form a sentence. Yup is not a sentence!" She folded her arms across her bosom and clamped her mouth shut.

He gave a rough yank on the reins and the buggy came to an abrupt halt. Sinclair slid forward and was nearly on the floor when he caught her. Before she could object she was nestled on Jefferson's lap. He tilted his wide-brimmed felt hat back and he knew there was good humor sparkling in his eyes.

Before she could utter a word, his mouth was scorching hers. His kiss was hot, demanding and her eager response nearly curled his toes. She went limp after a few moments and he thought maybe she was going to swoon.

He lifted his head to look into her eyes, now clouded with passion. "Does that answer your question, ma'am?"

Sinclair grinned up at him. "Yup, cowboy. It certainly does."

Chapter Thirteen

When Jefferson told her Lord Evan Billingsley was the richest man in Ghost Horse Gulch, Sinclair'd been prepared for a large, well-appointed house. But, nothing could have prepared her for "Heavenfield," his estate.

It was a fortress. Not quite a castle, but almost. The long driveway was bordered by groves of aspen and birch trees. The fragile new leaves fluttered quietly in the breeze, as if to greet the stream of guests arriving in carriages, buggies and on horseback.

People called out enthusiastic greetings, and Sinclair was aware of the curious glances thrown in her direction. She sat up and tried to remember all the lectures she'd received on proper deportment.

When they arrived at the carriage stoop, Sinclair paused to wait for Jefferson to jump down and assist her from the buggy. She gave him a warm smile as he bypassed her outstretched hand and put his hands around her waist to lift her down. It was a public display of his claim on her, and the intimacy of the signal made her blush.

A deep baritone voice greeted them.

"If my eyes do not deceive me, we are honored this evening by the presence of visitors from the Cripple Creek Ranch."

Lord Billingsley gave Jefferson a good-natured grin. "And McCloud, you do us the additional honor of escorting Miss Readford to my little gathering."

Sinclair turned to watch the people crowding the large stone steps and entryway into the house, if this was a small party she'd hate to see what constituted a large gathering in Montana.

Lord Billingsley rudely pushed Jefferson aside to gently grasp Sinclair's hand and bow down before her. His lips briefly touched her glove before Jefferson slid back into place between them.

"I'm very pleased to see you again, Lord Billingsley." Sinclair made a small curtsey.

"Please, call me Evan. We are in America, after all." He straightened to give Sinclair a brilliant smile.

"Quit showing off, Billingsley," Jefferson said with a growl.

Evan Billingsley ignored the rough manners of his neighbor and raised his eyebrows at Sinclair. She almost giggled as she realized Evan was having fun at Jefferson's expense.

"I'm delighted to see you again, Miss Readford, although I must confess I'm surprised this ill-mannered oaf hasn't managed to irritate you to the point of leaving our fair environs." He winked at her.

Jefferson put a propriety arm around Sinclair's waist.

"I promised Miss Readford an evening of music and dancing, Billingsley. I didn't come to chew the fat with you."

Lord Billingsley ignored Jefferson's caustic tone and continued to hover near Sinclair. "Nevertheless, I'm thrilled to see you, my dear. I was terrified I'd be forced to spend the evening entertaining an endless stream of witless chits and defending myself from their scheming mothers. Now I can dance with you." Evan offered Sinclair his arm.

Jefferson brushed by his friend, ignoring the offer of escort.

"Sorry, your majesty, but this lady is with me. You'd best figure on keeping company with that herd of heifers." Jefferson nodded toward a gaggle of brightly clad young women.

Sinclair glanced toward the group and noticed both men appeared to be the objects of admiration. Although their stares were bold, there was much giggling, gesturing and blushing among the women. It signaled a profound lack of breeding in Sinclair's eyes. Her gaze briefly brushed that of a tall brunette garbed in a peach-colored gown. Sinclair shivered at the icy stare that was returned to her, and briefly wondered at its cause.

"I beg of you, McCloud, please share some of the dances of your lovely Miss Readford, or I shall be tortured by husband hunters all evening long. She's quite possibly the only intelligent woman at this gathering."

Sinclair frowned. "It simply won't do for me to

196

hoard the attention of two eligible bachelors all night long. And two of the handsomest men in the territory, to boot!" She could see the men puff out their chests at her compliment. "You must both promise to ask other ladies to dance, or I'll become a wallflower myself."

She gathered her skirt to climb the stairs and worried that if these two spent the evening hovering over her, arguing about fetching refreshments and the next dance, it wouldn't take long for the other single women to take an intense dislike to her. She had enough working against her, with the stories of her escapades as the runaway hula-hula whore. She had come to this gathering with the intention of making friends. Despite Jefferson's attention, Maddie's progress and Lettie's companionship, she missed visiting with women her own age.

Arriving at the huge oak doors that marked the entrance to the house, her eyes swept the stone building in awe. It was three stories high, with twin towers flanking the doorway. She was reminded of a medieval keep.

"I swear, Lord Evan, this place is so authentic, I expect you must even have a dungeon."

Evan Billingsley nodded emphatically. "I'd be happy to put your escort there and then we could dance the evening away." He leaned forward and winked at her again. "It's where I put all my boorish guests."

McCloud gave him a cool glance. "And all this time I thought it's where you put your women when you got tired of 'em."

Evan stared at McCloud for a moment, then gave

a hearty laugh and roughly pounded him on the back.

"By God, my friend, it appears you've finally found your sense of humor again. Tell me, did Miss Readford locate it for you?"

Jefferson gave him a lopsided grin. "Let's just say it helps when you're dealing with Sinclair to have a *very* good sense of humor."

She wanted to poke him in the ribs, but knew she'd appear to be vulgar if she gave into the inclination.

Evan Billingsley laughed again as his hand swept the foyer of the house. "Come in, and enjoy yourselves. McCloud, you've been here enough to know the house. Now, if you'll excuse me, it appears that my butler is in need of some assistance."

The Englishman bowed cordially to her, then turned to walk toward a very tall, very stately man standing in the back hallway.

Sinclair put her hand to her mouth to stifle a giggle. She gave Jefferson an amused look. "A butler? In Montana?" Her gaze swept toward the winding cherry staircase that climbed up the levels of the home.

"I've been to England and this place is very authentic. But . . . it's so, unexpected. In Montana."

Jefferson shrugged. "Billingsley will be happy to chatter on for hours about his estate and his pedigree. Everyone else around here's content to own a ranch, but he's from some northern place in England. Guess he didn't like it enough to stay there, but he wanted some reminder of home, so he built this place."

Sinclair was very interested. She loved England.

"Where is his family from?"

Jefferson shook his head. "I don't recollect, ex-

198

actly. Someplace like North-umber-town, something like that."

"Northumberland?"

"Could be. Like I said, when he gets rattling on about his homeland, I ignore most of what he says. Except when he starts talking about bringing sheep in. That's a damn fool idea if I ever heard one."

Sinclair accompanied McCloud toward the back of the house, and found herself in a large dining room with cherry paneling, two crystal chandeliers and a table designed to seat at least twenty guests. The chairs had been removed, and the table was now piled high with food.

Jefferson gestured toward a plate with a large trout and sprigs of dill. "Are you hungry?"

She shook her head. "Not right now, although I confess, I'd love a glass of lemonade."

He nodded and circled the table, leaving her alone for a few moments. Glancing about the room, she admired the paintings on the walls and the furnishings. Lord Billingsley had a penchant for the gothic style, but he was careful not to overdo it and she admired his taste.

Jefferson returned with her drink, then edged her toward a small gathering and proceeded to introduce her. She met the town's banker; his wife, Harriet; another rancher and his wife, Bernice, and his daughter Marien. Sinclair smiled and made small talk, yet she noticed although the women seemed cordial, they were also a bit distant.

Sinclair imagined living such an isolated life made people naturally reticent. After all, when you knew everyone you came into contact with daily, it made sense it would take some time to accept a stranger.

They circled the room and Jefferson continued to introduce her, but he neglected to add the part about her being his fiancée. She'd need to talk to him about this oversight, because she was sure the additional information would help her in making friends that evening. Why, when the townspeople discovered she was supposed to marry one of their own, they'd probably overwhelm her with their offers of friendship.

Jefferson paused to take her glass. "Would you like to dance, now?"

His hand was still about her waist, and she brushed against him as they moved down the hallway, toward the stairway. He'd removed his Stetson and she couldn't help but admire the way the lamplight highlighted the sun-kissed streaks in his hair. When he glanced down at her, his eyes seemed darker. There was a warmth in them that made her feel special and treasured.

"That is what you invited me here for, isn't it?" She made her voice an enticing whisper.

He paused to pick up one long, blond curl and twirl it about his finger. "I've got a lot of invitations on my mind tonight, sugar."

"Jefferson McCloud, you low-down snake!"

They found their path blocked by the brunette in peach who had stared back at Sinclair with a cool gaze. She started to tap Jefferson's chest with her fan.

"You never once let me know you planned to be here tonight." Her voice was indignant and her pretty face held a playful pout. Her eyes were filled with adoration as she stared up at Jefferson.

"But, I suppose you've been too busy with the

roundup." She gave Sinclair a cursory glance, dismissed her and moved closer to Jefferson. "I've missed your visits to the Circle Bar T. You haven't been to see me in ages."

Jefferson looked uncomfortable, but Sinclair didn't feel like rescuing him; she was too interested in his relationship with the brunette.

When he tried to move away, the woman's hand moved quickly to rest against the broadcloth of his frock coat.

"And you were getting to be such a regular visitor. You simply must join us for dinner this Sunday." She had a predatory look in her eyes as she focused on Jefferson, taking another step to block his escape.

Jefferson managed to extricate himself from the woman's grasp, as Sinclair continued to watch the performance.

"Miss Maizy DeWitt, I'd like you to meet Miss Sinclair Readford. She's staying out at the Cripple Creek with us."

Sinclair waited for him to add to the introduction, but he appeared to be finished. His reluctance to give any justification for her presence at his ranch irritated her, but she'd have to wait until they were alone to remind him of his promise in the buggy.

Giving him a dark frown, she realized she'd have to take matters into her own hands and deal with this woman.

"How do you do, Miss DeWitt. I'm pleased to make your acquaintance." She extended her gloved hand toward the other woman, but Maizy DeWitt just stared at it and finally Sinclair let it drop back to her side. The ways of westerners continued to perplex her.

Maizy DeWitt studied her for a few moments with slitted eyes, then returned her attention to Jefferson.

"We never did take that ride up to Blue Lake. The wildflowers must be in full bloom by now." There was more in her voice than just an invitation for a trail ride and Sinclair decided she'd have to let Miss Maizy know who she was dealing with.

Sinclair squeezed closer to Jefferson and put a hand on his shoulder.

"I'm afraid I've kept Jefferson so busy lately, he's hardly had time for anyone else." Her honeyed tones didn't disguise the ill-will in her statement.

"He's been teaching me to ride, but I don't recall a place called Blue Lake. It certainly sounds lovely. Jefferson," she plucked an imaginary piece of lint from his coat, "we should plan a picnic there."

She could see a hot flush spreading across the other woman's cheeks and Sinclair felt a sense of superiority rush through her.

She leaned toward Maizy conspiratorially and said in a stage whisper. "I'm afraid I've been consuming all of his time. He's such an attentive instructor, we've been riding nearly every day."

Maizy looked at her dumbfounded. "In the middle of roundup? He gives you riding lessons?"

Jefferson now looked as if he'd like to jump over the two women and scurry out the door. Sinclair ignored his discomfort, tossed her head and gave a deep, feigned sigh.

"I know it seems like an inconvenience and when he comes back from the range just to ride with me, I think so too." She fluttered her lashes and gave Jefferson a look of adoration. "But, he's so insistent and you should see how well I can ride now." She rolled her eyes dramatically. "And to think before I came to Montana, I didn't even like horses."

Maizy's head was now twisting between Jefferson and Sinclair. She seemed to be having some difficulty comprehending everything Sinclair had confessed to her.

"He came back to the ranch, during roundup?" Maizy seemed too confused to flirt with Jefferson, and Sinclair thought she'd take advantage of the situation. She could hear the music floating down the stairs and the joyful, brash sound make her want to tap her toes.

"Don't like horses?" Maizy was looking at Jefferson with a look of shock on her face. He shrugged.

"Excuse us, Miss Dill-Wit." Sinclair pushed the woman aside and pulled Jefferson with her.

"DeWitt!" Maizy's voice was high-pitched now with anger. Sinclair leaned into Jefferson and glanced back toward Maizy DeWitt. "Jefferson has been promising to dance with me for hours . . . and I simply can't wait any longer."

Sinclair yanked on Jefferson's arm to pull him around the astonished Maizy DeWitt and up the stairs with her.

"I'm not sure what just went on, but I've got the feeling you just put that woman in her place." Jefferson gave her a lopsided grin.

Sinclair gave a small moan. "You desperately needed my help."

He straightened his shoulders. "I was doing fine. Maizy DeWitt doesn't scare me."

"Ha!" Sinclair laughed up at him. "That just shows how little you know. A few more minutes and she'd have you agreeing to dinner on Sunday and a spin in the buggy."

"Really?" Jefferson looked impressed. "Does that mean she has designs on me?"

Sinclair was tempted to push him back down the stairs, instead she paused to reach up and adjust the top button of his collar.

"If looks could kill, I'd drop dead and you'd bury me right here on this spot."

He tried to turn and look down the stairs.

"Don't look," she said.

He gave her a glowering frown. "You say something like that, then tell me not to look. It's enough to drive a man crazy."

"I suspect she's already picked out the names for your first three children." She lifted her eyebrows and gave him a playful pat. "You can look now."

A now composed looking Maizy stood at the bottom of the stairs waving her hand languidly in the air. "Save a dance for me, Jefferson," she called up after them.

He continued to climb the stairs. "I've hardly paid any attention to that woman. Her family invited me to dinner a few times and we met up on the trail one day, by accident."

Sinclair shook her head sadly. "By accident? I hardly think so. Believe me, I know the look of a predatory woman when I see it. Miss Maizy has you clearly in her sights."

"Hell," he muttered under his breath.

"You know, our agreement in the buggy could serve you just as well as me, Jefferson. If these unattached women thought you were getting married, they'd leave you alone."

"It might be worth it," he grumbled, glancing down once more at Maizy, then shaking his head.

She wanted to broach the subject of his introductions, and the fact that he was neglecting to mention her status as his intended bride, when they entered the ballroom.

It was a huge room with a polished wood floor. The middle was open and couples twirled about as a small band composed of a piano, a trumpet, a violin, a drum and a flute played. Sinclair could see chairs arranged along the outside walls and people were seated in small gatherings all about. She once again felt curious stares studying her.

"Would you like to sit down?" Jefferson's eyes scanned the room searching for an empty place.

Sinclair gave him a disgusted look. "Not on your life, cowboy. You promised to take me dancing and here we are." She pointed to the couples energetically spinning around the floor in a five-step waltz.

She put her hand on her hip defiantly. "Although, I don't for one moment believe you even know how to dance. I think this whole evening was just a ruse to get me alone." She gave him a challenging look.

Jefferson put his hand to his heart and adopted a wounded expression.

"Miss Readford, you can insult my cattle, call my men lazy, my horse stupid and my dog ugly, but don't ever tell a cowboy he doesn't know how to dance."

With that he led her out onto the dance floor, pulled her into his arms, grasping one hand tightly in his and placing the other one on his waist. He gave her a flirtatious grin and they started to waltz.

He moved with fluid grace and Sinclair found herself easily matching his steps, even though he was much taller than she was. He adjusted his gait until they moved in perfect unison. When he swung her in a circle, she found herself laughing up into his handsome face. They circled the dance floor several times, yet he filled her senses so completely, she was oblivious to anyone else in the room.

When the band finally stopped playing, she fell into his arms in laughter.

"You don't even have a dog." She gave him a playful punch. "But you certainly can dance. I apologize for the insult and your reputation in this arena remains unchallenged."

Jefferson grinned down at her. "My dogs stay with the cattle, where they belong. Now, if I could only charm you with some of my other talents. . . ."

She straightened herself, realizing that a slower waltz was now beginning.

"Shall we?" she invited, holding out her hand.

He gave her a mock bow. "Yes, ma'am!"

After three more dances, Sinclair begged for a respite. "I've never known any man who enjoyed this as much as you do, Jefferson. And where did you learn to be so graceful on the dance floor?"

He led her to a seat near an open window and she was grateful for the gentle breeze that stirred the curtain and cooled her warm face. She opened her fan and waved it to cool herself down even more.

"Bess taught me. She loved to dance and she'd get books in the mail that gave all the directions for the latest dances. Since the judge was never around, she practiced on me and the boys."

His motioned toward a small gathering of cowboys at the edge of the room. She could see several hands from the Cripple Creek standing together. They had clean boiled shirts, fancy vests and new-looking silk bandannas wound around their necks.

"The Cripple Creek Ranch is famous for her dancing cowboys," he stated matter-of-factly.

Sinclair couldn't help herself and started to laugh. She put her hand to her mouth in an attempt to smother it, but she just couldn't seem to stop. The image of those rough, tough, bronco-busting cowboys spinning around the dance floor was too much for her. Tears were beginning to form in her eyes.

Jefferson tried to ignore her and looked in the other direction.

"You gonna be all right?"

She swallowed hard to smother another round of laughter. "I'm sorry, but things in the West are so . . . incongruous."

"Incongruous. That's a five-dollar word if I ever heard one. I'd better write that one down for Ollie. He's making a collection of all your fancy words, in case he ever needs to go before a judge."

Sinclair started to laugh again. "Stop it, Jefferson. I believe you're doing this on purpose, so I'll look ostentatious."

Jefferson whistled. "Damn, Ollie should be here. That's ten dollars worth of words in only five minutes."

207

Deborah Schneider

Sinclair wished she could hit him with her fan, but two older women in dark black silk gowns were approaching them.

Too late Sinclair realized they were the same two women she'd seen in the mercantile on the day she'd been attacked by Hank. Her spirits plummeted.

"The Gibbon sisters," Jefferson whispered under his breath. "Dried up old crows who enjoy ripping people's reputations to shreds. Watch out!"

Sinclair barely had time to compose herself before the women were staring down at her.

"I beg your pardon, my dear. But, my sister Emily and I were just wondering. Didn't we see you in town a few weeks ago?"

Sinclair felt her throat dry up. She felt like she was standing on a train track with a locomotive bearing down on her, but she couldn't step off to escape.

"I was in town a few weeks ago, to visit the dressmaker."

One of the thin, birdlike women nodded to the other. "I told you, Emily, my eyesight is not failing me. She's the one, all right."

Jefferson started to intervene, but the woman named Emily snapped her fan at him.

"Mind your manners, Jefferson McCloud, and don't interrupt."

Jefferson clamped his mouth shut instantly and Sinclair had an inkling Miss Emily Gibbon has spent some time keeping schoolchildren in line.

The women inched closer. "We don't mean to be forward, miss."

"Sinclair Readford," she said automatically.

"But, didn't we also see you in an altercation with that horrible Mr. Borscht?"

Sinclair felt herself deflate and wished somehow she could fly over the heads of these old busybodies and disappear into the inky darkness outside. Instead she heard her deportment teacher intoning, "When in doubt, face the circumstances honestly."

"He attacked me . . ." her voice was barely above a whisper, and she cast her eyes to the floor in embarrassment.

"Mr. Borscht thought my fiancée was someone he knew. He was mistaken." Jefferson's voice held power and authority.

"Fiancée," the two old birds chattered with delight, "why, Jefferson, we had no idea."

Jefferson gallantly offered his arm to Sinclair. "We're making the announcement tonight. Right now, in fact." He started to drag her toward the bandstand.

Sinclair wanted to slap Jefferson senseless. This was not the moment to announce such a thing, she needed time to compose herself. But, before she could object, Jefferson was climbing up to stand next to the trumpet player.

"Friends and neighbors, I've got an announcement."

Everyone stopped talking and watched him with quiet expectation.

"Tonight, I'm happy to tell you that I've decided to get married." He folded his arms across his chest and grinned. "Yup, I'm gonna rope a heifer for life, and Miss Sinclair Readford is the lucky woman."

Sinclair gave him a startled glare. It was a totally inappropriate announcement.

"Now, I know you folks have heard some talk about her, but I'm here to tell you she's a fine woman and you can just forget all those rumors you've heard about her and the parlor house."

Sinclair wanted to cover her face with her hands and sink right into the floor. If people hadn't heard the rumors, they'd be sure to search them out now.

"We haven't exactly set a date, but she's staying out to the Cripple Creek and we wanted you to know it's proper and all. Sinclair's from Phillydelphia, so she's worried about such things." He unfolded his arms and nodded at the crowd, who stared back at him, some people whispering to one another. "Thank you kindly."

He climbed down from the bandstand to stand next to Sinclair. People crowded around them to ask questions and congratulate the happy couple. Sinclair felt like she was suffocating.

"Get me out of here," she whispered under her breath as a burly rancher pumped Jefferson's hand then kissed her soundly on both cheeks.

"We can't do that. We're the center of attention."

"That's exactly why I need to escape," she retorted, as she tried to smile at a young woman who offered her blessings.

"Well, honey, this was all your idea. You made this bed." McCloud shook the banker's hand and slapped him on the back in good humor when the man made a ribald comment.

She turned to leave. "I don't care. You've embar-

210

rassed me and I need to get out of here." Her voice held a note of dismay.

Before she could take a step, she felt his arm around her waist pulling her back toward him.

"You think that was embarrassing, sugar? Just you wait!"

Leaning her back over his arm, he kissed her with all the ardor and enthusiasm of an eager groom. She tried to resist him, but the warmth of his mouth seduced her, until she found herself responding to the kiss, her arms wrapping around his neck, her heart beating a quick cadence as the blood rushed through her veins.

When Jefferson finally lifted his lips from hers to set her on her feet, they were greeted with a roar of approval and applause. Sinclair wished she could somehow melt into the floor and disappear.

Chapter Fourteen

"You spent how much money on whores last night?" Jefferson gave Ollie a disgusted look. "I said to buy some information, not the services of every painted cat in the place."

"Hell, Boss, you know as well as I do that nothin' comes cheap at the Blue Willow." Ollie rolled the wad of tobacco in his mouth, then spit.

"Besides, I reckon it was worth the price if your future wife can find her beloved Aunt Matilda."

Jefferson didn't react to the teasing tone in Ollie's voice. His gaze scanned the low green hills lying before him, and he sniffed the clean, spring air. It was his favorite time of year. Time for new life and new beginnings. For the first time in many years, Jefferson found himself pondering what it would be like to watch the seasons change with pleasure, instead of regret. He was beginning to think he could learn, especially with a woman like Sinclair Readford at his side.

"Cost me extra for the questions, ya know. Whores hate answerin' questions, they just like it when ya get on with yer business." Ollie spat again. "Of course, it weren't really no chore, Boss, 'specially bein' with that Marmalade, you know, the one who can . . . ?"

Jefferson held up a hand. "Did you find out anything about Matilda Haynes, or did you just figure you were gonna soak me for an evening of pleasure."

Ollie gave a deep, booming laugh. "I tell you, for a man of my years, I can still manage to . . ."

"Damn it, Ollie, I don't want to hear about your adventures last night." Jefferson gave the man a glowering look.

Ollie laughed again, then shifted in the saddle. His horse lifted his head, glanced back, then decided he could finish munching on the small tufts of rye grass beneath his feet.

"I expect yer gonna be one happy bridegroom by the time the weddin' comes round. I see that look you get in yer eyes every time you even hear the swish of Miss Sinclair's petticoats."

Jefferson lifted his gun from the holster and pretended to be studying the barrel. "Maybe I should just shoot you, old man, and put you and me both out of our misery."

Ollie looped one leg over the saddle horn and leaned back, as if sitting in a rocking chair.

"Better not shoot me till you hear the information I got."

Jefferson seemed to consider his options, then shook his head. "Better spit it out before I get tired of your flapping jaw and shoot you just for the sake of peace and quiet."

The horses moved farther down the ridge and the men didn't bother to lift their reins. Range horses knew what they were about.

"Seems like the girls are real worried 'bout Miz Haynes. She just up and disappeared one day and they say she ain't never done that afore. They found a note what said she'd gone off to San Francisco, but they don't believe it." Ollie wiped his bandanna across his face.

Jefferson still studied the landscape. "Women get the urge to get up and go every day. What makes them think Matilda Haynes wasn't the type to set off in search of greener pastures?"

"Well, that's most exactly what I asked Polly. But she said these here pastures is pretty green. The girls are all makin' good money and they liked workin' for Miz Haynes."

Jefferson gave Ollie a hard look. "What exactly do they think happened to Matilda Haynes?"

Ollie pretended to study the landscape himself. "They ain't too sure, but all the ones I talked to seem to figger Hank Borscht has somethin' to do with her falling off the face o' the earth."

Jefferson had an idea the whores weren't too far off the mark. Hank Borscht was a bully and a snake-oil salesman. The kind of man who took from women, but never for a moment could spare them a kindness or a thought. He'd seen the type before. Whenever he remembered the way Hank had attacked Sinclair that day in town, it made his blood boil. More than once he'd regretted not putting a bullet in that bastard's heart.

"They have any ideas about what he did with her?" Jefferson put his gun back in his holster.

Ollie looked thoughtful for a moment. "They said he likely wouldn't kill her, 'cause the house is willed to some niece back east. Seems like Hank would lose his meal ticket if he killed Miz Haynes."

Jefferson removed his Stetson and ran his fingers through his long, dark hair. "Are you thinking Sinclair might be that niece?"

"You bet she is." Ollie shook his head and glared at Jefferson. "Miss Sinclair ain't no sportin' woman. She's a real fine lady and if anybody, includin' you says otherwise, I'd be inclined to put a bullet in their worthless hide just to rid Montana of another damn fool!"

Jefferson stared at his friend in surprise, then leaned forward to study him carefully. "I'm not going to swap lead with you over her, am I, old man?"

Ollie snorted in derision. "Don't know why an educated female'd want anythin' to do with a jackass like you, but since she told me herself she was promised to ya, I guess I'll have to start believin' in miracles again."

Jefferson laughed. "I'm glad to know you think so highly of my upcoming nuptials. But, we're not hitched yet, so maybe you still have time to make her see the error of her ways."

Ollie shook his head. "The way she's been liftin' her nose at you the past few days, I won't hardly have to tell her nothin' to convince her that marryin' a man who don't know what he really wants is foolish business."

Jefferson felt his jaw tighten. "You talk too much, old man."

Ollie put his leg back into the stirrup and pulled on the reins of his horse. He adjusted the brim of his hat, then turned toward the east.

"I know when I see a woman worth havin', but you better be sure you'll fight for her. Because you and I both know there's gonna be a helluva fight over this one."

Jefferson watched his friend ride off and he couldn't shake the sense of dread that crept into his heart. He couldn't tell Ollie that he'd made an agreement with Sinclair and their engagement was just a little play acting. The trouble was, as hard as it had been to adjust to the idea of even pretending to get married, as soon as the words were out of his mouth the other night at the dance, everything had seemed covered with a warm, calm light. He didn't mind the idea of marrying Miss Sinclair Readford as much as he thought he would. In fact, he was adjusting to the idea with enthusiasm. He just didn't know how to tell her that.

"Here kitty, kitty." Sinclair lifted the lantern in the dusky afternoon light and glanced around the hayloft. There was a dry, sweet scent that reminded her of summer afternoon buggy rides in the country. Most of the loft was empty, with hay spread across the floor and a few bales pushed into one corner. She placed her boot carefully on the top rung of the ladder and pulled herself up, being cautious of the lantern.

"Come on out, kitty." She tried to peek into the corners, but it was too dark to see if any of the litter of kittens Ollie had told her about were frolicking in the warmth of the loft.

"Is that you up there, Sinclair?"

She swallowed as she recognized Jefferson's voice. She wanted to scurry into one of the corners herself in order to avoid him, but realized it was too late when his felt hat peeked up over the top rung of the ladder, followed by dark eyes that glittered with mischief and that damn arrogant, lopsided grin.

"Whatchadoin'?"

She straightened her shoulders and tried to give her voice a cool, diffident tone. "I'm searching for a kitten."

Jefferson pulled himself the rest of the way up the ladder and followed her into the center of the loft.

"You need to be careful with that lantern up here, this place is dry enough to burst into flame with just the touch of a lucifer." He glanced down at her and grinned again.

"Got a mouse problem?"

Lowdown, sneaky rat might be more like it, she thought. She had tried to ignore him since the dance. She had never in her life been so humiliated as when he jumped up on the bandstand and acted like he was announcing an auction or horse trade instead of their engagement. Then, she'd had to suffer all through the night as every cowboy, ranch owner and businessman begged to dance with the future Mrs. McCloud. By the time they left after dawn, she'd been too exhausted to let loose with the full force of her indignation.

The following day she'd attempted to catch him in his office and demand that he retract the announcement, only to be interrupted by Ollie and Lettie, who hugged her and offered their congratulations. They had been so happy and supportive, so welcoming, that she had changed her mind about confronting McCloud.

Then he'd simply disappeared for more than a week. It irritated her that he could come and go with so much freedom, without even a thought to her feelings or plans. As if that wasn't bad enough, it seemed nearly everyone in the territory had descended upon her, with women from all the surrounding ranches and several from Ghost Horse Gulch coming to call. She and Lettie had to clean the parlor, polish the silver, make tea and desserts, so that Sinclair could spend nearly every afternoon playing the gracious hostess.

"I'm planning to give Maddie a kitten, for a pet." She turned and her eyes tried to see into the shadows.

"A barn cat would likely scratch the girl's eyes out. Might as well have me go get her a cougar kitten to play with." He folded his arms across his chest and watched her with interest.

Sinclair tossed her head, the long blond braid twitching to one side. "I don't expect you to understand the reasons a child needs a pet, but it has occurred to me that a special confidant might serve to break through to her. I feel like she's on the brink of a major leap forward, perhaps she'll even speak again."

She glanced back as Jefferson took a few long strides toward her, his face was bright with hope as he put his hands on Sinclair's shoulders.

"Don't fool with me, Sinclair. Do you really think Maddie could learn to talk again?"

Sinclair set the lantern down and made herself comfortable on one of the bales of hay. She gazed up at Jefferson, and as much as she wanted to vent her anger, she knew this was too important to him to use as a weapon to vindicate her own pride.

"I believe I've heard her talking several times in her room. The other night, when I came upstairs to go to bed, her bedroom door was ajar. I went to close it, and I swear, I heard whispering in there. When I looked in to check on her she seemed to be asleep. I know it could be my imagination, but I just have a sense about her, that there's more there than she's letting on."

Jefferson sat down beside her and removed his hat. She found herself admiring his hair as it fell in two long waves to the tips of his ears. He still wore it parted in the middle and even though his face wore a shadow of a beard, her heart fluttered at the beauty in the planes of his face. She never remembered thinking of any man as beautiful until she'd met Jefferson McCloud. Handsome just didn't seem to convey the highlights of his hair or the deep dimples when he smiled.

Pulling off his gloves, he tossed them toward his hat, then put his hands on his knees and grinned at her.

"Seems like a good time for you to give me the

tongue-lashing you've been holding in since Saturday night."

Sinclair gave him a startled look, then shook her head. "Then you knew I was furious with you?"

Jefferson rubbed the back of his neck. "I'm getting so I recognize that look pretty good, the one where your bottom lip sort of comes out a bit and your eyes sparkle like fireworks on Independence Day. Yup, I'm getting so I know that one when I see it."

She dug her elbow into his ribs and almost pushed him off the bale of hay. "Then why did you pretend that everything was just fine?"

He rubbed the stubble on his chin thoughtfully. "Because it was you who cooked this whole thing up and it seems to me that once you get cooking it doesn't matter what happens, you just gotta have your own way. I figured we'd just see what happens and so far it looks like you got what you wanted. I hear Lettie's been complaining for days about the steady stream of lady-folks coming out here to visit."

Sinclair put her elbows on her knees and rested her chin on her hands, contemplating the mess in which she'd landed herself.

"That's what I find so ... disconcerting. The whole point of our pretend engagement was to foster my acceptance into the community."

She glanced sideways at him and his eyes were clouded with confusion.

Jefferson scratched his chin pensively. "That's what I thought."

Sinclair sat up and touched his arm gently. He jumped a bit and edged away from her as he flushed deeply.

220

She made the tone of her voice serious as she continued.

"That was my plan, to deal with all those silly rumors and to give myself a social boost. And that's exactly what's happened. The women here have welcomed me with invitations to dinner and tea, to quilting bees and sewing circles. I've even been sponsored for the Ladies Aid Society."

Jefferson shook his head. "Sounds like serious trouble to me." The corners of his mouth lifted a bit.

Sinclair gave a deep sigh. "It's all gone exactly as I planned, and yet . . ." Her voice trailed off.

Jefferson sat silently for a moment, patiently waiting for her to continue.

She coughed, and couldn't keep a tear from sliding down her face.

He pulled her into his arms and gently kissed the top of her head.

"It can't be all that bad, sugar. These women will get tired of traipsing out here before long, then you can get back to normal."

She wiped at the tear and sniffed. "That's not the problem, Jefferson. I like these women. I like them more than anyone I ever knew in Philadelphia. They're so strong, they aren't afraid to speak their minds and they're kind and thoughtful. Did you know that Mrs. Helverson just gave birth to her third child and that several of these women were there for the birthing. Now they're taking turns to make sure the family has dinner, that the washing is done and that the other children are cared for so she can rest up. In the city, you have to pay a servant to do that."

Jefferson gently tucked a curl back behind her ear.

"It doesn't surprise me. Folks out here rely on one another, it's just the way things are. We don't mind asking a neighbor for help, because we know if they needed it, we'd do the same for them. But, I don't understand why all this neighborliness has you so upset."

Sinclair leaned into him and as he rubbed the soft skin just below her elbow, she shivered. Being close to him always made her so jumpy. She almost wished he would slide a few inches away from her again, but she enjoyed his support and she didn't think he really wanted to move.

"I'm getting attached to this place, Jefferson. To the mountains and the ranch, to Maddie," she paused and took a deep breath, studying him carefully, "and to you Jefferson McCloud."

He felt his chest expand and he could have sworn a firecracker must have exploded inside of him, he was filled with so much heat and light. He gazed down into her clear blue eyes. Eyes that always reminded him of the bright blue Montana sky, and touched her lips with the tip of one finger.

"I'm getting pretty attached to you, Miss Sinclair Readford, even if you do have the temperament of a wildcat sometimes. In fact, I've spent the past few days just thinking about coming home to you."

He could see the surprise on her face. "Really?"

He leaned forward to sweep his mouth over hers, just brushing her lips and whispered, "Really." Then his fingers gripped her chin carefully, he tipped her face up toward him, and scorched her lips with a hot, probing kiss.

Her arms crept around his neck, her fingers clasping together, as if she was afraid he might pull away from her. They melted together and Jefferson felt the heat of desire whip through him like a lightning bolt in a thunderstorm.

Without even realizing what he was doing, he pulled her down to the floor to settle her on top of him. She was all softness and curves, her feminine body filling all his hard male spaces. His hand found the gentle swell of her bottom and he cupped her, pulling her closer to him.

She finally lifted her lips from his, to gaze down at him, her eyes dark with desire and her lips swollen from the fervor of their kiss.

"You missed me?" she asked, her voice husky.

"God, yes!" He gently laid her down next to him so he could admire her. His hand traced the outline of her bosom and he could see her quiver at his touch. But when she didn't pull away, he was encouraged enough to begin to unfasten the buttons of her bodice.

His hands continued to work as his mouth traced a line from her earlobe to the small hollow of her throat. He loosened the tie of her chemise to discover the soft fullness of her breasts spilling from the top of her lace-edged corset. Plunging his tongue eagerly into the small valley between her breasts, he was rewarded when she gave a soft moan. He pulled the corset down to expose one soft, white orb.

"I can't sleep, can't eat. All I can think of is you, Sinclair. How much I want you." His tongue flickered across her softly puckered nipple, then he suckled deeply. His hand moved beneath her dress and found the top of her stockings. He started to knead the soft flesh of her inner thigh.

He was rock-hard and his body was screaming for release. His fingers fumbled and he knew he was being clumsy as he finished unbuttoning her bodice. The sides fell open to reveal the rest of the white lace chemise, and he groaned in frustration.

"Hell woman, why do you need to wear so damned many clothes?"

He roughly pulled the chemise off her shoulders and hurried to unhook the rest of her corset. Then he paused to lean on one elbow, enjoying the view of her flesh exposed to him in the golden light of the late afternoon. His fingers gently rolled one nipple, then the other and he watched her eyes close as she experienced the pleasure he was eliciting. He wanted to take his time, to make this lovemaking last for hours, but his body throbbed, his manhood thick and heavy with desire.

Her fingers were plucking at the buttons of his shirt, trying to unfasten them. He started to help her, but she smiled up at him and brushed his hands away. Inch by inch she revealed the muscles of his chest, then leaned over him and flicked her tongue across his nipples. He felt like he was going to rise up off the floor, the sensation was so incredible.

"Your hair," he whispered, his voice rough with need, "let it down."

She sat up and slowly raised her hands to pull the braid apart. He licked his lips as he watched her breasts jut out in invitation, and he traced his finger down one side, then the other. She shuddered as long, blond curls tumbled around her shoulders.

He pulled her down beside him again, his hands eagerly tugging her skirts and petticoats up around her waist. He glanced at the pantalets and stockings encasing her legs and he groaned again.

"Just too damned many clothes."

Gazing down at her, he realized this would have to be a hurried, eager mating. He simply couldn't wait much longer to feel her soft, moist heat surrounding him. He pulled himself to his knees and started to unfasten the top button of his pants.

"Fire," she said, her voice cracking. He thought, *she wants me so badly, she can barely speak*. He felt virile and powerful.

She swallowed and alarm entered her eyes. He tried to reassure her.

"I know, sugar. I'm on fire, too, and tonight, we're gonna build that fire until it's a mighty blaze."

Her head was shaking and he could see she was clearly alarmed now. Damn it all, he was moving too fast and now she was terrified. He swore under his breath as he withdrew his hand from the buttons on his pants.

"The barn," she said with a gasp. "It's on fire!" She pointed over his shoulder, and he turned to see flames edging across the floor toward them.

"Hell!" He jumped up and started to stomp out the blaze. "Throw me my shirt."

Sinclair was trying to quickly fasten her bodice, but she stopped long enough to toss him the worn denim shirt he'd removed just minutes before. He started to swing it through the air, attempting to put out the flames. He could see the kerosene lantern lying on its side, and he cursed himself for being such a fool.

He'd been so intent on seducing Sinclair, he didn't notice when the lantern was kicked over.

He could hear voices outside the barn now, yelling "Fire" and he glanced back at Sinclair. She was standing up, trying to adjust her clothing, but her hair was filled with bits of hay and he could see from where he stood that she was buttoned up all wrong. It'd be obvious to everyone what they'd been doing up here.

Smoke was filling the loft, and he pointed to the ladder. "Get down and get out. I'll handle this."

She stared at him, but when he stamped his foot and pointed to the ladder again she hurried over and started to scramble down. She didn't get very far when he heard one of his hands below.

"Why Miss Sinclair, what you doin' up in the hay-mow?"

A few minutes later Dakota Red came up the ladder with a bucket, tossing the water in it before he realized Jefferson was standing between him and the fire. Jefferson was soaking wet but Red's effort put out the last of the flames.

His hired hand gave him a funny look, glanced down at the lower level, seemed to consider the situation for a moment, then grinned at Jefferson.

"Didn't see ya standin' there, Boss."

Jefferson shook the water from his hair and glared back at his hired hand. "I was trying to put the fire out, Red."

Red gave him a knowing grin and raised an eyebrow. "Yup, Boss. I can see that now." Without another word he went down the ladder, and Jefferson moaned.

He didn't want to imagine the tales that would be told around the campfire that night. Before morning, every hand on the place would have heard that the boss was up in the haymow with Miss Sinclair, and whatever they were doing, it must have been hot, because they nearly burned the barn down.

He rubbed the grime from his eyes and ran a hand through his hair. He'd never live this one down and most troubling, his men would be gossiping about Sinclair. He didn't want anyone questioning her virtue, but he'd just insured that every tongue on the place would be wagging about her. He climbed down the ladder and flung his tattered shirt into a corner. Not much more than a rag now, there was no point in trying to wear it again.

He heard a loud hiss from one of the empty stalls, and turned to see Sinclair beckoning him. "Come here," she demanded.

He cringed, wishing he didn't have to discuss what had happened with her right then, but he'd best take his medicine and get it over with.

Her dress was still fastened haphazardly, her hair was wild about her face and she was flushed from all the excitement.

"Did you get the fire out?"

He stopped a few paces from her. "Yup, I did. But, well." He paused to consider his choice of words. "Dakota knows we were both up there, so I've gotta warn you, he's likely to talk about this to anyone who'll listen. He's worse than the Gibbon sisters when it comes to gossip."

She nibbled her lower lip and looked worried. "Do

you think they'll know we were . . . were . . ." She looked embarrassed.

"Making love? It won't take much imagination to put the pieces together." He stepped closer to her and started to unbutton her bodice. She slapped his hands away, and he grinned down at her.

"I'm not planning to take up where we left off, even if I will be riding sore in the saddle for the rest of the day. You'd better try to look fairly respectable when you get back to the house."

She glanced down, saw what was wrong and started to make amends. He pulled his fingers through her hair in an attempt to dislodge the pieces of hay. He marveled at the smooth softness that slid through his fingers.

She touched him and he felt that familiar tingle race through his blood. She had an incredible effect on him and he felt like a man crossing a desert, desperate for a drink. Except to his love-starved body, her kiss was the drink he craved.

He looked down into eyes, stormy with emotion.

"I could say I'm sorry for what happened up there, Sinclair. But I'd be lying to you. I'm not one bit sorry, except for starting that fire. Because if that lantern hadn't tipped over, I'd be pleasuring you right this minute. I'd be teaching you how incredible we could be together."

Her mouth formed a small "O," and she dropped her hand. He could see a rose-tinged blush climb up her neck and color her cheeks. Maybe he shouldn't have been so blunt with her, but if she didn't want him, she'd best not tempt him the way she just did up in the haymow.

"And what happened today won't stop me, Sinclair. It was just a little interruption. I mean to have you, but if you don't want me, then you best stay out of my way."

He turned and with several long strides he was out the door. He didn't look back. As far as he was concerned, the course of their relationship was all up to her now.

Chapter Fifteen

Sinclair paced her small bedroom like a caged animal, and for what seemed like the hundredth time that day, she paused to glance out the window toward the barn and corral.

She blushed as she recalled her last visit to the barn, the way Jefferson had stroked her body, kissed her and made her tremble with feelings she couldn't describe. She'd barely slept these past few days, tossing and turning, aching with a need she didn't understand.

And she'd managed to endure the ribald remarks and crude comments she'd overheard regarding her nearly disastrous encounter with Boss McCloud in the haymow. Even Lettie had been unable to resist the temptation to joke about the red-hot love birds.

It didn't help that McCloud had decided there were some cattle on the farthest edge of his spread in need of his immediate attention. He'd been gone two days and Sinclair couldn't decide if she was going to kiss him when he returned or shoot him for abandoning her.

She'd debated for days about the challenge he'd flung at her in the barn. He'd made it clear that it was her decision if they made love. Despite her strict upbringing and the endless warnings she'd received regarding the things a woman didn't do outside the bonds of marriage, she was confused.

She knew the consequences if a woman was seduced and left ruined, yet she couldn't stop thinking about the way Jefferson's hands had touched her, as if she were some rare and precious treasure, and the gentle way his mouth had explored her body. She'd been aroused and left wanting, yet he'd made no promises nor had he uttered even a word about loving her.

She leaned against the window casement and sighed deeply. She'd spent many hours these past few days wondering if she loved him. She could recall the way he walked, the deep dimples that appeared when he smiled, the combination of leather and pine that seemed to be his own personal scent, and the deep, dark sadness in his eyes sometimes, when he didn't think anyone was watching.

She was sure she did love him and that knowledge made her stronger. Jefferson didn't believe he was worthy of love, and she sensed he was afraid to trust anyone. His heart had been broken when both his mother and stepmother died in this western wilderness. He tried to insulate himself from loss by denying his own feelings.

Sinclair had spent years watching her father do the same thing. Jefferson had built a shell around his heart, because he didn't want to be hurt again, just like her father. But she could prove to him love wasn't always filled with pain and heartache.

She shook her head to clear it and smoothed the soft cotton fabric of her dress. Straightening her shoulders, she marched to the door and yanked it open. She had a plan of action, and even though it might backfire, in her opinion action was more important that words. When he returned home, Sinclair would confront him.

Until that moment, Sinclair had never considered herself a coward. She'd been proud of the way she faced problems head-on, managing somehow to deal with circumstances as they came. That night she sat on her bed, cowering in fear of what would happen when she finally faced Boss McCloud.

She knew he was back, she'd heard the commotion down at the corral after supper. The voices of the men carried on the late-afternoon breeze, their good-natured teasing reminding her that their escapades had not yet been forgotten. His return would just fuel the gossip even more, and she'd discovered there was little entertainment on a ranch as lively as a hint of scandal.

She'd finished putting Maddie to bed, settling her with a story, then crooning a lullaby to send her gently off to sleep. Sinclair had been alert ever since Jefferson's arrival, afraid he might come up to see her immediately, and she had tried to prepare what she would say. But, he'd gone to the bunkhouse to eat and she'd spent the remainder of the evening trying to work up the courage to approach him.

She'd had no preparation at the Shady Lawn School for Ladies of Quality for what she planned to do that evening. Nice young ladies didn't even speak of such things, much less scheme about how to accomplish them. But, Sinclair had a purpose and she'd decided earlier that day she would face Jefferson McCloud head on and tell him that she loved him. She just wasn't quite sure what his reaction was going to be to her confession.

"Time to take the bull by the horns," she whispered to herself, adjusting her lacy batiste nightgown. She had no idea if her plan would work, but what had Jefferson said about her? Once she made up her mind, she simply had to see a thing accomplished. Well, the best way to do that was to get the hard part over as soon as possible.

Slipping carefully down the stairs, she found herself hoping Lettie had turned in at her usual hour. She didn't want the housekeeper witnessing any of the events she had planned for that evening, or Sinclair's reputation would truly be ruined. Of course, her pretense of being Jefferson's fiancée provided some protection, as a couple nearly married could engage in behavior that might be considered inappropriate otherwise.

She crept silently toward the door to Jefferson's study, but was disappointed to find only a lamp glowing in an empty room. She paused to consider her options. If he'd gone to the bunkhouse, she certainly couldn't go traipsing out there dressed as she was, to invite him back to the house. Even she wasn't that bold.

She tapped her bare toes in disappointment, realizing that her plan would have to wait for another night. Despite her impatience, one couldn't rush things like confessions of love and vows of the heart.

She pushed open the screen door leading to the porch, deciding to get a little fresh air before she turned in. She stood gazing up at the huge moon, hanging like a giant silver piece in the black velvet of the night sky. She stretched up on her toes, savoring the beauty of the night sky with its stars twinkling like crystal pendants on a chandelier.

Breathing deeply of the fresh, clean air, she nearly choked when a voice spoke from behind her.

"You know, I can see right through your nightgown when you stand in the moonlight like that."

Her heels hit the worn pine of the porch with a thud, and she whirled to stare into the dark recesses of the porch. A deep red glow lit one corner and as her eyes adjusted, the form of a man began to take shape. Jefferson sat leaning back in one of the oak chairs, his feet perched on a small table. She couldn't see his expression, but his voice sounded lazy. She wondered if he'd been drinking.

"I . . . didn't know you were here." She moved closer and could see he was smoking a cigar.

"I got back around suppertime, but I didn't see you around. Guess you were busy with Maddie."

Sinclair licked her lips, which felt dry and parched, as if she'd gone days without water.

"I suppose that must have been it. And you didn't bother to come upstairs to find me?" Her voice held a note of recrimination and she lifted her chin a bit, offended that he appeared to be avoiding her.

"I thought maybe I was the last person you'd want to talk to, considering, you know, what happened and all." He sounded apologetic. "I hope the boys haven't been too hard on you with their teasing."

She took another step closer to him, putting her hands on her hips. "I never thought I'd hear any description that could surpass the runaway hula-hula whore but I've now been labeled 'Blazin' Brazen, the flame from Philly.' "

Jefferson laughed loudly and Sinclair resisted the urge to walk over and punch him in the stomach.

"I'm thrilled I provide so much entertainment for your ranch hands, McCloud. It must have been pretty dull around here before I arrived." Her indignation was apparent by the tone of her voice, and her toe began to beat a cadence on the porch planks again.

She could see his shoulders shaking as he continued to laugh. When he finally stopped, he brought a glass to his lips, took a drink, then coughed.

"Dull. This place was a damned graveyard before you got here. Now, I can hardly wait to see what you're gonna do next."

Sinclair narrowed her eyes and pursed her lips. "Really, so you want more entertainment, is that it, McCloud?"

"You aren't mad at me, are you, Claire?" She couldn't see his expression, but he sounded unsure of himself.

He'd never referred to her as Claire before and she paused to consider if it was an endearment or if he was so drunk he couldn't pronounce her name. She'd moved close enough to smell the whiskey, so she knew he'd been drinking tonight. Drinking quite a bit judging from the smell and his temperament.

"You nearly seduce me, ruin my reputation, make me a laughingstock, then abandon me, but of course, I couldn't possibly hold that against you, McCloud, now could I?"

"Nope, you couldn't, because you know what you are, Claire?"

"Besides a blazin' brazen runaway-hula-hula whore, the flame from Philly? I shudder to imagine how anyone could hope for more than that."

He was silent for a moment, as if trying to decide if he could improve on her title.

"You're a damn fine woman."

Sinclair shook her head sadly. He was drunk as a skunk and she'd have to postpone her plans for the evening. She'd better make sure he could find a bed so he could sleep it off.

She held out a hand. "Come on, McCloud, I think it's time to go to bed." She took the glass from him and watched as he tossed his cigar over the porch rail.

"I'm inclined to agree with you, darling."

Jefferson grasped her hand, then yanked on it hard, bringing her to him roughly. Before she could resist, he'd plopped her down across his lap and his face was buried between her breasts.

"God, you smell so good. Every time I get close to you, I think about riding through wildflowers in the springtime."

His tongue slid slowly across the edging of lace on her nightgown, then moved across her skin to the small dip beneath her collarbone. She swallowed and tried to pull away.

"I don't think you're in any condition for this . . . and I don't want you to wake up in the morning thinking I took advantage of you." She tried to decide what to do with the glass of whiskey in her hand. It seemed a shame to waste it, so she brought the glass to her lips and finished it off.

She coughed as liquid fire burned its way down her throat. How did men tolerate drinking such horrible stuff?

She felt him grin into her bosom.

"It takes time to develop at taste for it, honey, likely you should stick to tea." His fingers squeezed her bottom tightly. "I can't believe how soft and sweet you are. Like you was made from spun sugar."

Sinclair felt a rush of warmth suffuse her, as his tongue continued to explore and elicit sharp, delicious points of pleasure.

"But, I can't have you. Because you're too damn good and fine for the likes of me. You're a thoroughbred, Sinclair, and I'm just a wild mustang."

He paused to gaze at her and she could see the deep longing in his eyes. "Too fine," he repeated, trying to push her off his lap.

Grabbing him by the shoulders, she refused to move, then leaned forward to place her lips eagerly on his. Advancing her tongue, she forced him to part his lips, then she thrust its tip forward to unite with him in the soft, moist cavern of his mouth. He gasped, but seemed to decide he wasn't going to argue with providence.

His hands eased up the hem of her thin cotton

nightgown, heat following his touch, and she heard him moan deeply when he realized she was naked underneath.

When their kiss finally ended, she brushed her hair back from her face to gaze down at him.

"I didn't wear too damn many clothes this time, Jefferson."

"I can see that, darling." His voice was stronger, his words less slurred and lazy. "I still don't think we should do this."

She traced a finger across his cheekbone, her smile wise and knowing. "You said it was my decision, remember?"

She heard an intake of breath and sat silently waiting for his answer.

"That's what I said." His hand moved higher, now gently kneading the flesh of her thigh.

"And didn't you promise to teach me about all the secrets between a man and a woman? Didn't you mention something about pleasure beyond my wildest dreams?"

She could see a few drops of moisture sliding down the side of his face. His eyes were smoky and half-closed as he answered her. "I might have said something to that effect."

"And aren't you a man who honors his word?" She found herself breathless, anticipating his response.

His other hand gently nudged the neckline of her gown off one shoulder, to fully expose her breasts. He seemed to study her carefully for a moment, then she could see him close his eyes.

"I can't fight it any longer, Sinclair. I don't wanna want you, but I can't fight it anymore."

His mouth found one breast, one small bud of a nipple and as he suckled, she pulled her gown fully to her waist, encouraging him with soft, plaintive whispers of delight.

She felt wanton and powerful as his tongue teased and nibbled and created ripples of pleasure throughout her body. The cool night air should have chilled her, instead she felt feverish.

His hand moved from circling her thigh, to the opening between her legs, and he gently inserted a finger into her. She gasped in surprise as his thumb found a sensitive spot at the edge of the opening and he caressed her with a feather touch. She found herself lifting her body, moving to encourage his ministrations, the wild, enticing movements that made heat rise within her like a banked fire when a log is tossed upon it.

Their lips locked together as she continued to rock and moan, unaware of their surroundings and unconcerned about the noise she was making.

Jefferson pulled his hand away, and she cried out in protest. She wanted his touch, the building, the climbing to something she didn't understand but desperately desired. She couldn't tell him what she needed, she didn't understand it herself. She only knew that she never wanted him to stop the sweet torture his fingers elicited.

"More," she demanded, her kiss-swollen lips forming a pout.

Jefferson lifted her with one smooth movement to set her gently on the porch. He paused to brush the moisture from his brow before rearranging her nightgown. Glancing around them into the darkness, an expression of concern crossed his face.

"Not here, love. I'm not gonna put on a show for any hand who happens to wander by. Upstairs. I want to see you stretched across a bed, naked and whispering my name, just the way you did a minute ago."

Her hands trembled as she touched him. She wondered if he realized what he'd just said, or if his endearment was simply part of the moment, part of the passion.

"Let's go," she said, putting her hand within his and pulling him with her. They paused halfway up the stairs, unable to keep from touching each other, from sharing one more deep, hungry kiss.

He stopped at the top of the stairs, as if considering. She felt her heart flutter in fear, but she knew she'd need to make the decision for him. She turned toward the master bedroom, toward the room he kept as a shrine to Bess, and pulled him with her. He halted at the doorway, looking confused.

"You might never forgive me for this, Jefferson. But I want you to know, I did this because I love you. I know the kind of pain you've held inside yourself these past few years, afraid to take a chance on love or happiness. I know you don't think you deserve those things." She put her hand over the place where his heart was, leaning forward to feather a few small kisses on his chest.

She could see confusion clouding his eyes, but she couldn't let that stop her. "I want you, Jefferson. I won't make you give me empty promises or insincere vows."

She lowered her head and swallowed. "I don't expect words of love, but if we do this, I want you to at least be willing to let go of the horrible memories and move on with your life."

She lifted her clear blue eyes to capture the look of surprise in his golden-brown gaze.

She opened the door and beckoned him in. He followed her, walking slowly, uncertainty apparent in his posture.

"This is the bedroom of the master and mistress of this house. I don't need a marriage proposal or even words of love, Jefferson. But I need to know that you'll honor my love for you by letting go of the pain and the guilt."

He stared at the bed, which was covered with the quilt from her room. All of the furnishings had been changed except for the large cherry wardrobe and the carved bed. Moonlight filtered in through lace curtains at the window, and candles, resting on various pieces of furniture, flickered, casting them in a warm glow.

He stood staring around the room in silence. Sinclair felt her heart pounding, but she couldn't tell if he truly understood what she was trying to do for him.

"I love you, Jefferson. I want you to be happy."

He crossed the room in two long strides and grasped her shoulders. His face was hard and his eyes stormy.

"What makes you think you know me so well, Sinclair? That you know what will make me happy, or if I even deserve happiness?"

She reached out to touch him, but he pushed her

hand away, let go of her and turned back toward the door.

She couldn't just let him walk out on her. She had to convince him that they could be happy together.

"I know how much you love Maddie, even though you try not to let anyone see it. I believe you love me, but that you're afraid to admit it. People love each other, Jefferson. It's the chance we all have to take in life, because without love, we're lost." She could feel the tears in her eyes and hoped she could manage to keep them from falling.

"Love is the only thing that can save us, and yes, sometimes we can be hurt because of that love." Her words trailed off into silence.

He turned to glare at her.

"Hurt, Sinclair? Pain and suffering are just about all I've ever seen of love. My mother died from a broken heart and so did Bess. Love didn't save them, it made them lonely and desperate women. Love gave them silent days and solitary nights. My father wouldn't love them enough to save them, and I can't take a chance that I might be the same kind of man. I'd never want to do that to any woman and I'll be damned if I'd do it to someone as fine and good as you."

He paused to touch the tear sliding gently down her cheek.

"Loving me is just an invitation to heartbreak and unhappiness. I can't let you make that mistake." She could see the agony in his eyes, but she didn't know how to convince him that his love wouldn't destroy her.

Before she could say anything in response, he was

gone. She could hear the echo of each step down the oak staircase, but she couldn't move. What words could she offer him as solace? Could she promise their love would keep them safe? If they loved each other, was that a guarantee of happiness? Pain and loss were an inevitable part of life, but she'd always believed that love was the only thing that made it bearable. Love was the thing that helped a person survive the pain, but she didn't think she could ever make Jefferson believe that.

She stumbled to the bed and threw herself down as she felt all of her dreams shatter. Her mouth was bitter with the taste of heartbreak, and her throat hurt from the tears she needed to shed.

Jefferson was right about one thing, love did hurt. That night, it hurt like hell.

Chapter Sixteen

Sinclair had never realized how easy it was to survive, even when her heart was breaking. She woke up the next morning, her eyes red and swollen from the tears she'd shed, but she was determined to act as if everything in her life was normal.

When she dressed and met Maddie downstairs for breakfast, the child smiled up at her with such devotion, Sinclair fell to her knees to give her a hug.

She marveled at the wonderful changes in the little girl. Her eyes sparkled with vitality and she had a healthy glow from their daily walks. Her breakfast of flapjacks sat nearly finished in front her, with her fork perched on the edge of her plate.

"Hello, sweetkins, how are you this morning?"

Sinclair waited. Just as she waited every morning, hoping that this would be the day Maddie finally answered her.

Today, God, Sinclair prayed, *make it today, so that everything I've sacrificed could be worth something.* Losing Jefferson would almost be worth the pain if Maddie could talk.

A flicker of recognition seemed to light the girl's soft gray eyes, but was extinguished as she returned to her breakfast. Sinclair stood and brushed her skirts gently. Not today, but maybe soon. They had made so much progress these last few weeks, that Sinclair still hoped for a miracle. She wanted to hear Madison laugh and giggle with delight, she wanted to hear her talk, just like every other little girl her age.

Lettie came in the back door with a small package and handed it to Sinclair.

"Boss said you asked for this. He's off to see Ham Brewster about a string of mustangs and said to tell you he might be gone for a few days." She bustled over to the stove.

"You want somethin' to eat?"

"Just some coffee and a biscuit, please."

Sinclair carefully unwrapped the package and was thrilled to see a child's book with pictures of horses. She could hardly wait for lesson time to share it with Maddie. The little girl loved horses, and they'd been spending hours down at the corral watching the hands breaking them in and working with them.

Lettie set a cup and plate down in front of her, seemed poised to ask a question, then shook her head and went back to the stove.

"Jefferson didn't stay home very long, did he?"

Lettie slammed a pan down on the stove and turned back to face her, a look of indignation on her face.

"I know it ain't none of my business, but I might as well have my say so's I don't bust. That man is plumb crazy about you, Miss Sinclair. Ollie tells me Jefferson can't sleep when he's out on the range, and half the time he'd wander off and get lost like some young heifer if somebody didn't point him in the right direction." She rubbed her hands on her apron.

"The thing is, he always figgered he should have done somethin' more for the missus. She was sort of helpless and needed a man around to pay attention to her. Well, the judge, he was just startin' to ride the circuit and he couldn't be here most of the time. The boss tried to help, but he wasn't much more'n a kid, and he sure couldn't take sides a'ginst the judge."

Lettie crossed the room and pulled out a chair to sit down. Sinclair nodded, hoping it would encourage her to go on. Lettie wasn't usually much for conversation.

Her fingers rubbing the worn surface of the pine table Lettie seemed reluctant to go on, then she gave a deep sigh.

"I ain't one to pass on gossip, but the missus, she liked her laudanum. Seemed like the longer the judge stayed away, the more she took. Spent some days in bed, the whole day."

A look of disgust crossed Lettie's face.

"Like to have broken that poor child's heart." She threw a sympathetic look at Maddie. "She was just a little thing, but her ma didn't look out for her the way she should have."

Sinclair nodded. She could imagine the loneliness that had wrapped itself around this house, like a snake, slowly squeezing until all of the happiness and joy disappeared. It wasn't unlike what she had experienced when her own mother had taken ill. The need for quiet, the endless visits with the doctor and the whispering of the servants.

"I figger when Maddie went out on the roof that day, durin' the storm, she just wanted to see the clouds. She always loved lookin' up at the clouds. Darndest thing I ever did see, that little girl standing outside with her face up to the sky."

Sinclair wanted to reach over and touch Maddie, but the child seemed oblivious to Lettie's story. She kept her eyes on her plate, as she worked carefully to cut each piece of flapjack with her fork, then slowly lift it to her mouth. She seemed to be concentrating on her meal more than the conversation.

"I'm not sure this is the time to discuss this, Lettie." Sinclair threw a glance toward the little girl.

Lettie blushed and nodded. "Little pitchers have big ears. I just wanted to let you know, the boss, he figgers he could have done somethin' to keep the missus from havin' that accident. I know it eats away at him, but I was here that day. Seems to me that woman was killin' herself a little bit at a time. Ain't nobody can save a soul once they give up."

Lettie stood and looked embarrassed. "I don't usually go on so much. Just thought if ya knew, well, mebbe you'd understand the boss. He's a good man."

Sinclair felt a small tremor move through her, then she stood to lean forward on the table, her eyes hard and her voice like iron.

"Did anyone ever tell Jefferson about Bess? Does he know she was addicted to laudanum? That her condition was deteriorating?"

Lettie wrung her hands and shook her head sadly. "The judge told me to mind my own business, he wasn't gonna have gossip spread around about his wife. I reckon he just didn't want folks to know how much he neglected his family. He's got plans, the judge does. He had plans for the boss, too, politics, but the boss is a born rancher."

She leaned forward to whisper, as if there was someone to overhear. "Last time the judge was here, they had a big row, 'cause the judge wanted the boss to move to Helena. He'd made some kinda decision, and told the boss to let Ollie run the ranch."

She lifted her eyebrows and gave Sinclair a thin smile. "You can 'bout imagine how that went over."

Sinclair shook her head sadly. "So all this time, Jefferson has felt responsible for the accident that killed Bess, and for Maddie's condition. He was never told the truth and suffers every day believing he could have changed things." She stood.

"Lettie, when Jefferson gets back, I'm going to tell him the truth. The judge never told me to be quiet and even if he did, from what I've heard about the man, he doesn't deserve loyalty or respect. I will not stand by and let Jefferson McCloud throw away our chance at happiness because of a selfish old man. It's time we did some housecleaning here and the first thing we're going to do is throw open doors and let the secrets out."

She smiled, as a rush of memories flowed over her. She recalled the way Jefferson had stormed at her the first night they'd met, when she'd fallen on him outside the Blue Willow. She remembered the way he'd pointed his gun at Hank Borscht and threatened him if he ever touched Sinclair again. Images of the way he laughed, of the way his body had glistened the day she'd discovered him in the tub in the kitchen, and the way he teased her with incredible, breathtaking kisses that assailed her.

She put her hands on her hips and paced across the floor, small specks of dust dancing in the sunlight as she moved.

"He is a good, kind, loving, exasperating, arrogant, intelligent, bewildering man." Sinclair whirled around the kitchen and caught Lettie about the waist. "He thinks he can get rid of me, but we Readfords are a tenacious lot."

Lettie looked confused. "Get rid of you? Land's sake, the man is a fool if ever I knowed one."

Sinclair nodded in agreement. "Of course he is, aren't they all? Men think they have all the answers and they dismiss us as the weak and foolish sex. Well, I'll just have to prove to Boss McCloud that I'm not going to give in to his thick-headed demands. I've got a job to do and he's not packing me off before I'm good and ready to go."

Lettie stopped her suddenly, panic in her eyes. "You ain't goin' nowhere, are you, miss? Why, I don't know what we'd do without you 'round here. You can't let the boss scare you off."

Sinclair folded her arms across her bosom and winked at Lettie.

"Have you ever known any man who knew what was good for him? I'm going to stick it out just to prove Boss McCloud wrong." She straightened her shoulders proudly. "Nothing would give me more pleasure than proving to McCloud he doesn't know nearly as much as he thinks he does. Most especially about me!"

Sinclair felt renewed. She'd nearly let Jefferson convince her she shouldn't stay. Even if he thought he wasn't good enough for her, why should she allow him to run her off? And when she told him the truth, he'd realize she wasn't like Bess, she wasn't a spoiled, incompetent woman who needed to be coddled. Maybe she had been once, but she had changed. She was certainly capable of making her own decisions, and just because he refused to see how happy they could be, she'd didn't have to go running back to Philadelphia. All she needed to do was to prove him wrong.

Maddie finished her breakfast and stood. She studied Sinclair carefully, as is she wasn't sure what she should do next.

Sinclair grabbed the book and took Maddie's hand in hers. "I have something wonderful to show you, sweetkins."

Maddie walked to the door with Sinclair, then paused for a moment to look back. Sinclair could see she threw a perplexed look at Lettie as they went through the door and out onto the porch.

Settling herself into a chair, Sinclair opened the book and pointed to the first page. There was a beautiful illustration of a stallion, with his feet high in the air and his head regally thrown back.

"This must be Thunder, the horse the men were talking about. Do you remember what they said about him, that he was the king of the mustangs? I imagine this is what a horse who is a king would look like." Maddie studied the picture carefully, then she lifted her eyes to gaze longingly toward the corral. There weren't any horses in there today and Sinclair could see yearning etched on the child's face.

"I know, a picture isn't nearly as magnificent as the real thing, is it?"

Sinclair recalled her last ride on Brown Sugar. Despite their first encounter, she had become an adept rider and had developed an attachment to the horse. She wished Maddie could experience the wonder and exhilaration of riding.

Sinclair turned the page, but barely noticed the illustration as she considered the idea. Why not give Maddie a riding lesson? Certainly there must be a small horse somewhere on the ranch gentle enough for the girl to ride for a short distance. They wouldn't go far, perhaps down to the creek and back. It would delight Maddie beyond measure, and today, some delight was certainly in order, for both of them.

She closed the book and Maddie shook her head, indicating she wasn't finished yet. Sinclair held out her hand with one finger pointing up, her signal that she wanted the girl's full attention. Maddie paused to listen.

Sinclair leaned forward to put her face very close to Maddie. "I have a surprise for you."

Maddie made no indication she understood what the word *surprise* meant.

"Would you like to go for a ride on a horse today?"

Maddie's eyes immediately grew wide with wonder, and Sinclair nodded.

"If you promise you'll listen very carefully, we can do this."

Maddie nodded back at Sinclair, silent but her eyes shining with happiness.

Standing, Sinclair put the book carefully on the chair and grabbed Maddie's hand. They went down the steps and toward the corral so quickly Maddie had to run to keep up with Sinclair.

"Mr. Red?" Sinclair waved at one of the hands. He stopped in his tracks to give her his full attention. She was short of breath as she approached him, but she didn't pause.

"Could you manage to find a gentle little horse for my friend here? She would love to go riding today."

Red looked at her as if she was crazy, but Sinclair was too accustomed to that look to pay any attention. "In fact, we'd both like to go riding, if you could saddle up Brown Sugar too."

Red scratched his head, as if it would help him to consider the matter, then he spit out a stream of tobacco juice, another thing to which Sinclair had grown accustomed.

"Don't know if the boss'd like that, her bein' tetched and all."

Sinclair frowned, then waved the man's concerns away with a flick of her wrist. "Jefferson allows me to make all the decisions regarding his sister's care, and I would like to teach her to ride. We won't be going far, only down to the creek and back."

Red studied her more carefully. "Why, roundin' up two horses, saddlin' 'em and gettin' all their riggin' on ain't worth it for that lil' bit of ridin'."

Sinclair shook her head. "I don't care. We must begin someplace and Jefferson assured me that when

I made a request, his men would honor it as quickly as possible."

Red moved his hand from his head to his beard, and scratched there a few moments before answering.

"I s'pose I can do it, but it's gonna take me a bit. Hard to know where them horses could be."

Sinclair nodded in agreement. "It will take me nearly an hour to get ready, but when I come back down here, I expect the horses to be saddled and waiting."

Red shrugged as he leaned his shovel up against the barn. "I ain't makin' no guarantee, but I'll git right to it." He shuffled off, muttering under his breath.

Sinclair felt giddy with delight as she twirled Maddie in a circle. "You, sweetkins, are going to go for a ride today. We'll need to find you something that can serve as a riding habit, and of course, you'll need some gloves and a hat."

Maddie smiled brightly up at her, and Sinclair felt a sudden rush of affection. There were moments when she could imagine Maddie was just like every other child, that the world had never silenced her or plunged her into the darkness of pain and sorrow.

She'd been trying to give Maddie all the small things she'd loved as a child. The stories, lullabies, books and art materials. Every time she made a little magic for Maddie, she melted some of the heartache of her own childhood.

Sinclair realized that was the way healing love worked. You couldn't repair pain, you just had to create enough happiness to make the sadness fade. Now that she had spent time with Maddie, she treasured the love and delight of her own childhood. That was what she wanted to share with Jefferson, wonderful times of enchantment, moments that would sustain them when the hard times came. She couldn't promise miracles but she could show him how love worked.

They climbed the steps to the porch and went in the main door. The house smelled fresh and clean, as sunlight streamed into the parlor. Sinclair had insisted that the dark, dusty velvet draperies be taken down for a good cleaning when they'd first started to receive guests. The change in the rooms had been so profound, they'd never managed to get the draperies back up.

The light scent of lemon oil filled the air, and as Sinclair climbed the stairs with Maddie, she couldn't help but marvel at the way the light made the polished oak glow. The house seemed friendlier, more like a home. She couldn't quite figure out what the difference was, perhaps just that she'd found purpose and strength within these walls. What had seemed strange and cold before, now felt comforting.

She was impatient to get on with her plans for the day, and quickly dressed Maddie in a dark brown dress, short pants to protect her legs, and a matching jacket. She laced a bright red ribbon through her straw bonnet, and found soft kidskin gloves to match the dress. Once the little girl was fully dressed, they went to Sinclair's room.

Maddie sat on the bed as Sinclair quickly donned her riding habit. She smoothed out the wrinkles and buttoned the jacket with practiced ease. Grabbing her hat, she gave Maddie a smile.

"We'll be the envy of all the women in Montana, sweetkins, with our fancy clothes and fine horses. We'd better hope the cowboys don't see us, because they'll simply swoon at our loveliness."

Maddie watched Sinclair carefully, but didn't respond. It didn't matter, this was turning out to be too fine a day to worry about what could be. It was a day just to enjoy what was.

She was nearly out the door when Sinclair realized she'd forgotten her parasol. Even though they were only going for a short ride, and she couldn't put it up near the horse, perhaps they'd take a stroll when they got down to the creek. She remembered Jefferson's lighthearted teasing about her freckles. She should be prepared, just in case.

As she hurried down the stairs, it occurred to Sinclair they could truly make an adventure of this ride and they paused in the kitchen to gather up some fresh bread, two apples and molasses cookies still warm from the oven. She wrapped the food in a clean linen napkin and winked at Maddie playfully.

"We'll sit down by the creek and have a lovely picnic. The weather is perfect today to dilly-dally."

They nearly collided with Lettie as they came down the porch steps. She gave them a perplexed look.

"Now what are you up to, miss?"

Sinclair waved her hand at Lettie and gave her a brilliant smile as she pushed Maddie toward the corral. "Just a little equestrian training for Miss Maddie."

Lettie frowned after them, switching the wicker clothes basket to her other hip. "Equal-extry what?"

Sinclair ignored her as she rushed toward the barn.

She could see Red with two horses and she was delighted that he'd been much quicker about the arrangement than she'd ever expected.

Brown Sugar stood next to a small horse with the markings the hands referred to as paint. The horse's coloring delighted Sinclair, it looked as if someone had taken a brush to her coat, randomly putting splashes of dark brown over white.

Red held tightly to both sets of reins and he still looked uncertain. "I wish you'd let me get word from the boss 'bout this." He spit tobacco out of the side of his mouth and appeared to be ready to protest more.

Sinclair decided she would have to make sure he understood her position here at the Cripple Creek Ranch.

"Jefferson trusts my judgment," she said, sniffing elegantly. "After all, Mr. Red, this little girl is nearly my own sister."

Red seemed to consider her words carefully. "Yup, there is that, ain't there?" He handed the reins to Sinclair and offered a hand to help her up into the saddle.

"Give me a boost!" she exclaimed, as he assisted her. Her phrase for mounting always made the hands laugh, and Mr. Red was no different. Sinclair had grown used to the teasing and laughter. She delighted in saying funny and amusing things to the hands, just to see their reaction.

Sinclair watched as he carefully lifted Maddie and set her gently into the saddle on the back of the small horse. The child wore an expression of pure delight and Sinclair was immediately appreciative of the man's assistance.

She leaned forward as he handed her Maddie's reins and nodded.

"Thank you, Mr. Red. You've made a child very happy today."

She watched the older man step back and beam up at them.

"Yup, I guess I did. Can't say as I can remember the last I see'd that youngun smile."

Sinclair gave Maddie the sign to listen, then watched as the child sat up straight and settled her undivided attention upon her. "You must hang on tight and keep your feet in the stirrups. We are just going for a walk down to the creek, then we'll come right back."

With painstaking slowness, Sinclair clicked her tongue to give Brown Sugar the subtle signal to move forward. The small horse carrying Maddie moved with them, and they were off. Their pace would have been considered plodding to any cowboy, but it was sufficient to bring an even wider smile to Maddie's face.

The sunlight was warm and Sinclair was lulled into complacency as they moved in a slow rhythm. Maddie held tightly to the saddle horn, and she seemed comfortable riding on the horse. Of course, it made sense the child would be a natural. Jefferson seemed as much at ease on horseback as he was walking.

She imagined how adorable he must have looked when he was a little boy, learning to ride. And she found herself wondering what his son might look like on the back of his first horse.

She was lost in a daydream, imagining a little boy with dark hair and bright blue eyes. A child that was part Jefferson and part her. She felt a small ache in her heart at the wonder of such a dream.

She was shaken out of her reverie by a man's voice, coming from behind her. She realized they were nearly to the creek and out of view from the ranch.

"Damn, we finally got a bit of luck. It's her, ain't it?"

She turned to discover two mounted riders behind them, their faces covered by bandannas and guns pointed directly at her and Maddie.

Sinclair swallowed as fear rippled through her. She had a feeling she was about to finally meet some of the outlaws about which she'd read so much. But now she had a child's safety to consider, and that thought chilled her to the bone.

Chapter Seventeen

Sinclair wanted to scream, but knew it would be useless. They were too far from the barn for Mr. Red to hear them, and she was terrified the men might shoot her if she made any noise. She wasn't sure if anything more than a strangled peep would emerge from her throat anyway, it was so tight with fear.

She swallowed and glanced at Maddie. The girl was staring at the creek, seemingly fascinated by the light playing on the surface of the water, and oblivious to the danger surrounding her. Sinclair gave a small sigh of relief, if Maddie could remain that calm, she couldn't be aware of the peril.

Taking a deep breath, Sinclair briefly closed her eyes, whispered a small prayer asking for God's protection, then straightened her shoulders and decided to try to bluff her way out their predicament. Opening her eyes, she attempted to use her most authoritative voice.

"I cannot imagine what you men think we possess to make guns and disguises necessary in order to rob us. We're on our way to have a picnic and the only treasure we have is wrapped in a napkin." Lifting her chin in defiance, she glared at them.

"Stealing our lunch would hardly be worth the effort."

The taller man nudged his horse forward. Sinclair could see steely gray eyes, cold and distrustful, in a dark skinned face. He studied her for a moment, and she shivered as his gaze moved over her.

Without a word, he moved closer and snatched the reins from her hands. When she tried to protest, he leaned toward her and his eyes met hers with a inhospitable force that silenced her.

"Yer comin' with us."

He turned his horse, and began to lead them away from the ranch, appearing to keep his pace slow in deference to the child.

Sinclair panicked. Maddie couldn't ride with them on the high trails. She'd never been on a horse before today, and although she'd done extraordinarily well, she couldn't be expected to go off on a long ride through the wilderness surrounding the ranch.

"You've made a terrible mistake. I'm sure you've confused me with someone else. I'm Sinclair Readford, of the Philadelphia Readfords, and I'm employed as a teacher for this little girl here on the Cripple Creek Ranch."

He words didn't appear to have any effect on the two men. They continued to ignore her, which made

Sinclair more indignant than frightened.

"Did you hear me? I work for Jefferson McCloud, the owner of the Cripple Creek Ranch." She pronounced her words slowly and carefully, as if she suspected the two were dimwits. Didn't they know about McCloud and his temper?

"He will be very, very angry when he finds out we've disappeared. And believe me, you do not want to make that man angry." She shook her head. "He is not a nice man when he gets angry."

One of the men looked back at her, and she could see his shoulders shaking. Sinclair realized he was laughing at her and her indignation grew into affront. Well, she'd just let them find out for themselves. They would surely suffer when McCloud found them. If they thought dealing with him was some kind of joke, she wouldn't say another word of warning. Then she glanced over at Maddie and tamped down her temper. Just because she was offended, she had no right to endanger this child.

"Of course, he might just be happy to get his little sister back. After all, I'm only an employee and a troublesome one at that. If you let Maddie go now, he'd likely just forget about me." She shivered at the words, aware that McCloud was gone, probably for days. And she briefly wondered if he would come looking for her if she did disappear. Perhaps he'd think she'd gone back to Philadelphia. Perhaps he'd be relieved she was gone. She bit back bitter tears, she didn't have time for regrets. She had to find a way to save Maddie.

"From what we hear, McCloud won't be that happy to see you go. It don't matter though, we've been paid to catch you. The kid, she's just a little extra baggage." The smaller man had turned to answer her. His eyes were not as cold and hard as the other man, and in fact, he almost appeared sympathetic.

"Just do as yer told. We won't hurt ya. There's a man what paid good money to see ya again. You should be honored, ma'am." The smaller man turned back to his companion and shrugged. The other man remained silent.

Sinclair gave another deep sigh and slumped back in the saddle. She should be honored to be kidnapped, responsible for a child's safety and hauled off to God knows where. Oh yes, she'd just count her blessings right then. Why did it seem that lately every time she tried to do something good it had a tendency to come flying back into her face as a problem? Was she stupid or just unlucky? She didn't have time to ponder the issue, but perhaps if she managed to get out of this alive, she'd seriously consider her propensity for getting into trouble.

Maddie seemed to be enjoying the ride as she stared in wide-eyed wonder at the canopy of leaves and pine boughs shading the trail. Sinclair wished they were here under better circumstances, but at least Maddie maintained her equilibrium. Nothing could shake that child's world and Sinclair felt a stab of envy. Perhaps that was the reward for suffering the fate of living deep within yourself. You couldn't be terrorized, and certainly that was a definite benefit.

As they moved farther from the ranch, Sinclair tried to figure out the identity of this mysterious man who wanted to see her badly enough to pay outlaws to kidnap her. At least, they looked and acted like outlaws. Sinclair couldn't be sure who they were, but they certainly didn't appear to be taking her on a short jaunt to join someone for a tea party. She briefly wondered about Lord Billingsly. He did have a wicked sense of humor, but this just wasn't his style. He was, after all, a member of the aristocracy. He wouldn't think it funny to frighten a woman.

Her mind combed all the various possibilities, until she finally settled upon one cold, hard visage. Hank Borscht. He'd vowed vengeance upon her and somehow this kidnapping smacked of him. Sneaky and lowdown, that certainly sounded like Hank.

She stared at the two men riding ahead of her and tried to formulate a plan. She had a pretty good idea of what would happen if Hank finally managed to get her alone. He'd made his intentions clear on more than one occasion. Sinclair shuddered at the memory. After feeling Jefferson's gentle, loving touch, and experiencing the wonder of his lips moving over her body, she had no intention of succumbing to a filthy pig like Hank Borscht.

She glanced down at Maddie, who seemed to be studying the path carefully, watching each step her horse took with deliberate attention. Sinclair leaned over and whispered her name. Maddie looked up at her, and now Sinclair could see fear in her eyes. Maddie knew they were in trouble. Maybe that was a good thing.

"Listen, sweetkins. I know you're scared, but I need you to help me. I'm not sure if you can do this, but please, try. I'm going to create a diversion, um

. . . a surprise for these men. Do you remember, we talked about surprises this morning?"

Maddie glanced at the two men up ahead of them, then nodded slowly.

"When I surprise them, you're going to have a chance to get away. You'll need to pull the reins of your horse back." She pointed to the reins, aware that if she made too much fuss, the men would look back at them.

Maddie nodded again, and Sinclair hoped the little girl would be able to escape. Her idea was a great gamble, but it just wasn't Sinclair's nature to accept circumstances, fold her hands and whimper for sympathy. Even a long-shot gamble had a chance for a payoff.

Without drawing attention to herself she carefully pulled her parasol from the side of the saddle where it was fastened. She felt Brown Sugar shudder at the movement. Good, she was counting on the horse's reaction. "Don't let me down now, sugar," she whispered.

One of the men turned to look at them, just as Sinclair brought the parasol upright over her head. He studied her for a moment, then nudged his companion, who also looked back.

"What's that yer doin'?" the small man asked.

Sinclair tossed her head defiantly. "Just because I'm being kidnapped doesn't mean I intend to spoil my complexion. A lady can't look like some wild heathen who bakes in the sun." She made her voice impertinent. "Everyone knows a real lady should have a pale countenance, free of freckles." As if she even cared. But the men seemed to be satisfied, as they snickered between themselves, then turned back to watch the trail lying before them.

With careful deliberation, she slid the small mechanism partway up the shaft of the parasol. Then, with one swift movement she pushed it to the top. The spines pushed out, and, as the fabric unfolded over her head, she heard a loud *furump*. Brown Sugar jumped, gave a shudder and a sound emerged from her that was a cross between a scream and a whine. The horse then reared back on her hind legs and gave a heart-stopping whinny of displeasure. The men turned around in shock, and the reins of Sinclair and Maddie's horses slipped through the big man's fingers.

"Now," Sinclair yelled at the little girl, as she struggled to stay on her bucking horse. She could see Maddie leaning forward to grab her own reins, as Sinclair dug her heels into Brown Sugar's sides. She regretted upsetting the horse, but at this point, the more difficult Brown Sugar became, the better their chances of escape. She intentionally tried to put her horse between the men and Maddie.

The outlaws were trying to get their own horses under control, and Sinclair decided to take full advantage of the situation. She screamed and started waving the parasol dramatically in various directions. Brown Sugar became even more agitated, turning in circles in an attempt to get away from the offending device. Sinclair had gathered her own reins and worked to keep herself in the saddle. She just needed to buy some more time, so that Maddie could put as much distance as possible between herself and these men.

Deborah Schneider

"Whoa," yelled one of the men, waving his arms and trying to keep Sinclair's horse on the narrow trail. His bandanna had slipped, revealing more of his face. He seemed oddly familiar, and Sinclair realized she must have seen him in town before.

The taller man was sitting silently on his horse, as if patiently waiting for things to calm down. He seemed to be oblivious to the scene, until his eyes flickered back to the trail behind Sinclair. Recognition lit his gaze, as he yanked down his own bandana, kicked his horse forward and grabbed at Sinclair's reins. Nudging his horse close to Brown Sugar, he leaned forward and covered the mare's eyes with his large brown skinned hand, and softly mumbled a few words that Sinclair couldn't understand. The horse stopped bucking. With one swift, deliberate move the man snatched the parasol from Sinclair's hand and threw it into the woods. He glared at her.

"Damned troublesome white woman," he muttered, as he pointed behind Sinclair. "The kid's gone. You wanna go after her?"

The other man shook his head. "That girl is feebleminded anyhow. Everyone knows she cain't talk. Like as not, she cain't even find her own way home."

Sinclair followed their gazes down the trail, which was now empty. Maddie had escaped, but the man's words reminded her she might have sent the child off to a worse fate. It had never occurred to her Maddie might not be able to find her way back to the ranch. Terror flowed through her at the thought of a lonely, silent Maddie wandering the woods aimlessly, searching for home.

"Grab her reins and tie her hands to her saddle

somehow. Make her sit astride." The man she now thought of as the savage, because she recognized the Indian blood flowing through his veins, gave the curt, short order to his partner, then climbed down from the saddle.

"Ask her if she needs to take a piss. We ain't stoppin' after this." And he walked off the trail a few steps, turned his back and seemed to forget about them as he relieved himself.

The other man looked up at her, seemed about to ask her, then considered again. "Do you?"

"No," she spat at him, "not in front of you two." He seemed satisfied with her answer, then fumbled in his saddlebag for a moment. Pulling out a small length of thin rope, he gave her an apologetic grin.

"I'm sorry 'bout this, but I do what he tells me. Hoss is one mean son of a bitch when he gets riled. It's his Injun blood."

Sinclair flinched at the name. Of course, she remembered Polly mentioning the formidable Hoss. He was the man who kept the women in line at the Blue Willow. He had likely earned his reputation for cold-blooded violence under the tutelage of Hank Borscht.

"Can you, well, switch yer legs so you ride regular like?"

Sinclair gave the man a disparaging look. "Ladies always ride sidesaddle, but I suppose men like you wouldn't have experience with anything but the sad, forsaken women who occupy places like the Blue Willow." She pulled her leg over the pommel to let it hang down over the side of Brown Sugar.

He didn't say anything as he wrapped her hands

together with the thin rope, then tied them to the saddle.

"Leastways, you won't fall off if your horse decides to take off again."

Sinclair gave him a pinched look. "That is such a comfort to me. Thank you for your consideration." Her voice leaked vinegar.

The man backed off, looked up at her with a guilty expression, seemed about to say something, then simply swore softly under his breath.

"Damn bad business if ya ask me," he murmured, then mounted his own horse, pulling the reins of Brown Sugar behind him.

Sinclair's heart gave a small leap as she realized it was possible this man might be of some assistance to her. She suspected that he hadn't been fully apprised of what he'd be doing today, or who he'd be kidnapping. Perhaps she could make him an ally.

She called after him. "What should I call you? I know your partner's name, but if I need your attention, well, it's not very polite to simply yell out, 'You there!' " She pasted what she hoped was a winsome smile onto her face.

He turned back to her and seemed to lose himself for a moment. Then he looked down. "Just call me Corky. That's what everyone else calls me." He seemed embarrassed.

Sinclair thought these folks out West had some of the oddest names she'd ever heard, but she didn't offer any comment. She simply gave him that same sad smile and shrugged.

Sinclair's back ached and her arms were numb by the time they came over a small rise and paused to look down at a thin plume of smoke curling up toward them. She couldn't see any buildings through the thick brush and trees, but Corky assured her there was a small cabin beneath them.

"It ain't much, but it's dry." His gaze moved toward the dark clouds sitting on the horizon. "We're in fer a big blow tonight, so we got here just in time."

As the horses moved down the almost invisible trail, Sinclair thought about Maddie. Was she home yet? What would happen to the child if she were caught out in the woods in the middle of a storm? Would she be frightened? Would her small horse become terrified if there was thunder and lightning, throw her, and leave her alone and injured somewhere on the trail? Her mind reeled with the various scenarios: Maddie lying helpless and cold. Maddie wandering about the woods lost, the rain drenching her. And most terrifying, Maddie, her small body still and cold. Sinclair was exhausted, frightened and sick with worry. She didn't even bother to brush at the tears as they slid silently down her cheeks.

Corky helped her from her horse, but she was barely conscious of the small, rough cabin as she climbed a few steps to the porch. She could smell wood smoke mixed with the pungent scent of ham, onions and potatoes frying. Despite her exhaustion she felt her stomach give a lurch. She'd barely eaten all day and she was starving. She hoped there was coffee, as she was nearly numb with cold and fatigue and she needed something to revive her.

Hoss opened the door, indicating she should go in ahead of them. There was a pale yellow glow from a lantern, but otherwise the cabin was shrouded in dark shadows. She really didn't have any choice, so she stepped into the main room.

A woman stood at an ancient iron stove, stirring a large black skillet. She was handsome and stately, dressed in a gown of fine silk. Gold earrings winked at her ears, and she looked astonished to see Sinclair. Hoss pushed her into the room, toward the woman, and as Sinclair moved closer, she couldn't believe her eyes. The woman had golden curls, laced with a soft gray, but golden indeed. Familiar blue eyes, the same deep blue that stared back at her every morning in her mirror, met her gaze. Then a soft smile of recognition lit the woman's face and two arms stretched out in welcome. Sinclair stepped into the embrace and started to cry.

"Aunt Tilly," she whispered, between great, gulping sobs. "I've made a terrible mess of things."

Her aunt held her close and patted her back gently. "You never mind about that now, darling. Your auntie is here and I'll be damned if anyone's going to hurt you."

Her aunt's voice was sharp as she spoke to the two men. "Get your plates, fill them and leave us alone."

Sinclair saw a third man rise from a chair perched in a dark corner, and she cringed as a familiar voice rang in her ears.

"Now, isn't this nice? I'm touched by this sweet domestic scene. I guess you ladies should be thanking me for this poignant reunion."

Sinclair turned slowly to find herself facing the cold, hard eyes of Hank Borscht. She was reminded of the snakes about which she'd been cautioned. The ones waiting, curled up in the grass, for the best opportunity to strike.

He gave her a slow appraising look that chilled her blood, and the corners of his mouth dipped as his eyes grew even harder.

"I've gone to a great deal of trouble for you, Miss Readford. I've waited longer, been more patient and paid more for you than any woman, including Matilda." His gaze moved to the older woman, then settled back on Sinclair.

"Now, I confess, I'm reluctant to give up the opportunity to have you in my bed tonight, but if your aunt and I can come to terms, I'll agree to let you go."

He moved closer and gathered a small wisp of hair that had escaped from her chignon. Sinclair tried to pull away as he yanked her from her aunt's arms.

Hank twisted her about, placing her in front of him and wrapping his arms across her suggestively. He held the point of a knife against the lace at the throat of her riding habit. His grip was unyielding, and his breath was sour with the smell of whiskey.

Her aunt stood frozen, fear making her eyes wet with unshed tears, yet her body was straight and her shoulders lifted proudly.

"Bringing her into this mess just insures that you'll be dead before it's over, Hank. It's been between me and you, but now . . . you crossed the line. You can't threaten my family and get away it." There was a dark malevolence in her expression as she stared at Hank.

Hank pushed his face close to Sinclair's cheek, and she could feel the rough stubble of whiskers grate against her skin. He slowly moved the knife down to the swell of her breasts, then outlined their shape with the point. She didn't dare breathe, afraid that he'd plunge the tip into the soft sateen of her riding habit.

His lips moved against her cheek and she shuddered at his kiss, her stomach clenching in fear and disgust.

"I really can't decide if the money's worth giving her up, Matilda. I've waited so long, thought about it, planned what I'd do once I captured her again."

She felt him clench her tighter and his lips, wet and thick, moved across her skin once again. She whimpered softly, like a creature in pain, and she could feel him grow hard at the sound, aroused by her fear. It terrified her even more to know he derived so much pleasure from her panic and she closed her eyes, repeating the phrase her father had taught her: *Stop and think.*

Opening her eyes, she tried to relax and made her voice as calm as possible.

"If I'm going to be ravished this evening, I'd like to eat first. I'm starving."

The nonchalance of her own voice surprised her. But she could feel Hank falter, puzzled by her response. That was what she needed to do, keep him off-balance, be unpredictable. McCloud always said he could never guess what she would do next. She felt her resolve strengthen at the thought of Jefferson McCloud.

Of course he'd come for her. The man was crazy about her and she hoped the moment he discovered that she and Maddie had gone off riding, he'd slap his hat against his leg, get that wild-eyed look in his eyes and take off after them. She was counting on Jefferson to get rip-roaring mad and come in search of her. It might be her and Aunt Tilly's only hope.

Chapter Eighteen

Jefferson McCloud was nearly halfway to the Broken B Ranch when he realized he was behaving like a damned fool. Stopping his horse in the middle of the trail, he stared up at the mountains leaning against the horizon. He spent several minutes calling himself every foul name he could think of. He was the worst kind of lying, lowlife, polecat because he'd hurt the woman who loved him.

More importantly, he'd hurt the woman he loved. He hung his head in shame and swore again. What in God's name had made him say those awful things to Sinclair? She'd only wanted to make him happy, yet he'd rewarded her with anger and accusations. She'd reached out to him, and while he knew he sure as hell didn't deserve what she was offering, that was no reason to refuse her. Maybe if he lived long enough, tried hard enough and loved her enough, he could deserve her someday.

Yanking hard on the reins, he turned Old Pete around. He wouldn't be doing any horse trading that day. No siree, he was heading on back to the ranch in hopes that Sinclair Readford hadn't packed her bags and returned to Philadelphia that morning. And if she had, he'd follow her to Ghost Horse Gulch, follow her onto the train, follow her to Philadelphia if he had to. He never intended to let her go again.

He grinned and gave a small kick of his spurs to move Old Pete a little faster. Now that he'd decided to be happy, he could hardly wait to tell Sinclair. The moment he got back to the ranch, he was going to fall down on his knees, grab one of her small white hands and hold it against his heart. Then he'd ask her to be his wife, but not in some pretend, playacting-to-fool-folks way. He'd ask to be his wife for real. He'd plead with her if he had to. And he'd tell her he loved her, because he now realized those were the words that would finally set him free.

He cursed himself again for being a fool. It seemed he had a harder time figuring things out than Maddie did. All this time, he'd thought love was something he had to earn. The night before, when Sinclair stood in the moonlight, her eyes filled with promises and her body eager for him, he'd walked away.

He couldn't think of enough bad words to call himself. He'd been afraid of happiness, like some kid facing down his first angry bull. He'd run away from hope, just like he always tried to run away from the things that scared or confused him.

He shook himself. There wouldn't be any more running away. Sinclair loved him. She wasn't the kind of woman who'd offer herself to a man unless she did. She didn't ask for empty promises, and he didn't intend to make any. He'd give her his heart, his name, and the promise that'd he spend every single day of his life thanking God she'd fallen out of that parlor house window and onto him.

The more he thought about a life with Sinclair, the happier he became. The miles to the ranch seemed to fly by magically. When he finally rode into the yard, he could barely keep from leaping off the saddle and running up to the ranch house to find Sinclair and tell her the happy news.

He paused as he spied Ollie sitting on a wooden box near the barn door, slowly rolling a cigarette and looking downright disgusted. Jefferson knew Ollie well enough to see something was wrong and his heart plunged. She'd left, just as he'd feared she would.

Jefferson didn't waste any words. "What's wrong?"

Ollie rose slowly, spat and gave the younger man a look that said, *you ain't gonna like it.*

"More'n I can hardly say."

Jefferson lowered himself to the ground, his heart pounding. Sinclair had left, there was no doubt about it. She'd packed up, and as soon as Ollie finished telling him so, he planned to jump on Ole Pete and race after her as fast as he could. "Spit it out, old man, I don't have all day."

"Miss Sinclair, she took it in her head to take the girl out fer a ride today." Ollie gave him a long, measured look, then continued. "Old Red rigged up two horses before noon, and they ain't back yet." He glanced up at the sky. "It don't look too good fer bein' out tonight."

Jefferson took off his Stetson and ran his fingers through his hair. He couldn't believe Sinclair would take Maddie out on the trails, she knew the danger. There were mountain lions, snakes, even bears out there, and it wasn't like Sinclair to put Maddie in danger.

"That all?" Jefferson asked.

"Not by a long shot," Ollie replied.

Ollie fingered his smoke, but he didn't light it up. He gave Jefferson another dark look. "The judge rode in 'bout an hour ago. He's up to the house makin' Lettie's life miserable."

Jefferson stiffened. Why in hell was his father there? He hadn't been back to the ranch since Bess's funeral. He'd made it clear then he hated everything about the Cripple Creek, and if Jefferson intended to waste his life on ranching, he'd do so without his father's blessing. There had been missives sent from Helena, but no indication that his children were anything more than a bother. The judge was too busy with politics and making the right connections to worry about his family.

Jefferson straightened his shoulders and nodded toward Ollie. "Get me a fresh mount. When I finish with the judge, I want to be ready to go. Get my slicker out of my saddlebag and have Lettie gather up some grub. If that storm blows in, we might have to sit it out in a line cabin, so tell her to pack plenty."

Ollie put a gnarled, age-spotted hand on Jefferson's shoulder. "You all right?"

Jefferson put his hat back on his head and patted his old friend's hand as he gave him a grin. "More right than I've ever been, once I find Sinclair."

Ollie grinned. " 'Bout time you got some sense inta ya. That little lady is the best thing ever happened to ya. Thought mebbe I was gonna have to steal her away from ya to prove it."

Jefferson laughed. "Keep dreaming old man, because it's me she loves. I nearly kissed my chance for happiness good-bye, but I woke up in the nick of time. Now, I just need to deal with the judge and find her. That woman has a knack for trouble, and how she could get lost so close to home, well, it sure takes some kind of talent, doesn't it?"

Ollie winked at him. "Bet she's got more'n one kind of talent, so you'd better make fast work of the judge. Seemed to me he was spittin' mad, but you know him. Wouldn't know a good time if it kicked him in the ass."

Jefferson nodded in agreement as he turned toward the house. "More'n likely he's cooked up some scheme and needs money. He's been trying to milk me for a loan and to tell you the truth, I'm inclined to give in just to get rid of him."

His long strides slowed as he approached the house. He didn't look forward to seeing his father, that was for sure. The last time they'd been together, cruel words had been exchanged. His father had told him he was destined to be a failure, and he was disgusted with a man who'd waste his life on a cattle ranch when he could have a brilliant career in politics. Jefferson just couldn't convince the judge that he didn't want to be a mover and a shaker. Power wasn't important to him, the land was.

He opened the front door and could hear Judge Hamilton McCloud yelling down the stairs. "I asked for hot water, woman, and I meant today."

Lettie was coming out of the kitchen with a tin bucket, and he could hear her muttering under her breath. "Keep yer pants on, ya old fart, before I boil ya myself."

"How about if I take it up to him?" Jefferson said.

Lettie jumped at the sound of his voice. She set the bucket down on the parquet floor and started to wring her hands, all thoughts of the judge apparently forgotten immediately.

"They been gone all day, Boss. I'm right worried 'bout 'em, 'cause Old Red told me they was just goin' down to the creek. I sent him down there, but he said there weren't no sign of 'em. It ain't like Miss Sinclair, she dotes on that girl. She wouldn't do nothin' to put her in danger." Her words came out in a rush.

Jefferson leaned over to pick up the pail and gave Lettie a smile of encouragement. "Don't worry. Ollie's packing my horse right now. I'll haul this up to the judge, see what he wants, then go after them. Like as not, Sinclair just got lost." He gave Lettie a boyish grin. "You know she has no sense of direction whatsoever."

Lettie shook her head. "I don't like it, Boss. I got me one of my feelin's, and don't like it one bit."

Jefferson glanced up the stairs. "I won't be long. And don't worry." He turned to smile again at Lettie. "Finding Sinclair is the most important thing to me right now, and I won't let anything stop me."

Taking the stairs two at a time, he glanced down at Lettie one more time. "I'll find them, Lettie. No matter how long it takes, I'll find them."

Hamilton McCloud was a tall man, with thick, steel gray hair flowing over his collar and nearly to his shoulders. He was renowned for his cold, silver eyes. Eyes that could hold a man, capture him like a bug squirming on the end of a pin. He'd hung his share of criminals and sent many others to prison. He had a reputation as a hard man. He believed evil would flourish if society didn't maintain and enforce strict laws.

Standing in the doorway of the master bedroom, he watched Jefferson cross the hallway. There was a flicker of something deep in his eyes, then the cold-ness returned.

"I hope you know how far I've traveled to speak to you in person." His voice was devoid of emotion, as if he were talking to a business acquaintance.

Jefferson set the pail down and extended his hand. "Hello . . . Hamilton." He couldn't bring himself to call the man "Pa" but he'd be damned if he'd call him Judge to his face.

Hamilton McCloud looked surprised, but he moved aside and watched Jefferson carry the pail of water into the room. Jefferson faltered for a moment, remembering the last time he'd been in this room, and the terrible words he'd uttered there. Then he found his resolve. The sooner he could get this over with, the sooner he could be with Sinclair again.

"Why were there so damn many candles in this room? You having seances in here, trying to contact the dead or something?" The judge gave him an accusing look.

Jefferson took off his hat and turned to face his father.

"You didn't come all this way to ask me about candles. I need to get back out on the range tonight, so why don't you tell me what brings you to the Cripple Creek."

The older man dumped some of the water into a white porcelain bowl and rubbed a bar of soft, store-bought soap between his hands. He cleared his throat.

"I've heard about your shenanigans with that whore, Jefferson. I know you're a grown man and I can't tell you what to do." He scrubbed at his face, then reached for a linen towel to dry himself off.

Jefferson paced across the room to the window, glancing down at the rose garden. He was surprised to see a rainbow of color beginning to bud beneath him. He'd forgotten how beautiful the flowers were when they bloomed. He remembered the roses, the sweet scent perfuming the house throughout the summer. A warm, loving memory of Bess flowed through him, without bitterness or pain to dilute it.

With patience he didn't know he possessed, he turned back to face his father. "She's not a whore, sir. Her name is Sinclair Readford, and she comes from a very old, very respectable family. Her father is a professor at the University of William Penn in Philadelphia."

Hamilton McCloud crossed the room, pointing a finger toward Jefferson's nose. "I suppose she told you all those lies? Pillow talk, son, is not to be be-

Deborah Schneider

lieved. You're one of the most respected men in Montana territory, and made powerful by your connection to me. A woman like that could create an elaborate scheme to fool you. Women are not to be trusted and this one sounds like a conniving whore."

Jefferson frowned and tried to ignore the slur against the woman he loved. Why was the judge so concerned about his relationship with Sinclair? He'd never cared about such things, certainly never enough to come riding down from Helena to confront him about it. There was something else here.

Jefferson tried to look indifferent. "That doesn't really explain your trip down here, does it? Why all the sudden interest in the woman I'm keeping company with?"

Hamilton looked stunned for a moment. "Why, you're my only son. I need to look out for you, for your future." He paused to drop the towel next to the basin. "And the gossip about this, what do they call her . . . hula whore . . . or something? It could destroy your chances of finding a decent wife."

Jefferson shook his head sadly. "You're wasting your time arguing with me because I intend to make Sinclair Readford my wife. She's the most decent, honest woman I've ever known. If you came all this way to warn me to stay away from her, you've come here for nothing."

He started to cross the room, but his father blocked his way. Hamilton McCloud's face was red now, and his finger jabbed at Jefferson's chest.

"I've been working hard these past few months to convince Howard VanHorn that you'd be the best match for his daughter. It's all arranged, and in case

282

you've forgotten, Lydia VanHorn is the only heir to the Hornblower Silver Mines. By marrying her, you'll become one of the richest men in the state. Marry Lydia, then if you must keep this little whore, get her a house in town. Women like that are willing to be kept, it's a dream come true for most of them."

Jefferson shoved his father out of the way. "I'll marry the woman I love, not some heiress so you can build your political career. If Lydia VanHorn is so special, why don't you marry her yourself? Why do you need me to do your dirty work? You've never been afraid to use women, this is more your style than mine."

Hamiton grabbed his son's arm, his face livid. "She wants you. It seems you made a big impression on the little lady a few years ago when you came up to Helena. She's carrying a torch for you and has made it clear to her daddy that being Mrs. Jefferson McCloud is the most important thing in the world to her."

Jefferson tried to shrug off his father's grasp. "I don't even remember meeting her, so how could she know me?"

Hamilton stepped back, took a deep breath and pulled up his suspenders. "We can be rational about this, Jefferson. Who knows where women get their inclinations? She thinks you're some kind of dime-novel cowboy hero. You've got good looks and charm and the lady is smitten. She is a pasty-faced, skinny little thing, but with the millions that come with her, who cares? Think, boy. You can have it all, and all you have to do is say yes." He put his hands on Jefferson's shoulders.

Jefferson stared into his father's eyes, and he felt a sudden wave of sadness wash over him. Here was a man who didn't even care about his own children. He didn't care if Jefferson loved this Lydia, just that it would be a marriage to cement power, wealth and position. All his life Jefferson had tried to please his father, and yet doing the one thing that could insure his love and respect would condemn him to a loveless marriage.

He suddenly felt sorry for this old man who didn't value the love of his family. It was family that made all the sacrifices and pain worthwhile, wasn't that what Sinclair had tried to tell him? That without love they were lost, that love was the thing that saved them. It was true, and he could only hope he wasn't discovering it too late. He needed to finish this conversation with his father and find Sinclair.

"I love Sinclair, and I'm going to marry her. I don't expect you to give us your blessing, but I don't expect you to treat her with contempt either. I've found happiness, sir, and I'm not going to let it go. Sinclair Readford is the best damn thing that's ever happened to me and she loves Maddie."

Hamilton frowned and glanced toward the doorway.

Jefferson followed his gaze and narrowed his eyes. "I'll bet you haven't even asked about the girl, have you? It's so easy for you to forget about us when you're so busy thinking about yourself, isn't it? She's better, much better. And Sinclair's the reason. She cares for Maddie as if the girl were her own flesh and blood." Jefferson gave his father a sorrowful look.

"Funny how I never noticed before the way love

can heal folks. Sinclair taught me that, and I'll be damned if I let anyone take her away from me."

Jefferson pushed his way around his father, then paused in the doorway. "As for the ghosts of the dead? I'll be putting them to rest, too, not bothering 'em anymore. Life is for the living."

Jefferson walked out the door without even a glance back at his father, who yelled after him.

"You're a damned fool, Jefferson. You've been given the chance of a lifetime and you're willing to throw it all away for some lying, cheap little whore." His father's voice shook with emotion now. "You were a stupid, headstrong boy and you've grown into a foolish man. If you marry that whore, I'll never have anything to do with you again."

Jefferson stopped at the top of the stairs, pausing to consider the threat, his heart wrenching at the ultimatum, then he nodded in agreement. "That seems like a fair enough bargain. And leave Maddie here, too, since it's not convenient for you to remember she exists most of the time."

He heard the judge move into the hallway behind him. "Oh no. She's my daughter and I've decided to send her to a special school for the impaired in Ohio. Your little sister is still my responsibility, so legally I can make arrangements for her. I don't care if your whore has her reciting Shakespeare, she's being sent away to be with her own kind."

Jefferson felt his hands form into fists and it took every ounce of self-control to keep from turning around and punching his father.

"Maddie stays here, with us. She needs to be with

family, not with a bunch of strangers." Jefferson's voice was filled with rage.

"Perhaps we should discuss this in more detail, when you're not running away. That's what you do, isn't it, Jefferson? You never could face down your problems, you'd just climb on a horse, run off and wait for someone else to fix things."

Jefferson whirled back to challenge his father and found himself grasping the man's shirt in his fist, anger making him bold.

"That's how I escaped from you, and your beatings. But I'm not running away from anything today, I'm running to it. I'm chasing happiness. Don't believe for one minute I'd let you take Maddie or keep me from Sinclair. I'll kill you before that happens." With a cold, thin smile, Jefferson released his father.

"And the one thing you know about me is that I've never been a liar." With a quick turn, he strode down the stairs and out the front door. He ignored the curses trailing behind him.

There was a commotion down by the barn and Jefferson hoped Sinclair and Maddie had finally returned. After the confrontation with his father, he needed to hold them, to smell the wonderful floral scent that clung to Sinclair. He craved the feeling of Maddie's small, thin arms around his neck. He wanted his family. And the thought struck him like a lightning bolt.

Ollie was kneeling down, but Jefferson couldn't see who he was talking to until he came up behind him. He was shocked to see a sobbing, hysterical Maddie, covered with dirt and burrs. Pushing Ollie aside, he took the girl into his arms.

"It's gonna be all right, sugar. You're home."

He could feel Maddie's tears soaking through his cotton shirt and he reached for his bandanna. He recalled the many times he'd had to do the same thing for Sinclair. The memory made his heart plummet.

Where was she? Sinclair wouldn't let anything happen to Maddie. He needed to get on his horse as soon as possible, because he knew she must be lying someplace along the trail, injured. There was no other explanation for her abandoning his sister. Sinclair must be either hurt, or dead. His heart nearly stopped at the latter possibility.

Wiping the grime and tears from Maddie's face, he tried to soothe her. "Just settle down, sweetie. Let's get you up to the house. I'll bet you're starving."

He could feel the child trembling in his arms, and she shook her head vigorously. Her eyes pleaded with him. He set her back down on the ground, confused by her behavior.

Maddie pointed toward the creek and Jefferson nodded his head. "We know, Maddie. Sinclair took you for a ride, and I guess maybe the two of you got lost. I'm gonna go out and find her right now, so you never mind. Just go on up to the house with Lettie." He tried to push her toward the house, but she planted her small feet firmly on the ground, folded her arms and stared up at him.

Kneeling, he put a hand on her thin shoulder. He could see the concern in her eyes, and something else, something like terror.

She needed to tell him something, but she seemed to be searching for a way to do it. Finally, leaning forward, she gave him a wide-eyed, beseeching look.

"Bad . . . men . . ." she paused to take a deep breath, "tooked Claire." Her voice was a raspy whisper.

Jefferson nearly fell over in shock.

"What . . . the hell?" He turned to look behind him. Everyone had stopped, frozen in place by the words Maddie had uttered.

He caught Ollie's expression of disbelief. "I do believe hell mighta just froze over," the old man muttered.

Jefferson turned back to Maddie. His heart was thumping, but he didn't want to scare her. He made his voice as quiet and gentle as he could manage. One finger touched Maddie's face with love.

"Sugarpie, what did you just say?"

Maddie glanced toward the others, who were watching her as if she'd just sprouted wings. There was a low nickering from the horses, but everyone remained silent, waiting for the miracle to repeat itself.

Small, silver-gray eyes captured his gaze, and Maddie blinked once. "Bad men . . . tooked Claire and . . . me. She made a . . . surprise. I runned away." Her voice was stronger now.

Pandemonium broke loose in the barnyard. Ollie slapped Jefferson on the back so hard, he nearly toppled him over. Several people started talking at once and Lettie burst into tears.

Jefferson held up his hands, signaling the group to quiet down. He pulled Maddie toward him to give her a small kiss on her smooth, soft cheek.

"I'm so happy to hear your voice, sugarpie. I never

thought I'd hear you talk again." He hugged her roughly, but she pushed him away.

Her small face wore a serious expression. "Go get my Claire back, Jeffie. I made a trail, like Hansel and Gretel."

Jefferson was confused. "Hansel and Gretel? Who are they? Did they take Sinclair?"

Maddie stomped her foot in exasperation. "Bad men tooked Claire. I made a trail . . . you go get her back." As she took Jefferson's face in one fragile hand, he could see a tear roll down her cheek.

"I want Claire. Follow the trail, like the gingerbread house story." Maddie's explanation ended in a sob.

Jefferson shook his head as he patted her gently on the back. "I'm sorry, I don't understand, Maddie."

Lettie pushed her way forward to Jefferson. "I know what she's talkin' about, Boss. It's her favorite story. I heard Miss Sinclair read it to her lots of times. It's about children who get lost in the woods and they try to find their way home by leavin' bread crumbs in the path. Maddie must have marked the trail for you."

Jefferson felt a tremor of respect race through him. Not only did Madison know how to talk, but she was intelligent. God, how much had she missed? How was he ever going to make it up to her?

He stood to brush the dust from his dark wool pants, then pulled Maddie into his arms. He'd start making it up to her by granting her request.

"Don't worry, Maddie. I'll get Sinclair back. And we are never, ever gonna let go of her again!"

Chapter Nineteen

Sinclair sat staring at her aunt Tilly and for nearly the first time in her life, she was speechless. There were so many questions she wanted to ask, but she was afraid she'd offend her aunt. She tried to smooth the wrinkles out of her riding habit, shifted a little, then glanced about the room as if inspecting their quarters.

There was little to reassure her in the small box of a room. She noted the window was blocked by boards nailed across its width, preventing them from using that route as an escape. There was the small bed, a rough table formed from sticks nailed together, and a shelf that hung at an awkward angle from the wall. The only other furnishing was a large oak trunk that stood near the foot of the bed, the domed lid was open and Sinclair could see women's clothing peeking out.

She watched her aunt pace uneasily across the room, then she paused as if to consider her words carefully.

"I don't want to seem impolite, my dear, but exactly how did you manage to end up in Ghost Horse Gulch?"

Sinclair blushed at her aunt's honesty, then cleared her throat and shifted again on the bed.

"I found your letters and I was curious. Father never mentioned that I had an aunt living out West. He told me all of our relatives were dead or too distant to care about us." She blinked back tears.

"I never wanted to make trouble for you, Aunt Tilly. I just wanted to meet you. All the things you wrote about . . . Montana territory just sounded so exciting and wonderful." She paused to tilt her head back and close her eyes.

"I just wanted a little adventure." Her voice grew heavy with longing. "For once, I wanted to be the one keeping a journal of all my travels and exciting experiences."

Her aunt sat down next to her and gathered her into a strong, comforting embrace.

"It couldn't have been easy living with William," she said.

Sinclair leaned into her aunt's arms, the familiar scent of roses soothing her. It reminded her of her mother.

"Father just has so many . . . responsibilities," she murmured, enjoying the pleasure of talking with another woman. "He never really knew what to do with me. I always seemed a bother, just in the way of his

291

serious studies and adventures traveling all over the world."

Aunt Tilly made an odd noise. "I'm not sure he ever knew exactly what to do with his wife, either." Her voice carried a note of bitterness that surprised Sinclair.

"I always thought my mother was happy. At least she never complained." Sinclair looked at her aunt in confusion.

Aunt Tilly shook her head sadly. "Althea didn't complain. She was one of the strongest people I've ever known." Her eyes roamed across Sinclair's face. "And you're as strong and beautiful as she was."

Sinclair smiled and she wanted to put her head on Aunt Tilly's shoulder. She wanted to tell her everything about her new life in Montana. She wanted to talk about the Cripple Creek Ranch and Maddie. Most of all, she wanted to tell her only living female relative about discovering that she loved a man. A good, honest, exasperating, funny, charming, arrogant man.

But she suddenly felt as if her bones were melting. Exhaustion washed over her and she gave a deep sigh.

"We need to make a plan, Aunt Tilly. We can't stay here, you heard what Hank said when he left. Before noon tomorrow you're going to be a married woman."

Aunt Tilly rose to pace across the floor again. When she turned back to face Sinclair her mouth was twisted into an acerbic smile. "It's not the wedding I'm afraid of, honey. I've got an inkling I'm not going to survive the honeymoon."

Sinclair nodded in understanding. "If my assessment is correct, Hank plans to marry you to obtain control of your money."

Matilda Haynes nodded. "He found out that I was a woman of . . . means." She raised an eyebrow at Sinclair. "I'm sure you know what I'm talking about." Her thin smile returned briefly. "But when he couldn't charm his way into my affections, he decided to bring me out here and try to threaten me into cooperating with him."

Tilly gave a shake of one shoulder. "Up till today, that wasn't working either. But, honey, I can't take a chance that he'd hurt you." Her face went blank and her eyes flickered with fear. "I know that man. He can be ruthless. Let's be honest, it's one of the qualities that made me hire him in the first place."

Sinclair shuddered when she remembered the cold, calculating way he'd threatened her with the knife. Hank Borscht enjoyed hurting people, that much she knew. But she also sensed if her aunt married him, he'd arrange to become a widower as soon as possible.

Sinclair carefully pulled the pin from her large, velvet hat, then paused as she noticed how long and sharp it was. She immediately tucked it into the folds of her riding habit. Aunt Tilly watched her with interest.

Sinclair patted the skirt carefully and shrugged. "It might make a good weapon."

Tilly threw back her head and laughed, her eyes sparkling with pleasure.

"I can tell you're smart, just like your mother. And fearless, just like me."

Sinclair squirmed at the praise, but her lips formed a smile. "I never used to think things out very carefully, Aunt Tilly, but I'm learning that a little advance planning can make life a lot easier."

Her aunt sat down on the bed and started to remove her boots. She rubbed each foot and winced. "Remind me to buy bigger boots and to hell with fashion. Now, let's see what a couple of Haynes girls can cook up when they put their heads together, shall we?"

Sinclair leaned toward her aunt and rested her upper body against the woman's shoulder. "I never thought of myself as anything but a Readford. Father seems to believe there isn't any other family with nearly such an esteemed bloodline."

Matilda laughed again and the warm, boisterous sound made Sinclair hopeful. "Let me tell you, the Readford clan can't hold a candle to the Haynes family. The Readfords might have had the smarts, but honey, we've got the guts. That's for sure!"

Sinclair felt her spirits lift. "Do you think we can outsmart those men out there?"

Matilda glanced at the door and seemed to ponder the question carefully. "Well, it's only Corky out there. Hank took Old Hoss with him, in case the preacher needed some coaxing to come way out here."

They sat in silence, both thinking, until Tilly leaned over to whisper in Sinclair's ear. "If we can't poleax that fool, we deserve whatever happens to us, that man's stupider than a mule."

Sinclair giggled. "If I had to get kidnapped, threatened, and held hostage, Aunt Tilly, I'm sure glad it's with you."

Her aunt nodded wisely. "Me, too, honey. The Haynes women have to stick together." She patted Sinclair's arm gently. "We'll manage to get ourselves out of this, you can count on it."

Sinclair felt her fear evaporate like early-morning mist rising off a pasture in the spring sunshine. They might be women, but they weren't going to just sit there and wait for Hank to return. By damned, they were going to fight back.

Leaning toward her aunt conspiratorially, she kept her voice at a whisper. "Here's what I think we should do . . ."

It was close to dawn when Sinclair rolled off her side of the bed and stretched her sore muscles. Although she'd grown more practiced at riding, she still hadn't been prepared for spending hours in the saddle to travel to this isolated cabin. She put her hand in the small of her back and leaned forward, moaning as she felt the aching protest of her body.

The rain had stopped and she could see the early pink rays of dawn dusting the sky above the trees as she tried to peek out the window. The small piece of yard she could see through the dusty glass was deserted, but it did little to reassure her. She knew Hank would be returning soon.

Her aunt groaned softly. "Good Lord but I hate the morning. No civilized person should ever climb out of bed before noon." She sat up and shifted the blankets to cover her ample bosom.

"I'd give a hundred-dollar gold piece for a mug of

hot chocolate and one of the scones Lizzy makes."

Sinclair sniffed the air and shook her head sadly. "I believe the only thing we have to look forward to is coffee, but I'm so chilled, even if it resembles tar I'll be grateful for a cup."

Tilly grinned back at her. "I guess I'd better get up. I'll be so glad to be rid of this place, it's worth motivating my bones at this god-awful hour."

Throwing off the thin, faded quilt, Tilly put her bare feet on the floor. Her yelp of surprise made Sinclair rush to her side.

"Aunt Tilly, is something wrong?"

Her aunt looked disgusted. "Damn right there's something wrong. I have a perfectly fine bedroom back in town, with nice, thick carpets so my toes don't get cold when I climb out of bed. I hate this place, I hate that Hank has involved you in this mess and I'll be damned if I don't make him pay for what he's done to us."

She grabbed a boot by the laces and flung it against the wall. The other boot followed only moments later.

Sinclair tried to calm her down. "It won't be long now and we can escape. You need to be quiet, though. Corky might be stupid, but he's not deaf. We have to pretend to be meek, frightened women."

Matilda made a disparaging noise. "I can playact a lot of things, honey, but I don't think I can be meek."

Sinclair found her own boots and carefully laced them as she shushed her aunt again. "Just act natural."

They finished dressing and Matilda loaned Sinclair

a comb to remove the tangles from her hair. When they felt they were presentable, they carefully opened the door to their room to peek out.

The main room of the cabin was still dark, but there was a thin stream of light pouring in through the one small window. Sinclair could see Corky sitting at the table, facing their door.

Straightening her shoulders with pride, she glided into the room and paused to give Corky a brilliant smile.

"Good morning, Mr. Corky," she whispered in a husky voice.

He nodded at her, his eyes darting to look behind her. "Mornin', ma'am." He nodded again as he caught sight of Matilda. "You, too, ma'am."

"Well, you can ma'am us all you want, but what about breakfast?" Tilly glanced toward the stove. "Are there any eggs?"

Corky almost stumbled backward in his hurry to stand. "Yes'm, I got some bacon too. It's right there in that box."

He pointed to a wooden box that held provisions. Matilda moved briskly to inspect the contents, clucked her tongue and gave Sinclair a disgusted look.

"It might be edible, but it won't be tasty. Especially since I'm the cook, and even I have to admit, I'm lousy at it." She pulled a few items from the box, then turned to the stove to clank some pans together.

Sinclair tried to keep a straight face. She had offered to cook, but her aunt had insisted that Sinclair'd do a better job at distracting Corky, because she was younger and prettier. Her aunt had a mature, self-confident beauty that Sinclair envied, but rather than argue, Sinclair had agreed to flirt with Corky while Aunt Tilly put their plan into action.

"This cabin has a certain, rustic charm, don't you think, Aunt Tilly?" She gazed around the room with what she hoped was a rapt expression. "Just like the hunting lodges in Germany. Small, but cozy."

She could hear the bacon beginning to sizzle in the frying pan, and she moved closer to the stove. "I believe I'm going to have a cup of coffee. Mr. Corky, would you like some more?" She grabbed a small towel and wrapped it around the handle of the graniteware coffeepot. Her other hand scooped a large ironstone mug off a shelf as she strode purposefully toward the table.

Corky was sitting down now and he looked pleased to have Sinclair waiting on him. He leaned back in his chair to watch her, a contented expression on his face.

"Thank yuh, ma'am. I ain't used to havin' my meals with such pretty women, and havin' one to take care o'me is a pure pleasure."

Sinclair paused to glance at her aunt. She wasn't ready yet.

"Well, just because we've fallen into unfortunate circumstances doesn't mean we can't be civil. I believe common courtesy is one of the hallmarks of civilization." She looked toward her aunt again. This time she caught the signal and nodded.

"Let me give you a refill, Mr. Corky." She started to slowly pour the hot liquid into his cup. Her aunt carried the large cast-iron frying pan toward the table and indicated the pile of dishes sitting in the middle.

"Get one of them plates for the bacon, will you, Corky?"

Eager to please, he leaned forward to take the top plate off the stack and with great deliberation, Sinclair poured the hot, steaming coffee onto his hands.

Corky gave a loud roar of pain and stood. He didn't notice Matilda as she threw back her arm, then brought it forward with all her strength. The big black cast-iron frying pan whacked him on the side of the head, and he wore an expression of total disbelief as he crumbled to his knees, then fell to the floor with a loud thump.

The two women stood staring at each other in shock. Sinclair could smell something burning, but she couldn't take her eyes off the man lying at their feet.

"Aunt Tilly," she whispered, fear evident in her voice, "I'm afraid we've killed him."

Tilly bent over, quickly pulled his gun from his holster, and handed it to Sinclair. "I doubt we could commit murder with a frying pan. He's just out cold. Look at that, I can still see him breathing." She sniffed and glanced toward the stove.

"Sweet Jesus in the morning, the stove's on fire."

Sinclair dropped the coffeepot as she caught sight of the flames crawling across the surface of the stove. She took a step back as she saw the fire beginning to spread to the walls and the floor.

"Aunt Tilly, what did you do with the bacon?"

"I dumped it onto the stove. You don't think I'd

want to take the chance of burning myself when I smacked Corky, do you?"

Sinclair took another step backwards as the flames continued to rage unchecked.

"It didn't occur to you it might start a fire?" She was trying to keep the irritation from her voice as she spoke to her aunt.

Aunt Tilly slapped the frying pan down onto the table in disgust. "I told you I wasn't much of a cook. Now, let's get out of here before the place burns down around our heads." She headed toward the door. Sinclair started to follow, then paused to look behind her.

The fire was spreading quickly and she could see the flames inching toward Corky. She glanced at her aunt, considered her options, then called out.

"Aunt Tilly, help me carry Corky out. We can't leave him here." She might be a lot of things, but she wasn't a murderer, and she didn't think her aunt was one either.

Her aunt stopped in the doorway and coughed. The room was beginning to fill with thick, black smoke, and Sinclair found it increasingly difficult to breathe.

"Hurry up," she urged impatiently, "we don't have much time."

Matilda Haynes seemed to consider her options, then scurried back to grab hold of Corky's legs. She yanked on them, swore, and yanked again.

Sinclair lifted him beneath his shoulders and helped her aunt drag the unconscious man across the room. They could hear the crackling of the flames as the fire grew, and the heat was terrifying in its intensity. Dark clouds of smoke nearly blinded them.

They dragged Corky through the door, rolled him down the steps and paused to pull great, deep gulps of fresh air into their lungs. The fire was a conflagration now, as cinders filled the air, smoke poured out of the door, windows and chimney, and the flames rose toward the canopy of trees above them.

They rolled Corky far enough from the cabin to deem him safe. He groaned deeply and Sinclair was reassured he was still alive. But they didn't want to hang around long enough for him to regain consciousness.

Sinclair had a suspicion he'd be less than sympathetic with them, even though they had rescued him from the fire. Especially since they were in the process of burning the cabin down. She didn't know if it belonged to him, or to Hank, or if they were just squatters. She only knew they were responsible for starting the fire, and he wouldn't be very happy with them.

Grabbing her hand, Aunt Tilly pulled Sinclair toward the dark shadow of the woods. "Come on, before he wakes up and figures out what we've been up to."

They pushed through the underbrush, blackberry vines, burrs and branches tearing at their clothes. They stumbled into a clearing, where Matilda stopped so quickly, Sinclair bumped into her. They leaned forward, bending at the knees as they tried to catch their breath.

Matilda frowned. "Where's that six-shooter I took off Corky?"

Sinclair blanched at her aunt's question. She licked her dry, blistered lips.

"I had to set it down on the floor so I could help carry him out." She realized that her impulsive action to save their captor would likely end up costing them their lives. They were out in this wilderness with no horses, no provisions and no weapons to defend themselves. And most importantly, they had no idea how to get back to town or to the Cripple Creek Ranch.

Sinclair wanted to cry, but she knew it wouldn't do any good. Still, she promised herself, that if she did survive, she'd indulge in one of those wonderful, cleansing, soul-shaking crying jags.

Her aunt patted her on the shoulder gently. "Well, don't worry about it. We did the right thing. I don't believe I could live with a man's death on my conscience. Unless of course it was Hank. If it had been him in there, I'd have let him burn." She glanced toward the thick smoke pouring up toward the bright morning sky. "We need to put some distance between that cabin and us. Somebody's bound to see that smoke and get curious."

Sinclair nodded in agreement. As they continued on through the woods her only hope was that Jefferson might be the one to came in search of her. She recalled his face, the smooth handsome profile, the way his eyes crinkled when he smiled down at her, and the deep, beautiful dimples that framed that smile. The image calmed her. "Jefferson," she wanted to scream out into the forest, "come and find me. I'm frightened, and I need you."

As she stumbled through the woods, terrified, her

mind kept repeating her plea. "I need you, Jefferson. I love you, I want you and I need you." She prayed that the pleading of her heart would somehow reach him.

Chapter Twenty

Jefferson and Ollie rode the miles in silence. There weren't any words capable of relieving the pain. Each man grieved in his own way. Jefferson suffering because he'd neglected to tell Sinclair he loved her and he feared he was too late. Ollie suffered for the man he loved like a son.

They'd started out just before the storm broke the night before. It had been foolish, Jefferson should have waited, but he couldn't linger at the ranch, doing nothing while Sinclair was in danger. And there was no doubt in his mind that she was in dire straits. Maddie had described the men who kidnapped her and Sinclair. Masked riders wouldn't just grab a woman for no reason. He knew this was part of a complex plan to capture Sinclair, and he had an inkling Hank Borscht was at the center of the plot.

Ollie pointed toward the north. "Looks like the

lightning mighta set off a brushfire, mebbe we should take a look." He pulled his horse up and paused to wait for Jefferson to answer him.

"Damn it all to hell! We don't have time to be scouting out wildfires. We've gotta find Sinclair, before it's too late."

His words hung heavy in the air. He and Ollie both knew what he meant by too late.

"Could be headed for the range, and that'd be trouble."

Jefferson paused to take off his hat and run his fingers through his hair in agitation.

"We could split up, you go up there and take a look, I can try to pick up their trail."

They'd found the pieces of ribbon Maddie had left to mark her path. Once again Jefferson had marveled at her cleverness. It had made it simple to find the place the masked riders had captured Maddie and Sinclair, and they'd followed the tracks up to the high country. But, after the rain washed the tracks away, Jefferson felt like he was looking for a needle in a haystack.

"It's just over the ridge there, why don't we both take a look, then we can split up." Ollie opened a worn leather pouch, pulled out a plug of tobacco and bit off a chunk. Shoving one discolored finger into his cheek to settle the chew into place, he then closed up the pouch to return it to his vest pocket.

Jefferson rose to stand in the stirrups, trying to get a clearer view of the smoke. It wasn't much use, because the trees were too thick around them to see much.

After a few moments he nodded. "It's as good a

plan as any." There was anger and frustration in his voice.

Ollie spit a thick stream of tobacco juice out of the side of his mouth and glanced toward Jefferson.

"We'll find her. If I know that little lady, she'll leave us a callin' card."

Jefferson settled back into the saddle and gave Ollie a disgruntled glance. "It had better be a hell of a signal, because we're up against it now. I have an idea Hank Borscht is involved in this, and he's a cold-hearted bastard."

Ollie spit again and nodded. "He might be sneaky-smart, but Miss Sinclair, she's smart in more'n one way. Just give her a chance. She'll let us know where she is."

Jefferson's shoulders hunched forward as his horse picked his way over the rough, rock-strewn path. He couldn't forget the way Sinclair had looked that night in the moonlight. He could still see the passion shining in her eyes and hear the heat of desire in her voice. Heat that had stirred his blood until he couldn't think straight. If anything happened to her, he didn't think this was a world he wanted to live in. Shrugging off his dismal thoughts, he tried to concentrate on the direction of the fire.

It wasn't long before they smelled smoke and heard the crackling of flames. They came up a ridge and looked down. The remains of a small cabin blazed beneath them.

Ollie gave a whoop. "By damned that's a sign if I ever see'd one. I'm bettin' Miss Sinclair had somethin' to do with this, ain't it just like Blazin' Brazen, the flame from Philly to set somethin' on fire!"

Jefferson wasn't as thrilled to see a building in flames, even if it was a signal from Sinclair to notify them of her whereabouts.

"Well, we'd best be careful, because it sure looks like trouble." Jefferson studied the scene below them.

He didn't want to admit how terrified he was that Sinclair might be inside the burning structure. He'd been involved with her long enough to see more than one of her schemes kick back and end up in disaster. He nudged his horse down the steep incline, and gave a whistle for Ollie to be quiet.

They were just at the edge of the woods, when they paused to stare at the blaze in front of them. In the open space in front of the cabin, a man sat in the dust, looking stunned and confused.

"Wait here and watch my back," Jefferson ordered. He got off his horse, drew his gun and slowly crept up behind the man. The man didn't appear to hear him and jumped in surprise when Jefferson put the cold barrel of his Smith and Wesson in the middle of his back.

"I ain't armed," the man yelled.

Jefferson glanced down at the man's gun belt and could see it was empty. He stepped back to shove his own gun into his holster.

"You own this place?" he asked.

The man shook his head, as if to clear it, and Jefferson could see a thin trickle of blood rolling down the side of his face. It looked like he might have run into a wall or doorjamb in his dash to get outside.

The dazed man gazed up at him and shook his head again.

"What? I can't hardly hear ya. My ears are ringin'."

Jefferson crouched down to look the man in the eye. "I said, is this your place?"

The man looked up, fear in his eyes. "Nope, I was just watchin' it fer a friend."

Jefferson glanced at the flames as the roof caved in. "I don't think he's gonna be too happy about the way you took care of his place, what do you think?"

The man struggled to his feet, rubbing his head and wincing. "It weren't my fault, that witch hit me with a skillet."

Jefferson tried to keep his face blank. "You must have really pissed your woman off to make her do that."

The man shook his head again, stumbled a bit, then tried to regain his balance. He stood staring at the collapsing cabin in awe.

"She weren't my woman, neither. I was watchin' her."

Jefferson spit onto the ground, trying to seem unconcerned. "Seems to me you're not the sort cut out for watching."

The man glanced up at him, then shook his head sadly. "It was a bad deal right from the start, mister. I shoulda never got mixed up in it. Stealin' cattle might be one thing, stealin' womenfolk is another."

Jefferson stepped back, pulled out his gun and aimed it at the man's heart. "I'm looking for a woman who came up missing yesterday, and you'd best spit out what you know about her. She comes up to about here." He indicated the bottom of his neck. "She's got hair the color of sunflowers."

"Eyes like the sky early in the mornin'?" Corky looked a little lovestruck.

"Yup." Jefferson frowned.

"Yacks enough to give ya a headache just from listen' to her?"

"Sounds familiar," Jefferson said as he nodded, remembering all the times he'd wished Sinclair would be quiet.

"More trouble'n the devil hisself." Corky pointed toward the ground.

Jefferson stepped closer to grab the man's collar, putting his face close enough to smell the coffee on his breath. "That'd be my woman and I'm mad as hell that somebody took her."

The man looked surprised, then shook his head. "I don't know why any man'd want that much trouble, even in a fancy package, but she was here. Musta took off with her aunt after they knocked me out." He glanced down at the fist holding his shirt, then grinned up at Jefferson.

"She must be some kinda gal, huh?"

Jefferson let go as he took a long step back. "Yup."

The man held out both hands in front of him, pleading with Jefferson. "I'm Corky Brewster, and I mean to tell ya, it weren't my idea, none of this. I owed a man some money and he said doin' this little job would set us even." He spit on the ground and put one of his hands on the cut on the side of his head. "It were a bad deal right from the start, mister."

Jefferson scanned the trees lying beyond the small clearing. He didn't signal Ollie and Corky Brewster hadn't noticed the older man sitting in the shadows at the edge of the yard.

"What happened to the women?"

Corky shook his head slowly, then winced again as if in pain. "We was gettin' ready to eat breakfast, one minute she—yer woman, the youngun—was pourin' coffee. Next thin' I knew, she scalded me, then the other one whacks me up side my head with a skillet. I don't recall nothin' after that."

He seemed to consider the situation for a moment, then looked sheepish. "They coulda let me burn up, but they musta dragged me out here." He looked up at Jefferson with gratitude in his eyes. "I don't know many men that woulda done that, helped the person who was holdin' 'em prisoner. I reckon I need to thank 'em for that."

"You can do that by telling me who hired you to kidnap Sinclair." Jefferson tried to keep the heat of anger out of his voice, but rage whipped through him at the idea of her being brought out to the woods and held captive.

Corky looked frightened, glanced down at the gun, swallowed and seemed to decide to talk.

"That friggin' low down, weasel . . . Hank Borscht. I owed him money from a poker game." Corky spit and looked disgusted. "But I figger he cheated in the first place. I don't hold with nothin' he done, mister. But, I ain't got no idea where them women took off to." Glancing around him, he jumped as he caught sight of Ollie, then shrugged.

"They coulda taked off in any direction. Women is hard enough to figger. Scared women coulda done anythin'."

Jefferson wanted to hit something and Corky Brewster presented a likely target. He just couldn't justify it though, even if he had been part of the plot to kidnap Sinclair, so far Corky had also been co-operative.

"Who was the other woman who escaped with Sinclair?"

Corky rubbed his temple gently. "It was Mizzus Haynes, the madam over at the Blue Willow."

It verified Jefferson's first intuition, that this whole thing involved Matilda Haynes. But the reason for the kidnapping wasn't nearly as important as finding the women. Shoving his gun back into his holster, he nodded at Corky.

"You'd best get your horse and hightail it out of here before Borscht gets back." He paused, then raised an eyebrow.

"You got any idea where he went?"

Corky had started toward the barn, but turned back and grinned. "He was fetchin' the preacher, so's he and Mizzus Haynes could get hitched. I guess that's what all this was about in the first place. Kinda funny, him wantin' to get hitched so bad he had to steal the bride. Guess he's one'a them fellers just can't take no fer an answer."

Jefferson nodded, "Mebbe."

But he knew there was more to this than the story of a lovesick suitor who couldn't stand to lose the woman he adored. Borscht was too cold-blooded to let romance get in the way of making a dollar. He had something up his sleeve and Jefferson figured it was big enough for him to take a chance on spending a long spell in the territorial prison. Folks in Montana didn't appreciate men who mistreated womenfolk.

He paused to gather his reins from Ollie. The older man held his tongue and waited.

"It was her, weren't it. She lit this place on fire."

Jefferson nodded. "It appears she did, or at least helped Matilda Haynes do it." He pointed at the man moving toward the barn. "He helped them capture Sinclair, but he wants out. I don't have time to haul him into town and hand him over to the sheriff." He rubbed his chin thoughtfully. "He doesn't have any idea where the women are and I'll be damned if I can guess."

Ollie shrugged and pointed toward the ground. "I 'spect them little footprints in the mud could lead us to 'em, what'ya think, Boss?"

Jefferson felt his spirits soar and he threw himself onto his horse with one swift, efficient movement. He slapped Ollie on the back. "Let's go, old man, I guess you're not nearly as useless as I thought you were."

Ollie gave him a disparaging look. "Useless? Why, you couldn't find a herd if they was standin' in yer chicken yard without me."

Jefferson grinned at his old friend. "Well, let's go find us some women lost in the woods, that should be enough of a challenge for today."

Ollie snorted as they headed into the late-morning shadows beneath the tall trees. "Just remember, it weren't me that lost my woman in the first place. You just might learn to take better care of Miss Sinclair."

Jefferson thought wiser words of advice might never have been uttered.

* * *

Sinclair sat on a large rock and tried to pick burrs out of her hair. She was tired, thirsty and had no idea if they had run miles away from the cabin, or if they were simply wandering in circles. She wished she'd paid more attention when her father had lectured her about navigation. She knew how to find the north star, but it was broad daylight. She knew there was some manner of knowing direction from the way moss grew on the trees, but she couldn't remember what the direction was, or if the moss was on one side and the direction on the other.

Aunt Tilly sat opposite from her, rubbing her feet and letting loose with an outrageous stream of obscenities. Sinclair didn't know if she should cover her ears or give her an ovation. It certainly surprised her to hear a woman with such an outstanding repertoire of swear words.

"I promise, I will forget these damned French boots for the rest of my life. When I get back to Ghost Horse Gulch, I'm going to get Art Rollofson to make me some decent boots and I don't care if they are a size ten!" Matilda shook the offending boot as if she wanted to punish it for being too small and hurting her feet.

Sinclair wiped the moisture from her forehead and thought if she ever made it back to Ghost Horse Gulch, she'd sit in a tub for at least a day to soak out the dirt and relieve her sore muscles.

Pulling leaves and pine needles from her hair, she realized she'd lost her pins long ago. Dusty, blond curls tumbled down around her shoulders. She knew she looked a mess, but she was so dog tired, she didn't give a horse-haired-flying damn.

She smiled to herself and wondered what all her classmates at the Shady Lawn School for Ladies of Quality would think of her now. She thought of all the useless things she'd learned there, and shook her head. What a waste of time finishing school had been.

Her aunt stood to shake the dust from her gown. "I'm really sorry, honey. If it weren't for me, you'd be back in Philadelphia with all your friends, going to fancy parties and sitting at the opera."

Sinclair stood to face her. "Thank God I've been rescued from the boredom of that life! I've done more, experienced more and learned more in the past few weeks than I could ever have learned in a lifetime of living in the city."

She stretched her arms up toward the sky. "I've learned to be strong, to take care of myself and to take care of others before I even think of my own needs." She put her hands on her hips.

"Reading your letters lit a fire in me, Aunt Tilly. The stories you told about being independent, of making your own choices, it inspired me."

She stepped forward to wrap her arms around her aunt's waist. "I don't care if we are lost in the wilds of Montana, we're together and we're tough, resilient women. Someone will rescue us and we'll end up just fine. I know McCloud's looking for us, I can feel it." She put one finely boned hand over her heart. "And he's close, I know he is."

"Closer'n you think, sugar."

The two women spun around and Sinclair gave a squeal of delight, dropped her arms from around her aunt and ran across the small clearing. Jefferson McCloud stood with his arms stretched wide and Sin-

314

clair fell into them. As he pulled her close, she breathed deeply of the pine forest, clean air and leather scent that forever marked him in her memories.

She closed her eyes and leaned into his strong, broad chest. She could hear his heart beating a rhythm as fast as her own. For the first time in days, she felt safe and she realized that wherever Jefferson McCloud was, for her, that would be home.

Without a word he lifted her chin carefully, then covered her mouth with his in a hot, delicious kiss that made her shiver right down to her toes. She wanted the kiss to last forever, and she moaned deeply as his tongue pushed past her lips, seeking refuge, plundering the softness of her mouth.

She heard her aunt's voice through the buzz of desire clouding her mind.

"Jefferson McCloud, if you hope to live to see the end of this day, I'd better have a pretty good explanation as to why you're kissing my niece like that."

Reluctantly, Jefferson released Sinclair, but only to gently push her beneath his arm and face Matilda Haynes. He removed his hat in deference to the older woman who stood before them, her eyes blazing up at him.

Jefferson nodded at her. "Begging your pardon, Miss Haynes, but there's something I promised to do the moment I found Sinclair."

Without another word of explanation, he dropped to one knee, grasped one of Sinclair's hands and placed it against his heart. His dark eyes pleaded with her and she nearly forgot to breathe in anticipation of what he'd do next.

"Sinclair Readford, I've been the biggest darned fool in Montana, but I'd sure like to fix that. I love you, and while I know I couldn't ever deserve it, I'm hoping you love me too."

Her other hand touched the stubble of day-old whiskers on his face, and she smiled down at him. "I do love you, Jefferson, and we must have been destined for each other, because I don't see any other way I could have found you."

He gently leaned toward her and her fingers traced the soft outline of his lips. His eyes were shining with love so deep, it made her breath catch. This man, this good man, had become as precious to her as her own life.

"Would you be my wife, Sinclair?"

She touched the darkness of his hair and smiled, finally remembering to breathe again. She leaned down so that she was at eye level with Jefferson.

"Yup," she replied, her words nearly cracking with the emotion of the moment. His eyes danced with laughter as she leaned forward to kiss him again. Her lips were nearly to his when a voice stopped her.

"Well, since I got the preacher, maybe we should make this a double wedding. We got two brides and two grooms, what do you say to that, McCloud?"

Sinclair's blood froze as she recognized the harsh, cold tones of Hank Borscht. She stood, glancing around until her eyes found him sitting next to two other men at the edge of the clearing. She recognized Old Hoss who had a rifle aimed at Jefferson's back.

"Or maybe I'll marry one and take the other on the honeymoon. I'd like a fresh young thing to keep me warm at night. It's a long ride to San Francisco."

316

Three horses moved from the dimly lit cover of the forest into the bright sunshine of the clearing. Sinclair realized that the darkly garbed man with his hands tied to the saddle horn must be the preacher. She could see he was terrified, as he anxiously glanced from one group to the other. There was a bandanna gagging him, so she suspected he hadn't come easily or quietly.

"Turn around slowly, McCloud, and if you even act like you're gonna go for your gun, my man will shoot you."

Sinclair could see the rage in Jefferson's eyes, and she was afraid he was going to spin around and challenge the men to a shootout. Without a thought of her own safety she rushed past him toward Hank Borscht. She heard Jefferson cry out in warning, but she ignored him.

"Just take me, if that's what you want." She planted herself at Hank's stirrup. Tossing her head back and putting her hands on her hips, she gave him a saucy smile.

"If you think my aunt has money, you should see *my* inheritance. My grandfather invested in the railroads and he made a fortune." Flipping a blond curl from her eyes, she made her smile brighter. "I'll get nearly a million dollars when I marry." She twisted her head and looked over her shoulder, then stepped closer to put a hand on Hank's leg.

"Now, which do you think I'd prefer, to dry up and grow old before my time on a ranch in Montana, or to kick up my heels in San Francisco?"

"Sinclair!" There was a note of shock in her aunt's voice. "Don't do this."

She ignored her aunt Tilly and avoided looking at Jefferson. She was afraid of the pain she'd see in his eyes. She could only hope he would trust her.

Hank stared down at her, doubt evident in his face. "Why would you suddenly be so willing to go off with me? You've certainly spent enough of your time running away."

Sinclair formed her lips into a soft pout and tilted her head sideways. "Isn't it a woman's prerogative to change her mind? Maybe I just ran until you caught me, because the chase is so fun."

He frowned, then slowly a grin lit his hard features, almost softening his countenance. Leaning forward from the saddle, he gave her a long, slow perusal, then lifted himself back to sit tall.

"It doesn't matter why you've changed your mind, just get up here." He shifted his weight. "I planned to take you with me anyway, so this just makes it easier."

Sinclair moved toward the horse's tail, then turned to give Jefferson a small wave. Everyone's attention shifted to him, to gauge his reaction. It was exactly what Sinclair had hoped for. With a small jab, and a wince because she hated to do it, she drove the hat pin she had clutched tightly in her hand into the horse's rear flank, then took a giant leap backwards.

Hank's horse jumped straight up into the air and gave an earthshaking scream. His hooves never touched the earth again at the same time, as he bucked and jumped around the clearing. Sinclair dodged behind a granite outcropping, as the preacher's horse starting dancing in circles, trying to avoid Hank's horse. One shot rang out and Sinclair's heart skipped a beat. She was terrified to look, afraid she'd see Jefferson's lifeless body sprawled in a pool of blood.

Finally she carefully peered over the top of the rock, trying to see through the dust clouding her vision. There was a man lying in the clearing, and she could see he was bleeding. Her hand flew to her mouth to stifle a scream, then she realized it was Hank Borscht holding his arm and swearing at the top of his lungs.

"Shoot, you damned Indian, and I don't care who you hit, just shoot."

She could see Old Hoss sitting on his horse, his rifle at his shoulder, but he didn't move a muscle. Sinclair watched in amazement as his arm dropped and he tossed the rifle aside. She couldn't figure out what had happened. There was no sign of Jefferson, Aunt Tilly or the preacher.

Hank continued to scream, but Old Hoss ignored him as he urged his horse out into the sunshine. Sinclair's heart lifted as she spied Ollie behind him, a shotgun aimed at the Indian's back. She gave a sigh of relief and came out of her hiding place.

"Ollie, you are a sight for sore eyes!"

The old man grinned at her and she could swear he was blushing. "Howdy, Miss Sinclair, I'm right happy to see you ag'in too!"

"Keep your paws off my woman, old man, or I'll have to shoot you myself." Jefferson stood from behind a rock and brushed himself off. "It sure took you long enough to figure out what was going on."

Ollie spit and gave Jefferson a disgusted look.

"Why, Boss, I was just waitin' fer Miss Sinclair to

give me the sign." He nodded his head sagely. "I knew she'd have a plan, her bein' so smart and all. Sure'nuff, she did."

Jefferson's long legs carried him across the clearing in a few strides and without another word he picked Sinclair up and tossed her over his shoulder. She beat on his back in protest, but he ignored her.

Her aunt Tilly emerged from behind some bushes, brushing at her dress and swearing a blue streak. She stopped when she caught sight of Jefferson carrying Sinclair across the clearing.

"McCloud, what in damnation do you think you're doing?" she asked.

Jefferson lifted Sinclair onto his horse, climbed into the saddle behind her and yanked on the reins. He touched his Stetson and nodded at Matilda Haynes.

"I'm gonna go find that preacher. I figure I need to hurry up and marry this woman before she gets into any more trouble."

Sinclair snapped her mouth shut and gazed at him in wonder. He sat, waiting for her to say something. There was only silence.

He clicked to the horse and they moved off down the trail, the buzzing of insects and twittering birds creating a symphony around them. Still, she didn't utter a word.

After a few minutes, Jefferson began to chuckle, then he started to roar with laughter. She grinned back at him, but still remained quiet.

Finally he settled down, leaning forward to whisper in her ear. "If I'd known marrying you would shut you up, I'd have done it sooner."

Sinclair gave him a wicked grin. "If I'd known you

would marry me, I might have managed to shut up before this."

Without another word she pulled him down to her, closed her eyes and waited for his kiss. It didn't take long for Jefferson to comply.

The horse plodded along the wooded path, carrying the couple toward the Cripple Creek Ranch in a companionable silence.

Jefferson finally cleared his throat. "That was some tall tale you told back there, sugar. I can't believe Hank bought it." He shook his head. "Million-dollar heiress, whoa, but that's a good one."

Sinclair turned to glance up at him, her mouth forming a superior smile.

"It *was* quite a tale, Jefferson, but there's one little problem."

He planted a kiss on her cheek and his eyes glowed down at her. "There's no problem we can't solve together, you've taught me that, sugar."

Sinclair gave a sigh of relief. "I'm so glad to hear that, Jefferson, because I *am* an heiress, and when you and I get married, I'm going to inherit nearly a million dollars."

For nearly the first time in his life, Jefferson McCloud fell off a horse.

Chapter Twenty-one

"Claire, when you married Jeffie today, did you marry me too?"

Sinclair squeezed the small, delicate hand she held clasped in her own and leaned forward to kiss Maddie on the top of her head.

"We're a family now, Maddie. When the Reverend Brown said what God has joined together let no man put asunder, he meant that you, me and Jefferson are blessed to be part of the same family." She gave Maddie's hand another light squeeze.

"What are my two beautiful ladies whispering about over here?"

Sinclair lifted her eyes to find her husband beaming down at her, his handsome face lit by happiness so full and abundant, he almost seemed to glow. She took a deep, contented breath as she once again admired the way he looked in his formal wear. His dark frock coat couldn't disguise the broad shoulders and hard muscles beneath the broadcloth.

"Jefferson McCloud, we're gossiping about you and what a sinfully handsome cowboy you are." Sinclair gave him a devilish grin. "It certainly makes me appreciate becoming your wife."

Jefferson sat down on the oak chair next to her and glanced at his friends and neighbors gathered in the garden.

"I'm just lucky I decided to go to town that night you tried to escape from the Blue Willow." He shook his head as he caught sight of his father and Matilda Haynes wandering among the wedding guests with arms linked. He frowned and gave Sinclair a curious glance.

She shrugged. "Aunt Tilly has suddenly developed an interest in territorial politics." She gave him another impish smile. "Since your father discovered what a wealthy woman she is, he seems to have forgotten she's one of the most notorious madams in Montana."

Jefferson grinned back at her. "It didn't hurt your chances with him either when you promised to finance his campaign." He looked disgusted. "Now he brags to everyone he meets about his intelligent, beautiful daughter-in-law, the heiress."

Sinclair detected a note of bitterness in her new husband's voice, and she leaned over to rest her head on his shoulder.

"Your father drew up all those papers, just as you asked him to. I'm in control of all my own money." She wrinkled her nose at him. "But, you still can't prevent me from buying things we need for the ranch." She sat back up and straightened her shoulders. "I'm your wife and your partner. The success of the Cripple Creek is very important to me too." She blushed a deep red. "And it will be important to our children."

Jefferson leaned forward to whisper in her ear. "If we can't sneak away from this wedding party, there might never be any children."

Sinclair felt herself blush an even deeper crimson and stared down at her hands for a moment. She had been anticipating their wedding night for the past week. When Jefferson had finally found the preacher sitting in a small glade, his horse chomping on grass, Jefferson had been too upset with her announcement about being an heiress to discuss his marriage proposal.

She'd found Jefferson on the porch that night, pacing, drinking whiskey and angry as hell at her because she hadn't told him about her inheritance before.

It had taken all of her persuasive abilities, not to mention a large dose of feminine wile, to convince him they could deal with the money issues and that he'd just have to learn to adjust to the idea of marrying a wealthy woman.

Sinclair glanced out at the people gathered to witness their vows today and gave a deep sigh.

Jefferson watched her carefully, aware that there was sadness in the day as well as celebration.

"We could have waited until your father got here to have the wedding. I told you there was no rush, and I know you wanted him to give you away today."

Sinclair nodded sadly. "Every woman wishes for a storybook wedding, with her father walking her down the aisle." She entwined her arm with Jefferson's and smiled up at him.

"But, I was afraid you might change your mind in the time it would take for him to return to the country and come all the way out here. We'll see him after the fall roundup, when we visit Philadelphia." She gave him a reassuring look. "I'm your wife, and that's the most important thing."

Sinclair pulled her chair back from the table set with fine china, silver and linens and winked at Jefferson.

"I'll be upstairs waiting for you, sugar." She made her voice as sultry as she could and put a western drawl in her words, then swept the train of her gown back and started toward the house.

Jefferson sat watching the twitch of her skirts, then grabbed the glass of wine in front of him to quickly drain it.

Maddie watched him with interest. "Where'd Claire go?"

Jefferson poured himself another glass of wine and wished it was whiskey instead. He was as nervous about his wedding night as a young buck facing his first encounter with a woman. Of course, this would be the first time he was with Sinclair. And he wanted everything to be perfect. He hoped she'd be surprised when she went into their bedroom. He'd tried to plan every detail to make this night romantic and memorable.

Maddie sat watching him, patiently waiting for his answer. He blushed at the scrutiny of his little sister.

"Um, I think she's plum tired out and wants to go to bed."

Maddie frowned at his answer. "It's still daytime. Why would Claire want to go to bed in the daytime?"

Jefferson swallowed and tried to distract her.

"Why don't you eat some more cake, Maddie? I know how much you love cake."

Madison shook her head. "I already ate three pieces and Claire told me I'd get sick if I ate any more." Her face suddenly wore an expression of concern. "Claire isn't sick, is she, Jeffie?"

Jefferson turned to glance toward the upstairs bedroom window, thinking that right about now Sinclair would be stepping into their room. He wondered how she would react to the surprise he'd left for her.

Turning back to his little sister, he tousled her hair. "I don't think so, sweetie, but how about if I go up and check on her, just to make sure."

Maddie looked comforted. "Make sure she doesn't get sick, Jeffie." She leaned forward, a serious expression on her face. "I love her, Jeffie. Sometimes I pretend she's the mommy and you're the daddy, and you have lots of little babies for me to play with."

Jefferson McCloud kissed his sister on her soft, pink cheek and discovered there was a thick lump in his throat.

"Sometimes, I pretend that too, sweetiepie."

Rising from the chair, he started to cross the yard in long, easy strides. Several of the hands made ribald remarks, but he ignored them. One of his neighbors tried to stop him to offer congratulations, but Jefferson brushed the outstretched hand aside and kept walking. He was up the stairs and standing in front of the master bedroom when he finally paused to remove his hat, then knocked softly on the door.

Sinclair's voice was a bit strained when she answered.

"Yes?"

"It's me, sugar. Can I come in?"

He heard the rustling of her petticoats, then silence. He didn't know what to do. If he went rushing into the room, he might frighten her and he'd promised himself that he'd move slowly that night. He rubbed his chin thoughtfully, because he was already fully aroused, and he wasn't even in the same room with his bride yet.

Finally she answered him. "Yes, darling, you can come in."

He swung the door open and paused to gaze around the room. He grinned as he caught sight of her standing in the soft amber glow of the late-afternoon sun and candlelight.

"You look beautiful, sugar." Stepping fully into the room, he shut the door behind him, then leaned back on it, crossing his legs and enjoying the sight of her.

She'd removed the huge hat with the long, trailing ribbons and loosened her hair. Golden curls framed her heart-shaped face and cascaded down her back. She crossed the room to stand in front of him, and he could see tears shining on her cheeks.

"It's so beautiful, Jefferson. You remembered the candles."

He'd filled the room with candles and hoped she'd light them before he got there. The room glowed, and so did she as he touched her face gently.

"I was fool enough to walk away from you once, but I promise you, Sinclair, I'll never leave again without counting the moments until we're back together."

He leaned forward, his lips lightly brushing hers, then he stepped back. "There's something I've got to do."

Moving her gently aside, he went to the bed and bent over. He withdrew several boards, a hammer and a small tin can filled with nails. Sinclair stared at him in confusion as he walked to the window, closed it and proceeded to nail a board across it.

"Do you think I'm going to try to escape by jumping out the window, McCloud?"

He planted another kiss on her lips as he moved to the door, and nailed a board across it.

"You're scaring me, Jefferson. I've never heard of a bridal couple barricading themselves in their room. What if the house catches on fire?"

Jefferson tossed the hammer onto a small chair and started to unbutton his coat. "I suppose since I'm locked in here with Brazin' Blazin', the flame from Philly, there's always that possibility."

He dodged as she sent a shoe sailing in his direction, and laughed. "I'm trying to keep folks out and us securely locked in." He tossed his coat on top of the hammer and took a step toward her.

"Don't you think it's about time we got you out of that dress?"

Sinclair gave him a wide-eyed look of innocence. "I can't seem to unfasten it. Do you think you could assist me?"

Jefferson turned her gently around and went to

work undoing the pearl buttons climbing down her back to the bustle of her gown. As the fabric parted, he could see soft, rose-hued skin underneath and he paused to pull one sleeve aside and plant a languid kiss on her shoulder. She shivered.

He stood back to watch her step out of the gown and turn to face him. She slowly pulled the tie of her chemise, her eyes never leaving his as she unfastened it, then slid it off her shoulders. Now he could see the fullness of her breasts, as they nearly spilled out over the top of her corset.

He stepped forward and his arms circled her waist. Leaning down he found her lips. This time the kiss was hot, urgent and probing. He moved his tongue into her mouth, and she moaned deeply in response.

He lifted his face from hers as he felt her hands on the buttons of his vest. The idea of her undressing him made Jefferson nearly crazy with desire. He had to swallow hard and use all of his self-control to keep from throwing her back on the bed, pushing her petticoats up and taking her quickly.

Patience, he reminded himself.

Now her hands undid each small button of his linen shirt. Her fingers left a trail of heat in their wake. When she finished she rubbed her hands across his chest in wonder and he could swear the room must have burst into flames.

"I know I've said it before, Jefferson McCloud, but you truly are magnificent." Her fingers traced a line down the muscles of his smooth, flat belly, to pause at the top of his trousers. She gave him a questioning look.

Grinning down at her with a devilish expression,

he urged her on. "Don't stop now, sugar."

Sinclair could barely control the trembling in her hands. When she'd questioned her aunt Tilly about the wedding night, the woman had been frank with her. Her descriptions of lovemaking had not even remotely resembled the innocent speculation of her girlfriends in finishing school. Sinclair had decided then and there, if you want to know how to build a house, you should definitely ask a carpenter. She had spent several restless nights tossing and turning in her bed after that, imagining what it would be like to lie naked in Jefferson's arms and do the things her aunt Tilly had described.

Her fingers found the top button, fumbled for a moment, then unfastened it. She could see a patch of dark hair.

He stopped her suddenly and she noticed a thin sheen of perspiration on his forehead. "My turn," he said.

Reaching behind her, he undid the ties of her bustle, giving it an odd look. "I'll never understand why women wear these damned things," he murmured, tossing it aside. He paused to consider the laces of her corset, then grinned down at her.

"I remember seeing you that first night, hanging out that window in your underwear." His fingers slowly pulled at the lacing. "I do believe I wanted you right from the start, and Lord knows, I've been a patient man." He separated each lace, finally lifting the corset over her head. He paused to stand back and admire her.

Her breasts were full, round and ripe looking. Her nipples grew hard as he brushed one finger across them, her lips parted and her breath came faster. He was seeing through a haze of desire and he could barely control himself. Working the ties of her petticoats loose, they fell to pool around her feet. He stared at her pantalets and gave a groan.

"Too damn many clothes, Sinclair."

Sinclair slid the pantalets down her thighs, then kicked the clothes at her feet aside. She stood facing him in her stockings, then she started to roll down the garters. Jefferson lost patience and suddenly reached down to grab her around the waist and lift her into his arms. Carrying her to the bed, he fell to the quilt with her.

She laughed at his eagerness, watching as he shed his vest and shirt, then awkwardly finished unfastening the buttons of his pants. He stood up again, and she gazed in wonder as he removed his final piece of clothing.

In the warm glow of the candlelight, he faced her and Sinclair couldn't keep from staring at his manhood, thrust forward toward her. She'd imagined many things, and thought she'd had a pretty good idea of what a naked man would look like. Nothing had prepared her for the sight of her handsome husband, burnished skin aglow, his body hard and ready for her.

She leaned her head on her hand as she studied his heavily muscled physique. He didn't move as her eyes raked his body, but he gave her a lopsided grin when her gaze finally managed to lift to his eyes.

"Like what you see, Mrs. McCloud?"

She seemed to consider his question for a moment, then grinned back at him. "Get back in bed, Mr.

331

McCloud." Her voice was husky with desire.

He was quick to comply with her request. She gasped as his body covered hers, their legs twining, their skin hot as it touched. He traced a trail of kisses down her neck, across her collarbone and to her breasts. When his tongue circled the hard, rose-colored nipple, her hips lifted to buck against him. He turned to the other breast, and she tossed her head on the pillow, softly moaning his name.

His hand explored the velvety roundness of her body. She was all curves and silky softness, and he paused as he reached the triangle of blond curls nestled between her legs. His fingers gently rubbed her, and she responded by spreading her legs in invitation.

Sinclair was lost in a sea of sensation. Jefferson's mouth and hands were tracing patterns of desire across her body. Stretching, trying to bring him closer, she whispered encouragement.

"I want you, Jefferson."

He paused his sensual exploration long enough to kiss her, his tongue searing her mouth, exploring, then demanding. Her breath came in small pants.

She could feel his erection against her inner thigh, big, hot and hard. She briefly worried about the pain when he entered her, because Aunt Tilly had been silent regarding the matter of size. Sinclair had an inkling that her husband was well endowed in that department.

Jefferson gently parted the fragile petals protecting her womanhood and inserted one thick finger inside of her. He was rewarded by damp sweetness flowing from her, a signal that she was ready for him. Shifting his weight and balancing himself on his elbows above her, he focused on her face. He wanted to witness this exquisite coming together, this moment of joining. He wanted to see her expression when they became one.

With a slow, deliberate movement, he positioned himself, ready to enter her. He could see a flash of fear cross her face and he paused.

"I'd never hurt you, sugar, but . . . there's nothing I can do . . ."

Her fingers against his lips silenced him. "I know," she whispered. Her expression was confident now.

Pushing himself against her, the flesh surrendered to his assault and he slid into her. Her gasp was more surprise than pain, yet he hesitated as he felt the barrier and swallowed. Then he gave another push to thrust himself deep within her.

Sinclair gave a scream, but his mouth quickly came down on hers to capture it. With deliberate gentleness, he nearly withdrew, then moved himself deep inside of her again. The pleasure was nearly agony in its bliss. Repeating the movement, he could sense a change in her. He finally lifted his mouth from hers and paused.

"I'm sorry, love." He touched her cheek gently with one finger.

Her expression wasn't one of pain, but of rapt attention. "You're not stopping, are you?" she asked innocently.

"Do you want me to?" But, he wasn't sure if he could stop, even if she begged him.

She licked her lips. "That isn't all there is, is it?"

He laughed gently and moved into her again. He could feel her relax as he lifted her legs, to wrap them around his waist, allowing him to thrust even deeper inside of her.

Sinclair couldn't explain what she was feeling, as she adjusted to the shock of Jefferson pushing himself into her and the brief, tearing pain. But, that had been replaced by a throbbing, aching need that was new and baffling. As she experienced each hard, hot plunge, she responded by lifting her hips and moving against Jefferson. Delicious sensations flowed through her, as he thrust faster, deeper, harder within her.

She felt herself climbing toward something, each movement of their bodies pushing her closer, closer. They seemed enchanted, as they participated in an ancient rite of yielding. She couldn't think beyond the moment, couldn't respond with anything but primal instinct.

Jefferson held himself with every inch of self-control he could muster. She was tight, wet and scorched him with her heat. His thrusts grew longer and he slipped his hands beneath her, to hold her firm, round bottom in his hands as he lifted her to plunge, deeper and deeper to her sweet, succulent core.

His pleasure was so intense, he didn't think he could keep from spilling himself into his wife for even a moment longer. Plunging into her again, he watched in wonder as she writhed beneath him, moaning his name.

Sinclair was lost in a world of ecstasy, all reality growing dim as stars swept across the inside of her eyelids, carrying her to the heavens. She felt wave after wave of delightful sensation wash over her, and she didn't care if she ever returned to earth again.

A moment after hearing her achieve her pleasure, Jefferson allowed himself to go over the edge, a deep, guttural sound signaling his release. His body trembled with each hot, pulsating throb of his manhood, as he poured his seed into her. He wanted to collapse on top of her, to enjoy the feel of her tight sheath surrounding him, but he was afraid of hurting her. With one final, delightful thrust, he withdrew and fell upon his back.

Sinclair opened her eyes to gaze at her husband in adoration. He wore a huge grin of satisfaction as he stretched himself across the bed and put his hands behind his head.

"Now, *that's* all there is to it, sugar."

Sinclair nudged him with her elbow and laughed.

"I guess I should have asked for a special paragraph in that marriage agreement you made your father draw up. Something to the effect of satisfaction guaranteed."

Jefferson moved an arm to draw her closer and grinned even wider. "There was never any question of that, darling."

Sinclair slapped his chest playfully. "You are still one arrogant cowboy."

He opened his eyes and gave her a dark, smoldering look. "And I'm all yours, Mrs. McCloud."

She sat up, slowly perused his naked body and sighed deeply. "And for that, Mr. McCloud, I do believe I shall be eternally grateful."

Settling herself back against him, she put her head on his chest and listened to the gentle cadence of his heart beating. She closed her eyes, the dreamy glow of their lovemaking wrapping her in a drowsy cocoon.

She jumped when there was a sudden pounding on their bedroom door, followed by the crash of pots being clanged together. Jefferson yawned.

She could hear voices singing, at least she thought it was supposed to be singing, and she started off the bed to peek out the window. Jefferson captured one of her wrists and arched a brow at her.

"Sugar, do you think you should be standing in the window naked?"

She glanced down at herself in wonder. She'd nearly forgotten she didn't have any clothes on. It certainly hadn't taken much time for her to become a wanton woman.

The noise outside their door and window reached a crescendo, when she heard the familiar voices of several of the ranch hands. They were making ribald comments and Sinclair blushed.

Jefferson looked unconcerned as he pulled her back onto the bed, then drew a quilt over them.

Sinclair heard another crash, "What's going on out there?" she asked.

He closed his eyes but his hand started to fondle her again. She was distracted by another noise in the hallway and slapped his hand away.

"Shivaree," he said, simply putting his hand back again.

She sat up in bed and studied him carefully. He opened his eyes, focusing on the place where the covers dipped to just barely conceal her breasts. His hand moved again and she felt the flames of desire bank from a small glow to a raging inferno. She simply couldn't explain what this man did to her, but all of her inhibitions seemed to have disappeared. She lowered the quilt to her waist and his hand quickly cupped her breast, making her toss back her head and close her eyes.

"What's a shivaree?" she whispered, her voice husky with desire.

His mouth followed his hand, and as he suckled each nipple gently, her fingers combed his thick, dark hair.

Lifting his head to study her, he grinned. "It's a western custom. A serenade, sort of."

The clanging of pots had started again and she frowned. "It doesn't sound like much of a serenade. What's the purpose?"

Jefferson pulled the blanket even lower and sat studying her.

"I think it's supposed to distract the newlyweds." His hand moved down her thigh, reveling in the satiny texture of her skin. He was rewarded with a deep sigh.

"What can we do about it, Jefferson? I certainly don't think we're going to be able to sleep tonight." Sinclair was trying to smother a giggle.

He leaned her back onto the bed and positioned himself above her. He wore a playful expression.

"Well, you're creative and I've got stamina. I'm sure we can figure something out, sugar."

Sinclair grasped his face in her hands and smiled up at him. "I'd say that was an unbeatable combination, Boss McCloud. Between the two of us, we can take on the whole entire world."

Jefferson grinned down at her, his eyes sparkling with good humor.

"Yup," he said.

THE OUTLAW'S WOMAN
Tanya Hanson

Dena Clayter carries a secret. In the midst of a blizzard, the young widow harbored an outlaw. She fed and nursed the injured fugitive, frightened not of the man but of the longings he incited. She yearned for his touch, the comfort of his arms, his lips against hers, and their passion flared hot enough to burn away all her inhibitions.

Now Dena is racing across the West to try to save him from the hangman's noose. For more than just his life hangs in the balance—Dena's own future and that of their baby stands in jeopardy. And the expectant mother has to know if a bond conceived in winter darkness will be revealed as love in the light of spring.

EXTREME MEASURES
RENEE HALVERSON

NEW HISTORICAL VOICE CONTEST WINNER

If André DuBois were a betting man, he would lay odds that the woman in red is robbing his dealers blind. He can tell the beauty's smile disguises a quick mind and even quicker fingers. To catch her In the act, he deals himself into the game, never guessing he might lose his heart in the process.

Faith O'Malley depends on her wits to succeed at cards, and experience tells her the ante has just been raised. The new gambler's good looks are distracting enough, but his intelligent eyes promise trouble. Still, Faith will risk everything—her reputation, her virtue—to save the innocent people depending on her. It won't be until later that she'll stop to learn what she's won.

Sinfully
Delicious

Lora Kenton

A surefire recipe for true love: In a Texas whorehouse combine the two main ingredients—a New Orleans socialite and an ex-bounty hunter. Watch Kyra Lourdes and Cliff Baldwin's emotions bubble to the surface, as old feelings are stirred up in the childhood friends. Spice the mixture with danger from Kyra's vicious fiancé and threats from Cliff's disreputable past. Sweeten the dish with baking lessons that leave the pair hungry for each other. Let the heat from the couple's attraction develop into sizzling desire, until they roll together in a steamy union. Allow the lovers to bask in the afterglow of their passion. Season with tender endearments and wedding vows. The result: Home cooking that is sinfully delicious.

Dorchester Publishing Co., Inc.
P.O. Box 6640   5083-8
Wayne, PA 19087-8640 $5.99 US/$7.99 CAN

CHASE THE WIND
CINDY HOLBY

From the moment he sets eyes on Faith, Ian Duncan knows she is the only girl for him. But her unbreakable betrothal to his employer's vicious son forces him to steal his love away on the very eve of her marriage. Faith and Ian are married clandestinely, their only possessions a magnificent horse, a family Bible, a wedding-ring quilt and their unshakable belief in each other. While their homestead waits to be carved out of the Iowa wilderness, Faith presents Ian with the most precious gift of all: a son and a daughter, born of the winter snows into the spring of their lives. The golden years are still ahead, their dream is coming true, but this is just the beginning. . . .

Dorchester Publishing Co., Inc.
P.O. Box 6640
Wayne, PA 19087-8640

___5114-1
$5.99 US/$7.99 CAN

Please add $2.50 for shipping and handling for the first book and $.75 for each additional book. NY and PA residents, add appropriate sales tax. No cash, stamps, or CODs. Canadian orders require $5.00 for shipping and handling and must be paid in U.S. dollars. Prices and availability subject to change. **Payment must accompany all orders.**

Name: _____

Address: _____

City: _____ State:_____ Zip:_____

E-mail: _____

I have enclosed $_____ in payment for the checked book(s).

For more information on these books, check out our website at www.dorchesterpub.com.
_____ *Please send me a free catalog.*

KNIGHT ON THE
TEXAS PLAINS
LINDA BRODAY

Duel McClain is no knight in shining armor—he is a drifter who prides himself on having no responsibilities.   But a poker game thrusts him into the role of father to an abandoned baby, and then a condemned woman stumbles up to his campfire.   The fugitive beauty aims to keep him at shotgun's length, but obvious maternal instincts belie her fierce demeanor.   And she and the baby are clearly made for each other. Worse, the innocent infant and the alleged murderess open Duel's heart, make him long for the love of a real family. And the only way to have that will be to slay the demons of the past.
